The Preacher's Wifey

The Preacher's Wifey

DiShan Washington

www.urbanbooks.net

Urban Books, LLC
78 East Industry Court
Deer Park, NY 11729

ISBN 13: 978-1-60162-379-9
ISBN 10: 1-60162-379-8

First Trade Paperback Printing March 2013
Printed in the United States of America

10 9 8 7 6 5 4 3 2 1

Distributed by Kensington Publishing Corp.
Submit Wholesale Orders to:
Kensington Publishing Corp.
C/O Penguin Group (USA) Inc.
Attention: Order Processing
405 Murray Hill Parkway
East Rutherford, NJ 07073-2316
Phone: 1-800-526-0275
Fax: 1-800-227-9604

Acknowledgments

Where would I be without the Lord? It is in Him that I live, move, and have my being. I never would have thought I'd go through all I've been through the past couple of years, but the greatest part of it all is I survived it. I owe that to the Lord who has kept my mind on the many days I was sure I'd lose it. From thoughts of suicide, to being homeless, to days I had no food to eat and no money to buy any . . . I still survived. Jesus IS my life, and I'm rocking with Him until the day I die.

To my daughter, Alahna Rose Washington, you are the reason my heart beats. The days I would have taken my life, I looked at you and found every reason in the world to keep it moving. I waited so long for you and although I haven't been able to give you the life you deserve (yet), momma is working on it. There will come a day when nothing you ask for will be withheld from you. You are my saving grace. I love you.

To my parents, Pastors J.C. & Melinda Winters, thank you for being there. Thank you for the many sacrifices you've made for me. Thank you for believing in me when I stopped believing in myself. I love you to eternity. To my siblings, Detras, Harlan, Jerrell, and Beth, I love you with a love you will probably never know. We've all gotten so close over the past year or so and I'm grateful for the roles each of you play in my life. Let's keep doing the impossible.

To ALL of my family—especially my surviving grandparents, Sallie Williams & Jimmy Reese—I love you so much. I can't name all of you but just know you mean the world to me. I'll never forget from whence I came.

To my best friend, Shanna Fountain, thank you for the friendship. Thank you for rolling with me through thick and thin. It feels good to have someone in your corner no matter what. I love you, girl. To a special friend, Pastor Cheryl Moore, you've been like a sister to me. I will never forget what you've done for me. You put your money where your mouth was on the days I had nothing. You pushed me until I got up again. Forever in your debt. I love you. To my godmother, Victoria Christopher Murray, words cannot express what you mean to me. The late night phone calls, the encouragement, the prayers . . . it has all meant so much. Thank you. I love you.

To ALL of my friends, thank you. Some of you have been with me on this very difficult journey since *Diary of a Mad First Lady* was released, and I appreciate all of you. Whatever you've done to contribute to my life has not gone unnoticed. Much oblige. I love you, all. To all of my loyal readers and new ones, it is because of you I get to try my hand at writing. Thank you for being patient with me. It's been a while, but I'm back. Thanks for your support! I love you all from the bottom of my heart.

Myrondous, although our journey together ended, I'll always remember you were the reason I ever believed I could be an author. No matter what, love you, always.

~In Loving Memory of Rosia M. Reese~

Prologue

"And we now pronounce you husband and wife," Pastor Sprawlings said amid all our guests who had assembled at Cornerstone Baptist Church. "You may kiss your bride."

I looked into the eyes of my new husband, Byran Ward, as he leaned down and passionately sealed our nuptials with a kiss. The church erupted in applause as we both turned to face our onlookers with huge smiles plastered on our faces.

My eyes caught the gaze of my mother, whose expression made it clear that she was bursting with pride. I had finally done something right. Marrying one of the most eligible bachelors in Atlanta had done it. Up until I got engaged to Byran, no matter what awesome thing I did, my mother always made me feel that it did not count for anything. Today she was beaming—smiling her approval. Her happiness was not due to the fact that she thought *I* was happy. She was happy because she knew that she would finally get the prestige and recognition she had always wanted in life. She was now the mother-in-law of one of the nation's most prolific and well-known pastors. It was as close to her dream coming true as she would get in this lifetime.

"Baby, your smile should be a little brighter. You just came up," Byran said, turning my thoughts away from my mother.

Without responding, I simply smiled more. For good measure I leaned over and summoned Byran for a kiss. The applause of approval was deafening.

"That's it, darling. That's how you work the crowd," he said.

We made our way down the aisle, which seemed endless. Unlike most grooms, who would just make their exit with their bride, Byran—who was never going to pass up a moment to "connect" with his flock—insisted upon us stopping to speak to as many people as we could. It felt more like a Sunday morning than a wedding. But I did as he wished. I smiled. I waved. I shook hands. Already I was settling into my first lady role.

Finally, we made it to the back of the church.

"Pastor, the car is waiting out front to drive you to the other side of the campus for the reception," one of the deacons stated.

Byran nodded. "Thank you, sir."

That was another thing I had not wanted. I would have preferred to have my reception someplace other than the church, but Byran had insisted it was the perfect way for the congregation to feel involved, and as usual, I conformed to his wishes.

Byran carefully assisted me as I climbed into the black stretch Navigator limousine. My dress, which was a sleek white mermaid-style number and had a ten-foot, crystal-adorned train attached to it, was safely inside when he closed the door behind him and clicked the button that gave us privacy.

"You really need to do a better job at smiling, honey. It seems forced," he said.

"Baby, I do not know what you are expecting of me. I have smiled so much, my cheeks are close to being permanently frozen in a raised state."

"I understand the smiling gets a little tiring. But you still seem a little disconnected. Are you not happy? Is this not the wedding of your dreams?"

Was he really about to start an argument with me? On our wedding day?

"We have already been down this road. We both know this is not the wedding of *my* dreams, but this is what you wanted, and so this is what I have to deal with."

"I really hope I am reading you wrong, because if I did not know any better, I would think you would rather be someplace else than here at our wedding."

"Let's not exaggerate, Byran. Of course I want to be here. It *is* my wedding day. What bride would not want to be at her wedding day? I just have issues with you grilling me on how much I need to smile or *how* I should smile—all for the sake of people." I paused for a beat. "It just makes it hard to actually enjoy my special day when you are constantly nagging me about something I am doing or not doing. I understand image is very important to you, and it is also important to me. But at some point, you have to relax. Be yourself. And allow me to be myself."

"You are not getting paid to just be yourself. You are getting paid to be my wifey. So what did you think my expectations would be? This wedding, this relationship—it's an arrangement, Allyson. Please don't ever lose sight of that when you start to complain."

I could feel the blood running warm in my veins. I knew this was an arranged marriage, but why in the hell would he choose this moment to bring it up?

"Do you have to remind me? I know what I signed up for. I know what I agreed to. But can you just show some emotion today? Can you just at least pretend you are in love with me and that this entire thing is not a sham? Jeesh. Is that too much to ask?"

The limo rolled up to the Franklin D. Douglas Banquet Hall. Named after its previous pastor, who had been the pastor for forty-six years, until his death, it really was the perfect venue for a beautiful reception. Overlooking a sparkling eight-acre lake that was surrounded by many varieties of springtime flowers, it was the perfect backdrop for our wedding pictures and a would-be romantic evening.

As we exited the limo, several members of the church who had not had the opportunity to get a close-up were stretching their necks to get a view of my dress. I put on the biggest smile I could, and like any other celebrity would do, I waved to the onlookers.

I noticed a couple of local news trucks assembled on one side of the parking lot. On the other side were some of the nation's most elite and well-known pastors, along with their wives. I even caught a glimpse of some other celebrities making their way into the building. Our wedding had certainly spawned the latest tabloid-worthy buzz for the local area. From the day we announced our engagement, it had been one interview after another. The church's publicist had seen to it that we were featured on as many magazine covers as possible. The headlines of one of the magazine articles read YOUNG BLACK LOVE—THE CHRISTIAN WAY.

"Mrs. Ward, how does it feel to be married to one of the city's most prominent new pastors? A million women would have loved to be standing where you stood today and become Mrs. Byran Ward," said one of the reps from a popular online gossip site.

Everything isn't always what it seems, I thought. I wanted to say those words out loud, but instead I said what had been scripted. "It feels wonderful to be marrying my best friend. I am certain that any woman would love to be in my shoes today. Who would not want to marry a man who is as talented, gifted, and anointed as my husband?" I looked over at Byran, who was beaming brighter than the sun was on this spring day.

"Not to mention he's rich," said a blond-haired reporter representing Atlanta's Fox 5 News.

A few people chuckled at her comment. It was meant to be a lighthearted joke, but the truth was his money was exactly why I was marrying him. He had made me an offer I could not refuse. Would not refuse.

"His money is the least of my concerns. I have never given much thought to his wealth or his company. I fell in love with him, as a person."

"So if he was not wealthy, talented, and the new senior pastor of one of the largest churches in the country, would you still have married him?"

Hell, no.

"But of course. Again, I fell in love with him—not with his money or his title. Pastor Byran Ward is a wonderful man. I am very blessed to be his wife."

"Okay, everyone. I do not want to tire out my new bride by having her stand out here in this heat, answering your questions. I need her to save some of that energy for our honeymoon," Byran said, joking with the reporters.

"Speaking of honeymoon, where are you two lovebirds going?" another reporter, from Access Atlanta, asked.

Byran shook his head. "Now, now, you know I cannot divulge that information. We would never have our privacy. All of you would be following us there, and there is no way I am going to have you following my wife around while she is dressed in a bikini."

"Bikini? The pastor's wife . . . in a bikini?" the gossip reporter asked.

"Yep. And she looks great in one."

With that, Byran's assistants ushered us past the reporters. Inside, my mother and three bridesmaids were waiting to whisk me away so I could change into my second dress, which was a white, formfitting sequined number that stopped just above the knees.

Inside the designated bridal suite were all my bridesmaids. They all looked so beautiful in their lavender satin off-the-shoulder dresses. The ivory sashes tied around their waists gave them a very elegant, regal look.

I surveyed the room. Everyone seemed to be in their own little world, discussing the pleasantries of the wedding. The decorations, the single men . . .

"Allyson, you looked exquisite today," my mother said.

"Thanks, Mom. You looked beautiful yourself."

"Well, I did not want to outshine you on your day, so I decided to take it easy on you." She laughed.

I did not.

I wished I could believe that she was just joking, but I knew she was not. My mother had been in competition with me ever since I had had my first NFL boyfriend. She had made a mess with her own life and enjoyed living vicariously through mine. She was infuriated after each of my failed relationships with a ballplayer, a politician, and other persons of wealth and status. Somehow every breakup was my fault. At least in her mind it was.

"I'm glad you took it easy on me, Mom. We all know who the real beauty queen is," I said sarcastically.

"Glad you know it, baby girl. There is no mistake that you are strikingly beautiful with your model-like features, long jet-black hair, and hazel-green eyes. But it was your mama who made that possible."

She caught a glimpse of herself in the mirror. She was indeed beautiful. If it had not been for the almost twenty-year age difference, we could have passed for twins. I looked just like her. "Why don't you come and help me get into this dress? I'm sure Byran will send someone looking for me soon if I do not hurry and get changed."

"Yes, dear. And you certainly don't want to keep that gorgeous man waiting."

"Right."

"Girls, let's all help Allyson into this dress so we can go and enjoy the party."

Each of my bridesmaids rushed over to offer their assistance. Before long we were exiting the suite. In the hallway Byran and his groomsmen were standing there looking as debonair as any men could. As I neared Byran, I had to admit, I had landed a good one. Handsome, talented, and yes . . . rich. I was accustomed to dating men of status, but my previous relationships had never got serious enough for me to graduate from being either the side chick or the occasional lay if they came to town. Byran had been different. He was set on what he wanted shortly after meeting me. On the three-month anniversary of us dating, he popped the question.

"You look stunning. I'm going to enjoy taking that dress off later," Byran whispered into my ear. "So proud of you. Just enough seduction mixed with class."

"You speak as if I wasn't that way when you met me."

"You were okay. But this dress takes you to another level."

"Glad I can make you happy," I said, proud that I had finally done something right.

"No, I'm not happy yet. But I will be tonight. On our so-called honeymoon," he said playfully.

I smiled.

I knew they shouldn't have, but his words had slightly tugged at my heart. I had no idea why he kept feeling the need to remind me of what we both knew already. None of this was real!

The doors opened to the reception. Applause rang loud in the building. Byran and I, along with our wedding party, made our grand appearance.

"Ladies and gentlemen, please help us welcome our pastor and his lovely new bride, Pastor and First Lady Byran Ward," said the master of ceremony for the evening.

And for some reason it all suddenly hit me. The emotions I had pretended not to have for so long had chased me and caught me, and I was now feeling some regret about my decision.

As we walked to the center of the floor for our first dance, the startling truth was now a little difficult to swallow. While everyone stared at us lovingly, inside the moment had arrested my heart, and I secretly wished I had married for love.

Instead, I had actually become someone's . . . wifey.

Almost a wife.

But not quite.

Chapter One

One year later . . .

The waves beat against the ocean side. The Bahamian breeze was crisp, light, and refreshing. Byran and I walked hand in hand along the beach, stopping every few feet to pick up seashells that were buried deep within the sand.

"Isn't this a lovely evening?" I asked, hoping to end the silence that we had been experiencing for the past few hours.

"It is," he replied simply.

Not able to take it anymore, I asked, "Is something wrong? I noticed you have been really quiet since we arrived this morning. I mean, regardless of the reasons we got married, this is our one-year anniversary. Can we just enjoy ourselves and have a good time?"

"Baby, I'm sorry. I just have a lot on my mind."

"Is it something you want to talk about?"

"Actually, it is. But I will wait until dinner. Let's enjoy the remainder of our stroll."

Something in his voice told me *it* wasn't good. Well, no matter what he said, I had my own announcement that was sure to perk him up.

"Why don't we just cut this short and head in to get ready for dinner? I am a little hungry, anyway," I said.

"You sure? I know how much these long walks on the beach mean to you."

"Yeah, I am sure. Let's go back to the villa."

We turned and went in the direction of our two-bedroom oceanfront villa. As much as I loved walks on the beach, the villa was my favorite place to be. It was spacious and was decorated with vintage wicker furniture, the walls were splashed with shades of ocean blue and white, and beautiful hand-painted art complimented them. It was the perfect oasis for rest.

We slipped into the shower, then threw on our island clothes. I chose to wear a yellow sundress, and he, a white linen suit. We made our way to the casino to dine at Nobu, a Japanese restaurant, which we frequented whenever we were on Paradise Island.

"That sundress really compliments your skin. I love it."

Finally. He was back to being his charming self. As arrogant as he could be at times, it was this side of him that made it tolerable. I breathed a sigh of relief.

"Thank you, baby. I wore it for you. I know you love when I wear bright colors."

"Yes, I do. Honestly, you look great in anything you wear."

He sure was making up for such a sour morning and afternoon. Without even needing to look at myself, I knew my face was lit up as bright as the dress I wore and the matching flower in my hair.

"You do too, love. You are looking mighty handsome tonight in your white linen. You know I love it when you wear white. Sexy.com."

That garnered a smile from him.

"Are you all ready to order your drinks?" the waiter asked.

"The lady will have a glass of Moscato, and I will have a glass of Riesling."

"No, love, not tonight," I interjected. "I'll have a juice blend of pineapple, orange, and cranberry with a splash of Sprite."

Byran stared at me, no doubt wondering why I would ever turn down a glass of Moscato. It was my favorite wine of all time, and the fact that we were celebrating our anniversary was all the more reason to enjoy a bottle.

"Okay. The lady has switched it up on me tonight," he said, his eyes asking questions.

"Very well," the waiter said. "I'll be back momentarily to take your order."

"I know you are wondering—"

"You want to explain to me why you turned down Moscato? Are you sick?"

His questions came before I even had the opportunity to explain. "No, I'm not sick. Actually, I feel great."

His expression showed his confusion.

"I'm pregnant," I blurted out.

"Here are your drinks," the waiter said as he placed our drinks down. "Are you ready to place your order?"

Our eyes were glued to each other's. Byran looked as if his appetite had been ruined.

"Ma'am, do you know what you would like?"

I glanced down at the menu. I already knew what I wanted, and I was eager to turn my attention to something else. "I'll take the Sea Bass Fish and Chips."

"Great choice," the waiter said as he took my menu. "And you, sir?"

Byran forced himself to pull his eyes away from me and look at the menu. After a few minutes he said, "I'll have the Black Pepper Crust Sea Bass with Balsamic Teriyaki."

"Ah, another excellent choice," the waiter replied, also taking his menu. "I neglected to ask, but would you all like an appetizer? Tuna or Salmon Spicy Miso Chips? Or beef sashimi perhaps?"

The waiter's words were lost in the traffic jam of our thoughts. Realizing he was not going to get an answer to his last question, he dismissed himself from our table.

Immediately my stomach produced gut-strangling knots. The nervousness I felt threatened to consume me. Thankfully, Byran didn't prolong it.

"You're pregnant?"

"Yes," I said, hardly able to contain the excitement that was now beginning to seep into my nervousness.

"How far along are you?"

"I haven't had my first doctor's appointment yet. I don't know." I reached down into my black Birkin to retrieve the decorative gift box that held the positive test. I had not planned to blurt the news out the way I had, but it seemed to just roll off my tongue. I handed the box to him. "Happy anniversary, baby."

He took the box without saying anything, opened it, picked up the digital test, placed it back in the box, and put the cover back on it.

"I don't know what to say."

"Try telling me how elated you are. That would be a great place to start."

"Allyson, I wish I could tell you that and mean it. Truth is, I don't feel that way right now."

His words crushed me like ice. How could he not be happy that I was carrying his child?

Fighting back tears, I said, "Why not? Your flesh and blood, our flesh and blood, is growing inside of me. Byran, that is a beautiful thing." The tears threatened to overtake me.

"It's just not the right timing. I mean, I have been pastoring Cornerstone for only two years, we have been married for only a year, and what I wanted to talk to you about tonight . . . Let's just say this complicates things."

"That is so selfish of you to say. All of it. Who cares how long you have been the pastor at Cornerstone? What does that have to do with our child? And, just in case you didn't know this, married people have kids. Did you think we would be exempt?"

"I thought you told me you were on the pill."

"Come on. Are you serious? Do you think the pill is one hundred percent effective in preventing pregnancy? You have got to be kidding me."

"You didn't skip one, did you?"

"What?" I said, a little louder than I should have. The other patrons were starting to cut their eyes in our direction. In this moment I could care less. President Barack Obama could have been dining at the table next to us, and I would not have cared. This man had certainly lost his mind somewhere. "Please don't tell me you are suggesting I got pregnant on purpose."

"I'm just saying. We've been together for almost three years, been married for one, and you have never come up pregnant. I don't understand why now."

I wanted to pick up my knife and throw it right between his eyes. As classy a woman as I was, he was pushing me into the ghetto category real quick. Did he forget I had a contract? Why would I have a need to trap him?

"You are about to make me act in a very non-Christian manner in this restaurant. None of that is important. It is all beside the point. The fact of the matter is I'm pregnant. Point-blank. Period."

He studied me carefully. Then he took a sip of the Riesling he had ordered. Then he studied me more. And then another sip of the wine. His eyes played the cat-and-mouse game with his glass for several minutes.

"You have to get rid of it," he finally managed to get out. "It's just not the right time, Allyson. We have to be prepared to bring a child in the world, and we are not prepared. It would cause so many problems with so many things." He paused, as if to reconcile his final statement with his thoughts. "Yeah, you have to get rid of it."

My gasp was heard all over the restaurant. Every diner in the restaurant turned to focus his or her attention on us. But I could no longer help it. And just like the green beans my grandmother used to snap on the front porch, I snapped. I jumped up from the table, picked up my water glass, and tossed the liquid right into Byran's face. Not only that, but I threw the glass to the floor, causing it to shatter into little, tiny pieces.

"Were you prepared for that?" I shouted.

I stormed out, leaving a horrified, embarrassed Byran sitting at the table, looking as if the rapture had come and he had been left behind.

Who the hell did he think he was?

Chapter Two

His words played over and over in my mind. How could he ask me to get rid of our child, as if he or she was a piece of trash or something? Surely he was delirious if he believed I would go through with something like that.

The sound of the waves dancing along the beach was a calming factor. Ever since getting back to the villa, I had been lying in the comforting embrace of a white wicker chaise, crying. I cried so much, I was sure my tear ducts were drained dry.

Somehow I had seen the entire thing going differently in my head. I assumed he would be excited, and that whatever he was going through that had caused him to be somber would be temporarily forgotten as we celebrated the impending birth of our child. Not so.

I was so lost in thought, I did not hear the door to the balcony slide open.

"Allyson?"

Ugh. What did he want?

"Yes?"

"Are you busy?"

"Does it look like it?" His question was redundant and irritating.

"Listen, I know you are upset, and you have every right to be. There is no excuse for my attitude at the restaurant."

He had found his senses somewhere on his way back to the villa.

"You are exactly right. No excuse, Byran. How could you be so insensitive?" I sat up so I could turn to face him. "I am pregnant with your child, and you make me feel like I did it on purpose or all by myself. It takes two to make a baby, you know."

The tears started flowing again.

He walked over to me and wiped them away. His sweet gesture made them come faster, harder. I didn't know if it was my out-of-control hormones or the sensitivity of the situation, but before I could stop myself, I was bent over, weeping on his shoulder. He wrapped both arms around me and held on to me tightly. For the next ten minutes I felt like he really cared about me. I felt as if I was the woman he truly loved with his entire being, and not the woman he had an arrangement with.

"Allyson, I did not mean to sound so cold and callous. And I am sorry. Words cannot express how regretful I am for that coming out the way that it did. I can only imagine how it made you feel. Because no matter what, you are a human being with real feelings and emotions, and although neither of us married for love, I think we both care deeply for each other."

I remained silent.

He was right. Neither of us married for love, but after a year of being with him and pretending to be a happy couple, I had begun to believe our lie. Finding out I was pregnant with his child had only increased my feelings for him.

"Look at me," he said as he lifted my chin. "Stop crying, okay? We will figure this out."

"What is there to figure out? Do you really want me to have an abortion?"

"I cannot deny that the timing could not be any worse."

"But why? Things are going great with the church. Cornerstone adores you. Matter of fact, the membership is at its highest, and so is your salary. The car dealerships are doing well. The funeral home business in Chicago is booming. So I know it's not about money. You have everything just like you told me you wanted it to be when I first met you a couple of years ago."

"Baby, this is not about money."

"Then what is it about?" My level of confusion was increasing by the second. "Why is this a bad time?"

"I could never make you understand now. Prior to this baby, you would have understood perfectly. I will say our arrangement did not include kids. I needed you so I could seal the nomination to be the pastor at Cornerstone. I never even thought about having a family . . . with you. Remember? This was an—"

"Arrangement. I know. You just said that, and besides, you never let me forget it."

"But you were fine with it in the beginning. I asked you from the start if you would be able to keep your feelings at bay and see being my wife as your job—not your duty. And you assured me that you would. And I pay good money for you to be my wifey. You shop in the best stores. You eat at the best restaurants. You go on monthly excursions with the other pastors' wives in our circle. You live in a ten-thousand-square-foot home. You drive a BMW seven-sixty five days a week and a two-door Porsche Panamera on the weekend. You have unlimited access to my platinum American Express. You are on at least three of my bank accounts.

"Allyson, I have afforded you a very good life. You knew I was not in love with you. You knew that I probably never would be. This was all about me making my dreams come true. It was about me meeting one final requirement to become the senior pastor at the most highly sought-after church in the nation."

"But . . ."

"But you thought over time you would change me, didn't you? You thought that after living together and pretending to be a happy couple, I would somehow walk in the door and realize I was really in love with you. Allyson, I'm not. And you being pregnant just changes things. It confuses me. I am not sure how to feel about a child with a woman I am not deeply in love with."

"That still doesn't explain why this is bad timing. You are right. I knew you were not in love with me when we mutually decided I would be your wifey. You are also partially correct in that I figured over time we would be a real couple . . . actually in love with each other. But regardless of any of that, I am pregnant with our child. This child is innocent and has nothing to do with what can really be defined as our buffoonery. Not many people agree to have a relationship with someone based on terms and conditions. But we did it."

"I am not debating that."

"So what, then, is your point, Byran? Why does this have to be such a bad thing? How will this affect our contractual agreement, because in my mind it doesn't complicate things at all. What are you not saying?"

He got up and went to lean over the balcony. He stared out into what had now become the darkness of the night for several minutes before he spoke again.

"Do you really want the truth, Allyson? Because the truth often hurts."

"Let's not talk about what hurts. It can't hurt any worse than the hurt I've felt tonight."

"Don't say that."

"Byran, just spit it out. Stop the shenanigans and just say it."

"The woman I *am* in love with . . . is pregnant too."

Those words froze in midair like the characters from the film The *Matrix* before they hit my heart like 9 mm bullets. I shook my head in hopes of waking up from what I was sure was a horrible nightmare. Surely, I did not hear what I thought I just heard.

I convinced myself it was all a joke, and laughed incredulously. He could be such a comedian at times. I dismissed his statement, got up, and walked inside. I could feel his stares boring holes into my back. I went into the kitchen, took a juice glass from the cupboard, reached into the cabinet that held the liquor, and poured myself a shot of Macallan Scotch. I turned up the glass and swallowed the Scotch before it could splash my throat.

I poured another shot.

And another one.

By the time I was done, I had taken six shots.

My stomach immediately became furious with its contents, and I had to rush to the bathroom. I gripped the porcelain throne and released the Scotch from my insides. I stayed there long after I had thrown up in hopes of regurgitating the pain, the disappointment, the hurt, and . . . the baby.

"Are you okay?"

Was he still here? Why in the hell was he still here?

"Allyson?"

Without saying anything, I found the strength to make my way to the sink. I grabbed a towel that was hanging from the brass rack, turned on the cold water, and wet my face. Maybe the coolness of the water would somehow freeze the tears that were falling again. The scent of Byran's cologne, Gucci Guilty, filled my nostrils. Without even needing to turn around, I knew he had come into the bathroom.

He grabbed me by the waist and held on to me. I knew I should push him away, but I didn't have the strength to do it. It was then I accepted the truth—my truth—that somehow over the course of time I had fallen in love with this man. And even though he had just diced my heart like a ripe tomato, I had to fight for him.

For us.

For our child.

He put his face in the crease of my neck, and I lifted my head to see our reflection in the mirror. We were the perfect-looking couple. Our public showcase was a hit among our friends, our family, and even the people at the church. All I needed to do was convince him that he loved me.

He didn't know it yet, but I was going to make him love me.

I was going to make sure that before it was over, I became the real wife and not just the wifey.

Chapter Three

My mother and I sat on the patio overlooking my Olympic-sized pool, and she listened as I recapped the events of the past weekend. She didn't seem fazed at all that my anniversary trip had ended up being a nightmare from hell.

"Allyson, you have to look at this more than one way," she said as she sipped on merlot. "I know it hurt you to hear what he had to say, but the point is you are still his legal wife. It doesn't matter who he is in love with. You are *Mrs.* Byran Ward. He chose to marry you. Whoever is also pregnant by him is the sidepiece. The sidepieces never mean anything."

"That would be the case if he was or had ever been married to me for love. Technically, I am just a legal sidepiece. I have his last name. The other woman has his heart."

I stared into space as that reality settled into my brain. My husband was in love with another woman. And she was pregnant.

"Do you know who she is?"

"I have no idea. But I am certain she is beautiful. Probably successful."

"Let's not speculate. We need to find out who she is."

"That is my least concern right now."

"No offense, but if you intend to keep your man, you need to know who the competition is and what she's about."

"My contract with him basically states that the only way he can divorce me is if I embarrass him, expose our arrangement, or commit infidelity. None of which I intend to do. So I'm not worrying about *keeping* him per se. Actually, the truth is, I never had him."

"So you did not think to include that same clause for yourself? Because if this little secret comes out that he has another woman pregnant, it would most definitely embarrass you."

"Mother, I wasn't thinking about that then. Everything about the deal favors him. After all, he was the one who came up with it, and I was the one who agreed. I'm sure whoever this woman is, if she's in love with him, she won't be saying anything to anybody about him being the father of her child."

"I still say you need to find out who she is. We need to make her go away."

"Go away?"

"Yes, go away. Especially if she lives around here."

"I never even considered that she might live here in Atlanta. Oh my goodness. What if she does? How often does he see her? Is that where he is when he isn't here at home?"

It was too much. The thoughts. The questions. The what-ifs. All. Too. Much.

"Allyson, now is not the time to allow yourself to be frazzled. You are smarter than this. Byran is not the only successful man you have been with. You are accustomed to money and to men catering to you. You seem to be getting soft when it comes to him. First thing you have to do is push your feelings aside and handle this like business, because that's what it is—business. You made a mistake by allowing yourself to fall in love with him."

"Who said I was in love?" I said, trying desperately to hold back the tears.

"I am an old woman, and I have been around love's circle a time or two in my life. I know you think I am coldhearted, but I was not always this way. I know you are in love because you are crying. You are worried. Women who don't care . . . don't care. Let me ask you a question. Are you thinking about keeping this baby?"

"Excuse me? Of course I'm keeping my baby!"

She held up her hands in defense. "Calm down. It was just a question."

"No. It was not just a question. How could you ask me that? You act as if there is another choice."

"There is. An abortion."

My mother was losing her mind. No. She had lost it.

"Mom, I don't want to continue this conversation," I said as I got up to leave.

I put my hand on the doorknob to go inside the house, but her next statement stopped me in my tracks.

"If you have the abortion, you'll win his heart."

I stood staring at the door. She continued.

"This other woman . . . I'm sure she is thinking that by having his baby, she will keep him. Truth is, neither one of you can keep him with a baby. A man who's going to cheat will do so with or without a baby. And usually when a woman is pregnant, be it his wife—or wifey, as you call it—or the sidepiece, he finds a new piece of tail he can run to. Neither of you is fun to him anymore. He has chased and conquered.

"Sweetheart, if you have the abortion, he will see how selfless you are, and he will see the extremes you are willing to go to in order to keep him happy. You will use the same mind game on him that he uses on you. It will confuse him, and he will begin to question if he really even loves this other woman. As for her . . . well, she will get big and out of shape. She will be sick and in pain, while you and Byran continue on with your lives. He will come home more often, because who wants to be around a whining and complaining woman? I have been pregnant, and that is what most women do—whine and complain."

I gave what she said some thought. My mother had never steered me wrong. She was a genius when it came to men. If it had not been for her, I would have never landed my first athlete. It was because of her, and her long friendship with one of the ladies who attended the church that Byran was the pastor at before going to Cornerstone, that I even met him. She had taught me a lot, and it had gotten me everything I had wanted out of life. Except for one thing. Love. But maybe she was right. Maybe I needed to have an abortion and wait for Byran to *want* me to have his baby.

I turned to face her.

"What if you are wrong? What if I have an abortion and he still feels the same way about her? What if he caters to her and likes being around her while she is pregnant? How am I supposed to feel when he walks out of here to go see her or when she has the baby? What am I supposed to do when she goes into labor to deliver their child? Stay here and wait by the phone and congratulate him on the birth of his child?"

"You are most definitely in love," she sighed. "Who cares about all of that? This man comes home to you every night unless he is on the road, preaching, right?"

"I thought so. But at some point he has been with her. That's how she got knocked up."

"Maybe so. But doesn't he take care of you? Pay the bills? Afford you this luxury lifestyle? Allyson, I hate to keep reminding you, but there are a million women who would love to be in your shoes." She paused and turned to me. "Honey, you just have to trust your mother on this one. Don't make the same mistakes I made. I was once in love with your father. That man took care of me. He made sure I never truly wanted for anything. But when I found out he was cheating on me with multiple women, I left. My friends tried to tell me what a fool I was being, but I did not listen. They tried their best to tell me that all men were going to cheat at some point but to hang on, because one day he would get tired, come home, and stay home. But I wanted him all to myself and was hell-bent on it. Now I regret it. Because after we divorced, I struggled to take care of you and me, and I never again had the life that he afforded me.

"And that is why I don't want you to lose your good thing, your good life, because your man can't keep his thing in his pants. Trust me, he will remember that you were the one who stuck by him when times got tough. You were the one who agreed to marry him so he could live *his* dream. Men don't forget things like that. So if you have this abortion, he will again see just how much you are willing to sacrifice for him. He will have no choice but to fall in love with you."

I pondered what she said.

She had a point. Right?

Why would I give up the beautiful life I had to make a big deal out of Byran's extramarital affairs? Like she said, it was business, anyway. Why would I tie my life down trying to raise a baby he did not want? Even though he would more than likely hire a nanny, chances were the bulk of the responsibility would be on me. He would keep going right along with his life, and I would never be able to go anywhere. I'd be stuck at home with a screaming baby.

My mother interrupted my thoughts.

"And think about how repulsed Byran will be once you start showing. You have a video model's body right now. A baby will bring on stretch marks, sagging boobs, and your thighs and hips will explode like a volcano. Do you really want that? You know how obsessed you can be about your body."

She had another point.

My body was important to me, and I worked hard to make sure I stayed in shape. From starving myself to long hours in the home gym.

"Okay, I get it. Having a baby right now may not be the best thing."

"I'm telling you it's not. Listen to an old lady. You will regret it if you don't get rid of this baby."

Those words again.

Get rid of.

"If I am going to do it, I cannot prolong it. I know I will lose the courage. I have strong spiritual convictions about women who have abortions."

"I had three, and God still loves me."

"What!" I yelled. "Three? Mom, you have never told me that," I said, baffled.

"Why would I? It's not exactly something I am proud of. But all three times . . . bad timing. Wrong guys."

She quickly turned her head to look out across the glistening blue water in the pool. Although she didn't want me to see it, I saw something else glistening. Her eyes. I felt sorry for her in that moment, because who knows what else my mother had not told me? Who knows how many times her heart had been broken?

"Wow. I'm sorry, Mom. I had no idea. I just thought maybe you never wanted any more kids or possibly couldn't have any more kids. I never knew that there would have been four of us."

She kept her eyes fastened on the water. "Five. I had one miscarriage while on a boating trip with your father. I slipped in the boat and started bleeding within minutes. I was four months pregnant."

This time I saw a tear slide down her left cheek. I had not seen her cry since my grandmother died a few years back.

"That baby . . . I wanted. We had just found out we were having a boy. Your father was elated to be having a son. If only I had just sat down, as he asked me to. But, no, I wanted to stand while he was jumping the waves."

She dropped her head, and water rushed from her eyes, as if she was reliving that time all over again. I went and sat in the patio chair next to her and laid my head on her shoulder. I cried too. Her tears were for the baby she had lost, and mine were for the baby I was thinking of killing.

"Things were never really the same with your father after that. He blamed me and never really let me forget it. He was already cheating on me, but that made it worse. You see, I was counting on that son to change him. I had hoped that once he was born, our marriage would go back to being what it once was. Our family would be complete. Our little perfect world would be perfect again. It never happened."

"So that's why you don't believe in love anymore?"

She paused for several beats. "Love is what you make it. You can love anybody. But you only get one chance to be *in* love. One. You may love others, but it will never be the same."

"Are you still in love with Daddy?"

"Your dad has moved on with his life. It doesn't matter."

"You are right, Mom. Dad has moved on with his life. But you never did."

"Of course I did. How do you think those three abortions came about? I have since loved again, but no one has loved me the way your father did."

"Evidently, he did not love you. If he had, he would have never let you go."

"I left him. I let him go. I gave him permission to move on so he could be free. I loved him enough to release him to live the lifestyle he wanted to live. It was not his lack of love for me that led him to cheat. He just had no clue or example as to how to be a faithful husband. He saw his father cheat on his mother with his own eyes, and his mother stayed. She loved the things. She loved their life. And he followed in the steps of his father, not understanding why I was not like his mother. He could never comprehend that I wanted him—not the things. I was in love with him. Not our lifestyle."

Her tears returned, and the strong, often emotionless woman I had grown to know disappeared right before me.

"I don't know what to say. You've never been this transparent with me."

"I knew the day would come when I would have to explain some things to you. I have tried to keep you sheltered from the type of pain that comes when love has failed you. In hindsight, I would have shut my mouth just like his mother did, and I would have kept my family together. I would have grown to love him, even if I had to share him."

"But, Mom, you deserved more."

"Maybe so, but I ended up with less. I've had one failed relationship after the other, and I have nothing to show for any of them." She turned to me, prompting me to lift my head from her shoulder. "That is why I wanted you to be smarter. Love is for the birds," she said, the coldness returning. "If a man is taking care of you, then forget about love. Love will make you do some crazy things, and who wants to keep doing one crazy thing after the other? You will not end up like me—in your sixties, having to thank God that your daughter married up so you will not die destitute."

"Is that why you pushed me to marry Byran?"

"It had nothing to do with Byran specifically. It could have been Peter, James, or John. The individual person did not matter. I saw it as an opportunity for you to get more out of life than I did. Because at the end of the day, when you have all the things you have, who needs love?"

We both sat in silence for another hour.

Two women.

My mother, who had loved before but had gotten badly scarred and burned by the heat of it.

I, who had never loved but possessed the desire to do what all people did when warned against touching something hot.

To touch it, anyway.

Chapter Four

"Can I talk to you for a minute?" I asked Byran as I stood outside his office door.

"But of course. Come on in," he replied with the smile that had captured me the first day I met him.

"Are you busy?" I asked, noticing that he swiftly moved his computer mouse to click something off of the screen.

"Not really. Just working on my sermon for Sunday."

"Okay." I looked down at the floor, hoping to possibly find my next words buried somewhere in the fibers of the carpet.

"Is everything okay?" he asked as he leaned forward in his oversize, traditional tufted burgundy high-back executive chair. "Is something bothering you?"

I could hear the conversation I'd had with my mother blasting over the loudspeakers of my mind. I had to keep my cool. I could not let him see me cry.

I thought of flashing him my first lady smile—the same smile I used every week to warm and woo the congregants of Cornerstone. However, he was all too familiar with it and was sure to recognize it.

"Yes, baby, I am fine. I just wanted to quickly come in and let you know I have decided to go through with the abortion. I have an appointment tomorrow morning."

His silence was deafening. So many expressions were racing across his face, I could not decipher what any of them meant.

He cleared his throat. "What made you come to this decision? Last week, when I mentioned it, you made me feel like some kind of monster. Don't get me wrong. As a Christian, I do not agree with abortions, but I understand that sometimes you have to make that tough decision. Not to mention how awful it felt and feels to expect you to abort your first child. But why the sudden change of heart?"

"Let me be clear. I have not had a change of heart. I've had a change of mind. I thought long and hard about what you said, and I agree that maybe having your child is not the best idea. We have a business deal, and it did not include having babies or a real family. So I have allowed myself to come to grips with this, and thus my decision to abort the baby. Besides that, I am sure it has to be tough on you to have one woman pregnant, let alone two."

He seemed startled that I mentioned the other baby. But it was no sense to try to overlook the very large and very pink elephant in the room.

"I don't know what to say."

"It's no big deal. I'm just the wifey," I said, plastering on the first lady smile, though I had tried to avoid doing so. "I have no right to get real *wife* feelings for you. I get paid to do a job, and that is what I am going to stick to doing."

The words coming from my mouth were as dumb as I sounded. But this whole situation was ignorant. There was no other way of saying it and no need to put candy coating on chaos.

"You make it sound so bad. Allyson, I never meant for any of this to happen. When I met you, I recognized you were a woman of sophistication, smarts, and beauty. I also knew you had an over-appreciation for nice things. And I knew that with your track record of dating high-profile individuals, you would make the perfect 'wife' for me. You knew how to handle yourself with a man of status. You looked the part. You dressed the part. It was simple. It was easy. It was the perfect plan. You assured me the day we agreed to do this that you had no interest in falling in love. I believed you."

"I never expected to love you, Byran. I guess over time I developed these feelings. I am not saying I am *in* love with you, but I do care for you deeply. I would defend you if I had to. I would stand by you if something were to ever go down, but I don't have that type of love yet that makes me feel as if I could not live without you."

"You just described how I feel."

"Do you feel that same way about the other woman?"

"I really don't want to bring her into this. She has nothing to do with how I feel about you. I would appreciate it if we not talk about her."

"I don't know how you expect me not to talk about her or want to at least know how you feel about her."

"Easy. She has nothing to do with you—or your job as my wifey."

I felt anger rising in me. I sat down on the couch. "She has a lot to do with me. Because you told me in the Bahamas that you loved this woman. She is pregnant with your child. How is that going to affect my life? Should I be worried about my future? Will you come in here one day and announce that my position has been terminated and you are leaving to go be with her and your child?"

"You already know the contract prohibits me from doing that. It clearly states that I can divorce you only for—"

"Embarrassment, my exposure of our arrangement, or infidelity on my part," I said, cutting him off. "I got that."

"Okay, then. So why would I come in one day and announce I am leaving you? Do you think I would have gone through all of this trouble to marry you for the purpose of becoming the pastor of one of the largest churches in this country, only to screw that up and become just a regular preacher with a couple hundred members? I am not a 'couple hundred members' type of pastor. I was born for the masses. Besides that, I am sure I do not have to remind you of the clause that states if I do leave you for any other reason, I will have to pay you an insane amount of money for the next twenty years. I hope this doesn't sound insensitive, but it really is cheaper to keep you." His phone vibrated. He reached to pick it up and must have forgotten to turn the feature off that announced the caller.

"Call from Leah," the voice said.

He pressed IGNORE, but he might as well have answered the phone. The expression on his face said it all. Leah was the other woman.

"Do I need to step out?"

"No, you're good," he replied while appearing to send a text. "Finish what you were saying."

"Aside from the agreement we have, this is a little difficult for me. I signed up to be the wifey, but I never signed up to be disrespected."

"If I'm not really your husband, how is it disrespect?"

"So what does Leah have to say about all of this?" I asked. "Is she okay with knowing you will never be able to be seen publicly with her or be married to her? Is she okay with being the other woman?"

"Allyson, I told you I don't want to bring any other woman into this conversation," he said, careful not to confirm who Leah was. He released a sigh filled with frustration. "This is complicated, okay? As I said, I care very deeply about you. I have just gotten myself into a situation, and there is nothing I can do about it."

"How long have you been seeing her?"

He released another sigh. "I've known her for years. We were high school sweethearts."

I almost fell off the couch. "What? This is a woman from your past? Well, if you loved her, why didn't you just marry her? Why did you even get involved with me?"

"For one, she would have never married me. She would have made me spend time I did not have proving to her I was marriage material. It didn't matter that I had money, prestige, or anything else. She knew I was not capable of giving her the one thing she wanted. The one thing she asked for over and over throughout the years of our relationship."

"And what was that?"

"Faithfulness. All she wanted was to be my only woman."

This time I released a sigh. This situation seemed to be getting worse.

"So, let me guess. You repeatedly cheated on her, broke her heart, and you went after her again because you never really stopped loving her. You just couldn't have her. And because she's still in love with you, she fell for your advances, and in the process she got pregnant. Am I right?"

He got up, slipped his phone into the pocket of his black Armani slacks, and went and stood in front of his bookshelf. Again his expression said it all. Without him needing to articulate it, I knew if he could really have what he wanted, his perfect world would include Leah and their child.

"Yes, you are correct," he said, sounding defeated.

"So when you found out she was pregnant, you never suggested to her to have an abortion, because in some small way you feel like you owe her for everything you put her through. The baby is the only part of you she will always have, no matter what. And in turn, the baby keeps you connected to her."

With one hand resting on a shelf, he dropped his head, but it wasn't before I saw tears forcefully escape his eyes.

He really loved her.

If I wanted information, I knew now was the time to get it. He was open and would probably answer any question I had.

"How far along is she?"

"Four months."

That was easy. Next question.

"Does she live here? Does she go to our church?"

"Yes. No."

"Is she excited about the baby?"

I knew I was pushing it, but I just had to know. I was getting rid of my baby in the morning. I wondered how she felt about hers.

"She has mixed feelings. She knows we will never be together now that I have this arrangement with you. She is not exactly enthused about having to raise our child in separate homes."

At least she was not overly excited. I could not bear to imagine her being elated about her child while I grieved mine.

"Understandably so. So this contract with me and your image at the church mean more to you than being with the woman you are obviously in love with?"

"Allyson, you will never understand. There are other things about me that you do not know, and I am too deep into this life I have created. It is about more than an image. This is my life. I am one of the few pastors who get called to CNN and MSNBC when tragedy strikes and they need a religious figure to weigh in on it. I am one of the few who are called when the president has a meeting and needs clergy in attendance." He stopped and exhaled. "If this was fiction, I would just rewind the hands of time and start all over. But this isn't fiction. This is real life.

"She has finally accepted I am not the knight in shining armor who will rescue her from love's dungeon. And, unlike in the storybooks, we will never have our happily ever after. So I have decided I will make the best of whatever ending I get." He moved back to his desk. "I'll always love her. But I will have to continue what I have been doing for years, loving her from a distance."

He sat back down in his chair and, with the click of his mouse, gave me the signal that the conversation was over.

The doors to his heart were now closed, and unfortunately, I was not the woman who could open them up again.

Chapter Five

My navigation system guided me through the one-way streets, which were the headaches of most downtown areas. While I knew my way around downtown Atlanta, I was as lost as a bat in downtown Augusta.

"You have arrived. Your destination is on the right," the GPS lady announced.

I pulled into the parking lot and parked my car. I lowered my Moss Lipow sunglasses and took a glance at the gray, dingy building, which wore no sign or any indication that it was an abortion clinic. I surveyed the people who were walking by. I knew none of them. Augusta was outside of Atlanta just enough for me to feel comfortable going to have this procedure done, and I was certain I would not be recognized. The last thing I needed was to get an abortion in Atlanta and have an intake nurse who was a member of Cornerstone or the cousin of a member of Cornerstone, or a friend of a member of Cornerstone. I shuddered at the thought.

Severe cramps ambushed me, temporarily taking my focus off of the abortion clinic. I leaned my head back against the headrest and waited for them to subside. After about ten long, agonizing minutes, the pain was tolerable enough for me to get my bearings and prepare to go inside. I grabbed my Hermès bag, slid my sunglasses back up, and exited the car. The quicker I got inside, the quicker I would be on my way back home. I needed this to be over with so I could go back to living my life—and being emotionless.

I walked into the building, and surprisingly there was no one in the waiting room. That meant either not many people had abortions in Augusta or not many visited this facility to have it done. I looked around the room. It felt cold and uninviting. It had no warmth whatsoever. It was almost as if you could feel death hiding behind the walls, in the corners, underneath the floors. I wondered how many souls of babies had cried out to be saved.

I shook away that thought and made my way to the registration desk.

"Hello. Please sign in, select the type of abortion you are having today, and complete this paperwork. After you have completed the paperwork, bring it back to me and I will get everything set up for your procedure," the receptionist stated.

"Okay. You mentioned the *type* of abortion. I am not familiar with the types of abortion."

"This clinic offers two types. The one most commonly done is called the aspiration. The other is the D and E."

"Which do you recommend?"

"Ma'am, I really can't provide any input or opinion. It is totally up to your discretion which you prefer."

The little heifer didn't have to be so curt about it. This was hard enough on the patients who came in this place for an abortion, and dealing with a not so nice receptionist did not help.

I sat down in one of the metal chairs, which reminded me of the chairs that we had in my home church's basement. The same chairs I sat in as a child in Sunday school. How I wished I was sitting in a church chair now.

I scanned the paperwork. It included the usual consent forms, privacy forms, and medical history questionnaire. I filled out the information and flipped to the other pages detailing the abortion procedures. After reading over the two options for the abortion, I selected the aspiration. It was only a five- to ten-minute operation, was the most common, and had fewer risks.

The door to the clinic opened, and an older woman walked in. She appeared to be in her mid- to late forties. Her hair was pulled into a ponytail and wrapped into a ball on top of her head. If it were not for the bags and the wrinkles plaguing her eyes, she could have passed for a much younger lady. Wearing a pink and purple velour suit, she made her way to the front desk. Assuming she was a part of the staff, I focused my attention back on my paperwork to make sure I had completed it all.

"Hello. Please sign in select the type of abortion you are having today, and complete this paperwork. After you have completed the paperwork, bring it back to me and I will get everything set up for your procedure," the receptionist stated.

My head shot up. Was she talking to that older woman? *She* was here for an abortion too? Nah, couldn't be.

The older lady made her way past me to sit down. She reached into a worn leather purse and retrieved her glasses. *Women her age can still get pregnant?* She caught me staring at her and turned her body slightly away from me. No doubt she was probably as embarrassed as I was. But for some reason I could not pull my eyes away from her. She had the most intriguing and stunning look.

"Do I know you?" the woman asked. It caught me off guard, because I was not expecting her to say anything.

"I . . . I . . . I don't think so," I stammered.

"Then why are you staring at me? For goodness' sake, didn't your mother ever teach you that it was impolite to stare at people?"

I cleared my throat. "Yes. Yes, she did. You just have this stunning beauty about you," I said.

"Next time just say that. You make a person feel uncomfortable when you gaze at them."

"You are right. I apologize."

"It's fine." She glanced down at my lap. "Are you done with your forms? You should probably go and take them to Cindy."

"Cindy?"

"Yes, Cindy. She's the receptionist."

"You know her?"

"Not on a personal level. Hell, I don't think anyone knows her on a personal level. She comes in here, does her job exactly by the book, and leaves no room for cordialness. She has the same script for everybody, no matter how many times she's seen you."

"You . . . you . . . you come here . . . often?"

She dropped her head and cast her eyes to the floor.

"I'm sorry. That's none of my business," I said, hoping to ease my way out of her business.

"No, it's okay," she said as she picked up the pen to begin filling out the forms. "I opened myself up for that question. Yes, I've been here more times than I care to admit. Eight, to be exact."

My hands flew to my chest in shock. *Eight?*

"Wow. I don't know what to say."

"I don't, either, anymore. I am forty-six years old, and I continuously ask God why He keeps allowing me to get pregnant. There are so many women out there who would love to be able to have children and never do. Or they struggle to. Me? I've killed eight babies, and this will make nine. I do not want kids and never will."

Her words held little to no emotion at all. Neither did they contain any remorse. This seemed like a regular doctor's appointment to her and not a shameful act.

"What does your husband think? Does he know you keep, um, killing his babies?"

"Husband?" She laughed hysterically. "I don't have a husband. I have not had a husband for almost twenty years now. My husband walked away from me when I was thirty. He left me for another woman and her kids."

"I am sorry to hear that."

"Don't be sorry. He made his choice. I am happy with myself."

"So your boyfriend . . ."

"No real boyfriend, either. Look, honey, you probably know nothing about the lifestyle I live. Look at you. The Christian Louboutins you are wearing cost more than my car outside. You are a woman of status. A woman of class. You have no idea about the street life. Matter of fact, I cannot imagine what you would be doing in a place like this."

"I am here for the same reason you are—to have an abortion. In here you and I are the same. It doesn't matter that I have money, status, or class. In here I am a woman killing my baby."

Saying it in that way pierced my heart. *I am a woman killing my baby.*

"Why are you doing it? I can look at your face and tell you don't really want to go through with this."

"I don't, but my husband is not ready for a baby. It's a long story."

"But what do *you* want? Do you have a say-so in this matter?"

"Not really. It would cause more problems than I am willing to deal with."

"Do you ever want to have kids, though?"

"Most definitely. I just don't know if I ever will."

"I started having abortions the year my husband left me. I was pregnant at the time he walked away. He had gone on and on about not wanting kids, so when I got pregnant that year, I immediately had the abortion. Imagine how I felt when I found out the woman he was leaving me for had kids. It was a hard slap in the face, because at that time I still wanted to have kids. Well, after we got divorced and he moved on, I eventually moved on as well. Well, I tried to. I've never really moved on, because one thing about it, I loved that man. Would have died for him."

"Why didn't you fight to keep him, then?"

Her story was beginning to sound like my mother's. And it seemed they both had one thing in common. They didn't fight to save their marriages the way I was going to fight to win Byran's heart. Some things and people are worth fighting for. Especially the ones you loved.

"Oh, I fought. I fought the way I knew how, but she had what he was looking for at the time. And no matter what I did, it was not enough. I mentally checked out of the marriage, and eventually he left."

"Either of you ladies done with your forms? We have a slew of appointments coming in in just under an hour," Cindy said.

"We'll be there in a minute," the woman answered.

"What's your name?" I asked.

"Helen. Yours?"

"Allyson." She held out her hand, and I shook it. "Nice to meet you, Helen."

"You, too, little girl. So are you going to go up there and get this show on the road? You will be fine. It doesn't take that long. You'll be out of here in no time."

Good.

"Yes, I guess I will go on and get this over with."

"You can always walk out that door. You do not have to do this. This is still your choice. I choose to be in here today, and I chose it every other time I came. I have been a professional side chick, as they call it, since my husband walked away. So basically, I make a living and sustain my lifestyle by sleeping with other people's husbands. And every time I get careless and slip up, I find myself in here, doing away with yet another child."

"Did you say a professional side chick?" This woman was honest to a fault. Who would actually admit that to someone out loud?

"Yes, that's what I said. I have learned to be happy and content with getting the financial benefits of sharing a man versus having him as my own. They cater to me when they are in town, or on the weekends their wives are out of town, or on the days when they are supposed to be at work. I live a good life. My bills are paid, and I have a few things I want. I'm good with that. Who needs love, right?"

Her words were empty, yet full of emotion. She sounded more like she was trying to convince herself of what she was saying.

"We all need love, Ms. Helen. Even those of us who kill our babies," I said somberly.

"Well, I had my one shot at it. And it slipped out of my grip."

"Don't close your heart to it. It might just find you again."

"Ha. Doubt it. I am too old now."

"Ms. Helen, you are not too old." I laughed. "Forty-six is the new twenty-five."

That made her chuckle, and for the first time since I started talking to her, I saw a little light in her eyes. I reached into my purse and pulled out a pen and a piece of paper. I wrote my number on it and gave it to her.

"If you ever want to talk to someone, call me. I would love for us to continue our conversation," I said, smiling, hoping she would take me up on the offer. "I live in Atlanta, but I wouldn't mind driving back down here for lunch or something."

"Atlanta? No wonder you are all prissy. You didn't strike me as a woman who lived here," she said jokingly. "Why did you drive all the way here for an abortion? I'm sure there are tons of clinics there."

"Long story."

"Didn't want to be seen, huh?"

"Exactly."

"I understand."

"Ladies?" Cindy called out again.

"We are coming," Ms. Helen snapped. "Don't be rushing us."

"It was nice talking to you. I hope to speak to you again soon," I said as I stood up.

"Go on now, child. Ms. Helen too old to be crying," she said, half joking . . . half serious.

I gathered my things and walked toward Cindy. There was something special about Ms. Helen, and I silently prayed that she would call me. She needed a fresh hope, and maybe I was the one to give it to her.

Cindy flipped through the forms to make sure they were all completed.

"Come around through this side door. We need to do some lab work, followed by a physical and an ultrasound."

I followed her directions and went through the door, which led me to a small examining room.

"Here's a robe. Strip down, and put this robe on. Dr. Carson will be in momentarily. Celeste will be your nurse," she said and walked out of the room.

There were no pictures on the wall, no diagrams of the female reproductive system, no posters of smiling women. There were only pamphlets and brochures about different methods of birth control.

I took off my clothes and draped them over the chair that was sitting, isolated, in the corner. I slowly climbed onto the exam table. And waited.

Finally, after what seemed like forever, the door opened and a tall, very handsome doctor entered the room.

"Allyson?"

"Yes?" I answered, mesmerized by his light brown eyes and smooth, semisweet chocolate morsel–like skin. My pride wouldn't let me fan myself, but I wanted to.

"I'm Dr. Seth Carson. I and my nurse, Celeste, will be performing your procedure today."

Back in the day, I would have jumped at the chance to spread my legs for him, but I was a changed woman. However, this man was fine—in every sense of the word. And it did not help that I was feeling vulnerable.

"Here is what's going to happen," he continued, almost with the same attitude and personality—or lack thereof—as Cindy. "Once Celeste does your lab work, your physical, and an ultrasound, I'll come in and examine your uterus. If there are no roadblocks to be concerned about, I will administer you a sedative and place a numbing medication at the opening of your cervix. I will then proceed to open your cervix, insert a tube, and use a suction device to empty the uterus of its contents. Once I get started, it'll be over in ten minutes or less. Do you have any questions?"

"Yes."

"What are they?"

"There's only one. Is it too late to change my mind?"

Chapter Six

"Ms. Ward, you can elect to do whatever you choose. Just consider all the reasons you chose to get an abortion in the first place. If those reasons still exist, then I would advise you to follow through with it."

He had a point.

"I just do not want to live with the guilt of killing my baby. What if I am unable to have any more kids? I will forever blame this abortion."

"We do understand those concerns," the nurse said. "We have a list of counselors that we can recommend to you that will help you maneuver through your feelings once this is over. Trust me, I have been where you are—on that very table. I know it's not a walk in the park, and I would be lying if I did not warn you of the many emotions you will have afterward. But it gets better. You are here because in your heart you know this is the right thing to do."

She, too, had a point.

But although both of them had valid points, I still had reservations. My mind wandered back to the conversation I had just had with Ms. Helen. Did I want to end up like her? Did I want to run from the problems I had created with my very own actions? Did I want to keep killing innocent babies for selfish reasons? I knew that if I started, it would get easier each time.

Dr. Carson glanced at his watch. "I don't want you to think you are not important, but I do have other patients waiting for me. I know this is a difficult decision for any woman to make, so do you want to leave and take some time to think about it? Cindy can reschedule you to come back another day—after you have had more time to think this through," Dr. Carson said. This time he actually sounded concerned.

"Ms. Ward, before you answer Dr. Carson, I would just like to ask if you have discussed this with your boyfriend. I know it's harder to make the decision when you have not had the opportunity to talk it out with your significant other."

Boyfriend? Why does everyone keep assuming I have a boyfriend and not a husband?

"My *husband* and I did talk it over, as a matter of fact. He is the reason I am here," I said as tears threatened to fall.

"Nurse, please give me a moment with Mrs. Ward," Dr. Carson stated.

The nurse left the two of us alone.

"I normally do not get involved in the psychology side of this, because it is not my place. So I hope you don't mind the questions I am about to ask you. If you do, just simply say that and I will leave you alone. Do you mind if I get a little personal with you for a minute?"

The tears were fighting to win, but I held them back. However, I knew where his questions were going to take me. Straight down teary lane.

"Why in God's name would your husband be the reason you are here?"

I knew it. The million-dollar question.

"He isn't ready for a baby. And, to be honest, the more I think about it, I'm not, either."

"Is that the truth?"

"Is what the truth?"

"That you aren't ready for a baby. Or are you just saying that to cover up how you really feel?"

Dr. Carson really could have been a psychologist or a mind reader, because he was all in my thoughts. Was I that easy to read?

"Doctor, my situation is complicated. It really is. There is no right or wrong answer in my scenario. So, as I said, I don't think I am ready for a baby—especially because of the things going on in my life."

He studied me. His piercing gaze penetrated my eyes, causing me to look down into my lap. Those tears were pushing harder.

"I see. Sounds like you are married to a jerk, if you ask me. But, hey, who's asking me?"

"He is not a jerk," I said defensively. "That man has done a lot for me. He takes care of me, gives me anything I desire, and he is a good friend too."

"So why has he convinced you to kill your baby? What kind of man does that? What kind of husband does that?"

He was starting to piss me off. I hadn't minded the questions at first, but the insults were beginning to get under my skin.

"No disrespect, but the same could be said about you. You kill babies for a living. Exactly how does your wife feel about that?" I shot back.

"First of all, I am not married. Secondly, this is a job. This is how I make a living, pay the bills, and set myself up for the woman that I will one day marry and the family I will one day have. So let's be clear about that. What I do for a profession has nothing to do with my own personal convictions about it."

"Obviously, you have no convictions about it. You do this every day, as if it is a normal thing to do."

"I do have convictions. That is why I am not in there performing a procedure on another patient whose mind is made up. But I am in here with you, hoping to help you make the best decision for you."

"Whatever. You get paid to take lives. Only a cold person can take money with blood attached to it and walk around as if he or she deserves it."

I might not have been sure about getting the abortion, but I was sure about getting the hell up out of there. I held the robe closed as I got up to get my clothes. He reached out and grabbed my arm.

"Excuse you? I want to put my clothes on and leave. This was a mistake," I said, pulling my arm away from him.

Suddenly he softened his tone. It was almost as if he could see straight through the mock defense shield I was desperately trying to keep up.

"Allyson, you love him way more than he will ever love you. Can't you see it? He doesn't really love you. I am a man. When a man is in love with his wife, he *wants* her to have his child. He wants to see a beautiful product that was created from their love," he said as he moved closer to me. "And as beautiful as you are, who wouldn't want you to have their child?" he asked as he pulled me into his arms.

He was so close, I could feel the heat from his words. I knew I should have gotten my belongings and run, but I could not pull myself away from his words—his embrace. The truth was I needed this.

"You are so beautiful, Allyson. If I were your man, I would give you the love you deserve."

"How do you know what I deserve?" The tears had won and were now flowing freely down my face.

"I am a good judge of character. You may not be a perfect woman, but you are a woman with a good heart. And you need a man who can handle it with care."

His words were like water to a dry and thirsty land. I knew it was naive of me to put any stock in what he said—I had seen his type before. However, just like in times past, I fell for his type.

I used my right hand to brush away the falling tears, and my left to push away from him. I was becoming unglued and needed to pull myself together.

"Thank you, Dr. Carson, for . . ."

"Call me Seth."

Startled, I said, "Thank you, Seth, for being concerned. I really appreciate it. Can we move forward with the procedure, please?"

He looked at me for several minutes before he spoke again. "Are you sure? If you want to keep this baby, then keep it."

"No, I am sure. Can we please just get this over with before my mind falls back into limbo again?"

"I'll get the nurse."

When he disappeared on the other side of the door, I unleashed all the tears. They crashed against my face like waves on the beach. Not to mention, those terrible cramps from earlier had returned. *Great.* First, pain in my heart, and now pain in my body. This day could not get any worse.

After what seemed like a day, the door to the room opened again.

"Allyson, we are ready to perform your procedure. May we come in?" Dr. Carson asked, and this time comfort laced his words.

"Yes, I am ready."

The nurse opened the cabinets and took out everything they would need.

"Mrs. Ward, please lie back. We're going to draw some blood and perform an ultrasound. Once the ultrasound is performed, I am going to examine your uterus," Dr. Carson said in a professional tone. "Do you have any questions so far?"

I shook my head no.

They did as planned, and when the nurse rolled the ultrasound machine over to me, my heart starting beating faster. I decided I would close my eyes, because there was no way I could look at my baby on a screen and then kill it. No way.

The nurse spread a cold blue gel over my stomach, and Dr. Carson rubbed the probe across it.

"It is not uncommon for us to not be able to see anything unless you are further along than you think," he said.

"Okay," I said, still refusing to look at the screen.

He maneuvered the wand around my stomach in silence for a few minutes before speaking again.

"As I thought, I don't see anything in the sac. Not even a heartbeat."

"Are you going to the do the vaginal ultrasound?" the nurse asked.

"Yes," he answered. He grabbed another wand, a skinnier one, and put some gel on it. "Mrs. Ward, I am going to insert this inside your vagina. Open your legs and relax."

I followed his command, but with hesitation. After the moment we had shared earlier, I felt some type of way opening my legs for him.

"Allyson, we have a slight problem. Well, not a problem to be alarmed about, but this abortion may not be necessary," he said.

"Huh? I do not understand."

"You are bleeding. This could be nothing, or it could mean you are in the beginning stages of a miscarriage. Not that a miscarriage is any better, but since you were having reservations earlier about having an abortion, this may be to your benefit."

Huh? Miscarriage? Was this a blessing or a curse? After what seemed like the longest five seconds ever, I breathed a sigh of relief. He was right. I would much rather be having a miscarriage than an abortion. If I was losing the baby on my own, then it was a sign this baby was not supposed to come into the world in the first place.

He inserted the wand, and this time I looked at the screen. To me, everything looked black and fuzzy. I strained my eyes in hopes of seeing something more, but it was no use.

"I do not see a heartbeat. Do you?" he asked the nurse.

"No, sir. I don't see one," she replied.

He moved the wand around some more, which produced some discomfort.

"I am pretty confident—about ninety-nine percent confident—that you are indeed having a miscarriage." He removed the wand. "We can go ahead and perform a D and C since you are here, and remove any remaining remnants of the pregnancy from your uterus. You will more than likely bleed for a few days, maybe even longer, and you might experience some period-like cramps."

I'm already experiencing beyond period-like cramps. Tears of relief and sorrow merged and trickled down my face. I was happy that I was not going to have to live the rest of my life carrying the guilt of having killed my first child. On the other hand, knowing that my baby had died all by itself was heartbreaking. My body had defied me.

The nurse walked over, handed me some tissues, and I lay there, numb, as they performed the D and C. I was lost somewhere in thoughts of Byran, our deceased child, and Dr. Carson when he let me know it was done.

It was over. The baby's remains had been sucked into a vacuum-like contraption.

"Other than anything emotional, how are you feeling?" he asked.

"I feel fine," I stated solemnly.

"Okay. Well, everything is taken care of. You can get dressed and stop by the discharge desk and get your discharge information. I am going to prescribe you a pain medication just in case you need it," he said as he stood. He extended his hand toward mine. "It was a pleasure serving you, Mrs. Ward. I do hope everything works out for you."

"Me, too, Mrs. Ward," the nurse said sympathetically.

"Dr. Carson, can I speak to you privately for one second?" I asked.

The nurse cast a questioning glance at him to make sure it was okay for her to leave. After nodding his assurance, she exited the room.

"What can I do for you, Allyson?"

I slowly sat up on the exam table, swung my legs over the edge, and reached my hand out for him to take. He took it, and I pulled him closer.

"You can make me forget," I said as tears once again began to sting my eyes.

He leaned down and kissed me passionately, and our lips welded together as the kiss deepened. If I did not know any better, I would have thought he meant it.

I would have thought he loved me.

But I knew that was not the case.

Nobody loved me.

Chapter Seven

Was I seeing things? Was a pregnant woman walking out of my house, holding my husband's hand?

I opened the door to the car and slowly stepped out.

This is not what it looks like. This man does not have his pregnant mistress at your house. No, he is not that stupid.

Byran looked as if he had seen a ghost when he saw me approaching them. Was he so caught up in this woman that he totally missed me driving up and then sitting in the driveway?

"Allyson, um . . . this . . . this . . . is Shatrice," he said, stammering.

I exhaled and was grateful her name was anything other than Leah.

She extended her hand. "Nice to meet you, Allyson. I was just leaving." When I looked at her hand as if she had leprosy, she quickly realized I was not in the mood to be cordial. Giving up, she turned to Byran. "I'll see you later."

"Be safe getting home," he told her.

The lady walked by me and went to her car.

She was about my height, with a bad weave, and nothing about her wardrobe said designer. Her clothes looked as if they had come straight out of the clearance section of Value Village. She was not an ugly girl, just plain. Not Byran's type at all, which convinced me even the more that she was not *the* woman.

"Is she a relative?"

"We will get to who she is. I want to know how you are. How did things go today?"

Remembering the argument we'd had earlier this morning about him not going to support me in a decision I made solely because of him, I got angry all over again, and the memories of this dreadful afternoon came rushing back.

"The baby is gone."

Silence.

More silence.

Ending the standoff, I walked past him and into the house. All I wanted to do was get to my bed.

"That's it? That's all you're going to say?" he asked, following me inside.

I whirled around. "What else do you want me to say? I left here to kill our baby, and the baby is dead. I don't know what else can be added to that," I snapped.

"Why do you have to say it so callously? I know you are upset because I could not go, but you already knew I had a previous appointment. I asked you to reschedule for tomorrow, and you insisted on today."

"The point I was making this morning and will continue to make is there are some things you should do for me just because you care. Not because it is a part of my contract or agreement, but just because I am your friend, Byran. At least before we got married, you treated me like a person. You treated me like I mattered. It has only been a year, and already you are treating me like some ho you met on the street. Is that how you see me? Because if I had known that I was going to be treated like an accessory, I would have never agreed to this arrangement." I plopped down on my cherry velvet sofa. "There was a time when it wasn't all business between us. What happened?"

He walked over to the cabinet that held the liquor and poured a shot. He quickly downed it before walking over to the windows to look out.

"Do you think any of this is easy for me? I mean, really? Do you think I get joy out of seeing you hurt? Do you think I like feeling like a slimeball all of the time, or staying awake, tossing and turning, asking myself if any of this was worth it?" He turned to me. "Because if you think I do, then you are wrong. So wrong. Real wrong. I hate feeling this way. I hate disappointing you time after time. I hate that I was selfish enough to marry you for my own personal reasons, knowing my heart truly belonged to someone else.

"How do you think I feel each time a young couple at our church comments on what a beautiful couple we make or how we are their role models? It makes me feel like a hypocrite. When we first agreed to do this, it seemed like the perfect idea. You said you wanted a certain lifestyle, and I had the means to provide it." He went and poured another shot.

"I guess it's true. Money can't buy you love," I commented.

He turned to me again. "But that's just it. We never wanted love. Money was good enough for you in the beginning, and status was good enough for me. It was a match made in heaven."

"Or hell."

He sighed. "What do you want from me? What do you want me to do?"

"I just want you to act concerned. No, I want you to be concerned for me when times get tough. I want you to actually show you have a heart. I want you to care about me as your friend, if nothing else."

Suddenly a pain attacked my stomach, and I screamed. Byran rushed to me immediately.

"Are you okay? What's wrong?"

It took a second for me to capture my breath. "I'm fine. The doctor told me I might experience some cramps. That was one of them."

He wiped the sweat that had quickly formed on my forehead and pushed a strand of hair away from my face. I looked into his eyes, which were fixed on me.

"You are so beautiful, Allyson," he said as he continued brushing and stroking my face with the back of his thumb. "I'm lucky to have found you. I'm blessed to have you as my . . . friend."

"I'm your wife!" was what I wanted to scream, but I knew it would not make a difference. His heart was someone else's, and my energy to argue was nonexistent. I searched for words and could not find them. This had been a horrible day, and it seemed to be getting worse.

"I'm going to bed. I want to pretend today never happened," I said finally.

"I understand. I'll be up soon. Do you need anything? Have you had dinner?"

"No and no. I have no appetite. But if you don't mind, I have a prescription for pain medication in my purse. Go get it filled for me, please."

"Sure, anything you want or need. If you think of anything else, just text me. I'll go do that right now."

He helped me up from the sofa, as if I was fragile, and I climbed the stairs to our bedroom with him at my side. Just as I got to the top, I remembered something.

"Byran?"

"Yes, babe?"

"Who was that woman that was here earlier?"

Silence.

A moment later, he said, "Oh, that was . . . that was my cousin."

I stood for a second, trying to recall if I had seen her at our wedding. With the pain racking my body, and the memories of the day and the past week, I could barely remember if I was coming or going. So I definitely could not remember everybody who attended our wedding.

"Why was she here?"

"Babe, get some rest. I'll tell you later. I'm gone," he said as he turned to walk back down the stairs. a few moments later I heard the chime that signaled he had walked out the door.

Thoughts of the woman and why she was here faded as I walked in my bedroom and the soothing chocolate and gold hues greeted me. The smell of my lavender plug-ins tickled my nostrils, and immediately I felt my body begin to relax. I walked into my closet and sat down on the leather ottoman that was positioned in the center of the floor. I removed my earrings and placed them on the marble island in front of me. I reached down and pulled open my mini-refrigerator and selected a smartwater. I popped the top and took a few sips as I surveyed my closet. Gucci this. Gucci that. Gucci everywhere. Nothing was basic. From the shoes to the blouses to the jewelry—everything was designer. The items in just this closet alone had to be worth more than a hundred thousand dollars, if not more.

I dropped my head. All of this stuff and none of it was making me happy, as I had hoped. I stood, opened one of my drawers, and pulled out a tiny gray box. I lifted the cover and removed the picture that was inside. It was a picture of me, Mom, and Dad when I was younger. When they were married. When they were happy. When they were in love.

I studied the photo for a minute before I carefully placed it back in the box and lifted the gold herringbone necklace. It was the first piece of jewelry I had ever owned. My dad had scraped together enough money to purchase it for my thirteenth birthday. I smiled as it brought back memories. . . .

"Allyson, come in here. I have a surprise for you," my dad said.

I bounced into the living room, where Dad was sitting. Mom was in the kitchen, putting the finishing touches on my strawberry birthday cake.

"Yes, Dad?" I said as I plopped down in his lap and planted a huge kiss on his cheek.

"You know I love you, right, baby girl?"

I was cheesing. I loved when he called me that.

"Yes, Daddy, I know. I'm your bestest girl in the whole wide world."

"That's right. And don't you let anyone tell you anything different. Now, I might not live here anymore with you and Mom, but there ain't nothing I won't do for you. Okay?"

"I know that, Daddy. Now, what did you get me for my birthday?" I asked, unable to contain my excitement.

He pulled a long black box from behind him. "Happy birthday, suga."

I squealed in excitement. I grabbed the box and broke through the bow in two seconds flat. Every girl in my class had the one thing I wanted, and I knew my dad would not disappoint. I opened the lid to reveal the shiny gold necklace. I squealed again, this time grabbing my father around his neck. I squeezed him so tight, he pretended to be choking from suffocation.

"Thank you, thank you, thank you! You are the best dad ever," I shrieked. "I am never taking off this one-hundred-karat gold herringbone in my life. Not even to wash my neck."

He laughed. "It's not one hundred karats, Ally."

"Well, I don't care. I am never taking it off."

I smiled at the thought as I placed the necklace back in the box. I had kept my promise for a long time. I wore the necklace so much, it left a mark on me. Six years later my first rich boyfriend, NFL player Damon Hall, convinced me that gold was for little girls and diamonds were for grown women. He replaced the gold herringbone, which had once meant so much to me, with a platinum necklace that held yellow and white diamonds. It was the most beautiful piece of jewelry I had ever seen. It was also on that day that I realized simple was no longer good enough for me. I needed extraordinaire. I needed the bling.

I put the lid back on the gray box, and on my memories, and put the box back in its place. If only I could go back to the day of my thirteenth birthday and start my life from there.

My phone ringing in the other room interrupted my trip down memory lane. I walked over to it and picked it up to see an unfamiliar number. I didn't feel like talking to anyone right now. I just wanted to relax. I sent the call to voice mail and decided to do just that. I didn't even bother to put my clothes away properly. I let my skirt and blouse fall to the floor.

Wearing just my panties and bra, I pulled the satin comforter back and tried to bury my entire body in the fibers of the sheets.

The phone rang again. Same unknown number. *What city has a 706 area code?*

I sent the call to voice mail again.

I closed my eyes and exhaled. Tomorrow morning the thoughts of this day would be long gone. Just as I was preparing to drift off into the land of sleep, the phone buzzed. Whoever had called had left a message.

I debated listening to it, but ultimately curiosity got the best of me.

"Allyson, this is Seth Carson. I, um, just wanted to check on you to see how you were feeling and to check and make sure you had made it home safely." There was a pause before he continued. "I know I am way out of line, but I want to see you again. Away from the office. I'm coming to Atlanta in a couple of weeks for a medical conference. I thought about what you said, and I think it's time for me to explore another area in my field. Thanks for being an eye-opener. So, hopefully, you will call me back. I'm sure you saw the number on your caller ID. It's my cell. Call me."

My heart was beating rapidly. I wasn't sure if it was because he had actually called or if it was because he thought enough of me to check on me—to show concern. Or it could have been the heat building up within me when I thought about the kiss we shared. Whichever it was had me giddy and confused.

I contemplated calling him back, but I had no idea what to say. A part of me wanted to see him again, and a part of me knew it was wrong to even consider it. Then again, was it wrong? My marriage wasn't a real marriage. It was a business arrangement, as I had been reminded of a lot recently. But I was still on my mission to get Byran to love me. No, I couldn't call back.

I touched the button on my phone that led me to my screen for texts. Texting was safer than calling.

Seth, sorry I missed your call. Don't really feel up to talking right now. I'll try to reach out to you some other time. Take care & all the best, Allyson

I waited for his reply, and it never came.

It was for the best.

Chapter Eight

"Good morning, Lady Allyson. As always, you look gorgeous. That St. John knit was made for you," said Damita, my assistant at church.

"Thank you. You know your pastor loves to see me in my knits," I said, smiling my best first lady smile.

"Indeed he does."

"Pastor, don't forget you and First Lady have breakfast this morning with the deacons and their spouses. Everyone is there except for Deacon Walters. He isn't feeling well this morning and won't be attending the breakfast or service," said Renae, Byran's assistant.

"Thank you, Renae. Can you go into the conference room and let them know that I am on the premises and will be there shortly?" Byran replied.

"Yes, sir. Do you want apple, orange, or cranberry juice this morning?"

"Cranberry. But I also want a cup of—"

"Coffee. Two sugars and two creams," she said, finishing his sentence for him.

That irked me. The little heifer was always walking around bragging about how well she knew him. It was obvious to everybody around that she had a thing for Byran. Oh, well. She was too simple. He would never even look at someone who looked like her.

"You have a great memory, Renae," Byran said.

"That's not a testament to a great memory, Pastor. Anybody could remember how you take your coffee if they prepared it for you several times a day, every day," Damita said, looking directly at Renae.

Renae shook her head. "Oh, hush, Damita. You are such a hater. But I am not going to let you steal my joy. Because the joy of the Lord is my strength. I bet you don't even know where that is found in the Bible, do you?"

"I am sure you are going to tell us all," Damita said, rolling her eyes.

"You are right. It is in the book of Nebuchadnezzar, chapter eight, verse number ten," Renae said proudly.

We all immediately stopped walking. Damita and I exchanged a glance, as did Byran and I. The three of us were waiting on the burst of laughter that was sure to come from Renae at any moment. Instead, she looked at us as if we were the ones who had uttered something so ridiculous.

"You just showed your stupidity, Renae. There is no such book in the Bible. You meant Nehemiah," Damita said.

Embarrassment flooded Renae's face. She had been serious. "Of course I know that. I was just playing," she said, laughing nervously. She turned to Byran. "Pastor, you know I was just playing, right?"

"Don't make our pastor lie when you know he has to preach this morning. Our pastor is a man of integrity, and causing him to lie shows just what kind of woman you are—let alone an assistant," Damita said.

I knew she was talking to Renae, but Damita's words caused me to grimace. Little did they both know we were both already liars. We lived a lie.

"Renae, it is fine. We all make mistakes. I am confident that you knew there was no such book in the Bible called Nebuchadnezzar," Byran assured his assistant.

"I bet she didn't," Damita shot back.

"Damita, it does not matter. Let us not highlight our sister's weakness, if that be the case," Byran said, totally taking control of the situation. He was great at being a pastor. "Both of you ladies are my stellar students in Bible Study. I am proud of the progress you have both made. That is why you both get to have positions that a thousand others would love to have. Only the best could assist my wife and me. And you two are the best."

He had successfully squashed the beef and had made both ladies feel affirmed. He was quite the charmer.

We walked into our joint office, and Byran darted into his restroom to put on his tie. I walked into my space in the office and went directly to my floor-length mirror to check the status of my perfection. Still satisfied with the reflection I saw, I went and sat down on my oversize, lemon-colored chaise, which flanked one side of the room. It was my favorite piece of furniture in all of the church. No sooner had I sat down than Byran popped in and announced he was ready to head to the breakfast.

We walked into the conference room, where the deacons and their spouses had already begun eating. I surveyed the breakfast choices. From grits to hash browns to pecan waffles . . . there was everything you could imagine.

"Good morning, everyone," Byran said.

"Morning, Pastor. So glad to have you and our stunning first lady join us for our first Quarterly Deacon's Breakfast," said Deacon Stanley, the chairman.

"And we are indeed honored to be here," Byran replied, grabbing me by the waist and pulling me closer. "I see you all have already started partaking in this heavenly feast. My, my, my, this is a lot of food. Who on earth prepared all of this?"

"I would have you to know my wife and Deacon Sparks's wife made everything you see here—and from scratch," Deacon Stanley said as he looked proudly at his wife, who was sitting next to him.

"Yeah, Pastor, my old lady here is a monster of a cook," Deacon Sparks added. "That's how she got me."

The light moment caused laughter to erupt throughout the room.

"Well, First Lady and I are ready to dig in, aren't we, honey?" said Byran.

I nodded. "Yes, Pastor. I'm famished."

"First Lady, you do look amazing this morning. Actually, you do every Sunday, but that turquoise color really brings out your skin," complimented Deaconess Adams, one of the younger deacons' wife.

"Thank you, darling. You look radiant yourself," I said as I sat down in my seat.

As soon as Byran sat down, two ladies from the kitchen staff entered the room. One went over to Byran and the other to me to find out what we wanted to eat. They prepared our orders and brought us our plates. The food was delicious.

"Pastor, again, we appreciate you and First Lady joining us this morning. We are blessed that we get to meet with you on a weekly basis to handle the business affairs of the church, but we also wanted to have a time to get together to fellowship with you outside of business. Also, our wives haven't had the chance to spend any time with you and your wife. So that's why we are here this morning."

Byran nodded. "I think this was a great idea, Deacon Stanley. I look forward to these quarterly meetings."

"First Lady, I know it has only been a year, but all of us ladies are just dying to know when we can expect an addition to the first family," Deaconess Stanley said as the other ladies chimed in, in agreement.

The water I was drinking spewed from my mouth and landed in the center of the table.

All eyes fell on me.

It was an innocent question, but the timing of it could not have been worse. Unbeknownst to them, I had just lost my baby a few days ago, and to be asked about children unnerved me. I was tempted to lose my composure and add tears to the water I had spit across the table, but I remained poised. I went into my first lady role immediately, forced a smile on my face, and gave them an explanation.

"I do apologize, Deaconess Stanley, for my outburst. Your question caught me off guard."

"No, I apologize, Lady Allyson. I did not mean to pry or offend."

"Oh no. You did not offend me at all." I picked up my linen napkin and wiped the corner of my mouth. "I want children. I wanted my baby."

Byran nearly choked on his piece of bacon. This time all eyes were on him. He quickly grabbed his juice and took a huge gulp.

"As I was saying, I wanted my baby."

"Honey, do you think this is the time to be sharing this?" Byran asked through gritted teeth.

"These are some of the leaders of our church, honey. If we cannot be transparent with them, who can we be transparent with?" I looked across the table at Deaconess Stanley. "Am I wrong? Can we trust you all to be transparent with?"

Everyone eagerly nodded their agreement. By the looks on the ladies' faces, they could not believe their luck. Their ears were perked up out of a desire to hear this gossip, which was sure to spread throughout the church like wildfire.

Byran frowned. "Still, I do not think it is wise to involve them in our private affairs."

"No disrespect, Pastor, but we are a part of your family now," Deaconess Sparks quickly stated, hoping to dissolve any reservation he had.

I studied Byran. His facial muscles were rock solid, and his left eye was jumping. He was hotter than a country day in Alabama. *Good.*

"First Lady, what were you going to say?" another deaconess asked.

"For the third time, I wanted my baby."

"Wanted? *Wanted* is a past tense word. You speak as if there was a baby at some point," Deacon Sparks said.

"There was up until a few days ago. I—"

"Allyson! Don't go there," Byran shouted, his tone warning me of possible severe consequences if I kept speaking.

"I had a miscarriage," I continued, then released an unexpected sigh.

Saying the words for the first time since that god-awful day at the abortion clinic was actually an unexpected relief. While I had not planned to say them in front of the entire deacon board, the opportunity had presented itself, and in some odd way I felt like it was a chance to get back at Byran. Until this moment, I did not realize I had an innate desire to make him pay, but I guess I did. Had it not been for him and all the stress he had put me under, I would not have miscarried, nor would I have been at the abortion clinic in the first place.

I stole a peek at Byran. His rage had intensified. He hated surprises and to be caught off guard. Again . . . good.

The silence was loud in the room. As a result, I found solace in staring at the food left on my plate.

"I'm so sorry to hear about you-all's loss," Deaconess Stanley said, breaking the ice. "First Lady, I know things like that tend to have more of an effect on a woman than they do on a man. And I think I can speak for all the ladies here when I say if you need anything, and I do mean anything at all, please don't hesitate to call on us. We are here for you, if only just to be a listening ear."

"Thank you. I . . . we appreciate it."

One by one, each of the ladies came over to hug me, and not even meaning to, I fell into their comforting trap. The tears snuck up on me and attacked me faster than I had time to wave them away.

"I think it's safe to say that breakfast is now over. Please excuse my wife and me. We are going to our office to regain our composure before it is time for worship. Deacons, again, I look forward to our future meetings and thoroughly enjoyed this one." Byran pushed his chair back and stood up. "Ladies," he said, addressing the deaconesses, "thank you for being a shoulder for my wife this morning. As you can imagine, this is a difficult time for both of us, and we appreciate your support."

"You are welcome. Please let us know what we can do, if anything," Deaconess Sparks added.

Byran nodded. "We will."

With puddles still lingering in my eyes, I hugged each of the ladies before Byran grabbed my hand and we exited.

"Pastor, you all are done early. I wasn't expecting you to be out so soon," Renae said as she struggled to keep up with the fast pace at which we were walking down the hall.

"Yeah, I was thinking the same thing," Damita said, agreeing with Renae for once.

When we reached our office, Byran stopped them both in their tracks. "First Lady and I need a few minutes alone. Give us a minute, please."

"That is so sweet, Pastor. I just love watching the two of you express your love for each other," Damita gushed.

"I don't know how you got that out of what he said. Because if you knew him like I know him, you would know that tone isn't a good one. Trust me, I have heard that tone before, and it was only when he was pissed off about something. Sounds to me like First Lady is in trouble," Renae snickered.

If we were anywhere else, I would have slapped that outdated gold tooth down her throat. I made a mental note to get rid of her as quickly as possible.

Byran ignored both women and led me into our office. The door had barely closed before he went off.

"You want to explain to me what just happened in there? Because for a minute, I thought you had lost your mind. Are you okay? Because something has to be wrong with you if you for one second considered telling them you had an abortion." He all but whispered that last word.

"I was never going to tell them I had an abortion. Because I didn't."

"What?" He shook his head in confusion. "What do you mean, you didn't have an abortion? I am as lost as a blind man on a dark road right now. Did you not go to Augusta the other day to have an abortion? You kept the baby? What are you saying?"

"If you'd stop asking so many questions, I can give you the simple answer. And the simple answer is, yes, I went there for an abortion, but I did not have to have one, because I miscarried while waiting. Go figure."

I resumed my earlier position on my chaise. I was developing a headache the size of Texas. I looked up at the flat panel that hung on the wall adjacent to my desk as the live feed from the service came through. I could see parishioners filing into the massive eight-thousand-seat sanctuary as the praise and worship team began singing Tasha Cobbs version of "Smile."

People were clapping and swaying to the beat of the song, while others found their seats. I wanted to smile, but I could not.

"Why didn't you tell me? Why have you allowed me to walk around carrying the guilt that you had an abortion when indeed you naturally lost the baby?"

If he had any idea how I was about to go off, he would dismiss himself from my presence. Knowing that nosy Renae was just outside the door kept me calm, cool, and collected.

"Byran, let's not talk about guilt. Because where was your guilt when you asked me to get the abortion in the first place? I don't recall you showing any remorse when you all but demanded I get rid of the baby. I am the one who should be feeling guilty. I should have never agreed to such a thing. And the only reason I did was to show you how much I loved you and how I would do anything for you. I was going to do it because I wanted you to love me back, and I figured if I did what you asked, then you would. But everybody plays the fool, right? I should have known that love really don't love nobody."

A knock at the door cut into the heated moment.

"Pastor, are you all okay in there? It's almost time for you to come out," Renae said in her most irritating voice.

"You need to get rid of her. I do not like her," I said through clenched teeth.

He went to the door. "Renae, we will be out shortly. Go and tell the associate ministers to have prayer without me this morning. I'll see everyone inside the sanctuary."

"But, Pastor—"

"Just do it, Renae. No questions. No comments. No buts," he said with a voice laced with frustration.

She got the hint and scurried away.

He walked over to his desk, picked up his iPad, and focused his attention on the screen.

"You see those people in those pews? They come here week after week for *me*. I cannot afford to have a bad week. I cannot afford to be 'off' one single Sunday. They come here because they know I am one of the best preachers and psalmists in this country. And every week I stand before them, I make it my business not to disappoint.

"You may not believe this, but when I was growing up, I was one of the shyest kids ever. No one listened to me. No one cared to know what I was thinking. No one cared to try to understand what I felt—about anything. I tried for years to make my presence known, but with no father figure in my life, it wasn't until I went to Morehouse that I got in touch with who I was. My self-esteem skyrocketed, and for the first time in my life I felt important. I felt I mattered. It did not take long for me to become successful after that, because once I realized there was something special about me, I became confident. Some may classify it as arrogance.

"Nonetheless, from then on I always got what I wanted. At. Any. Cost. Even if it meant someone else getting hurt in the process. And I've hurt a lot of people getting to where I am now. But I am here. I am right where I've always wanted to be. So, Allyson, this attitude, this demeanor I have, it didn't just start with you. I have been like this for a while now, and it is the only way I know to be." He scrolled through something on his iPad before resuming. "You wanted the truth about me. There you have it." He popped a Halls cough drop in his mouth. "Now, are you ready to go out there and do what we both do best?"

"And what is that?"

"Pretend, Allyson. Pretend."

Chapter Nine

Church had been awesome, and Byran's soul-stirring message on forgiveness had gotten people up and out of their seats, shouting amens and hallelujahs. We had done our usual meet and greet after service, and after hugging and kissing a slew of old people and babies, we had finally left.

Now I was standing in my master bathroom mirror, wearing a white, fitted Nike T-shirt and some black boy shirts, posing in every way I could, taking pictures for Byran. Of all the uncertainties in my life, I could always count on every Sunday night being our freak session. There was something about getting done preaching that made him want sex the most. It was also a part of my responsibility as his wifey. However, tonight the most I could do was take pictures. I was still bleeding slightly, and if the truth be told, I was not in the mood for sex. As much as I was attracted to Byran, a huge part of sex for me, as with any woman, was emotional. And my emotional bank was in the negative.

I took about ten pictures before I decided there was absolutely no other pose for me to do. From sitting on the counter to lying on the counter to doing tricky handstands . . . I'd done all I could do for one night.

I heard a knock at the door.

"Allyson, may I come in?"

I hesitated before I answered. Honestly, I did not want to be bothered. I had planned to run myself a steaming hot bath and soak until my problems dissolved.

"Yes, you can come in."

The door opened slowly. He eased his head around the door before coming all the way inside.

"You busy?"

"No. I just got done taking pics for you."

"I know," he said, smiling from ear to ear. "I saw them. That's why I'm here. I wanted to see you in person."

"Oh, okay."

He walked over to where I was sitting on the side of our tub, and he began kissing me on my neck. That always demobilized me. My will, my anger, and my disdain all vanished whenever he was passionate toward me. The combined scent of his cologne and his body wash tantalized my senses. The dance his tongue did up and down the side of my neck would have intimidated the most skilled salsa dancer.

"Byran, before you get too worked up, I am not able to have sex tonight."

He kept kissing me. "Why?"

"Because I am still recovering from the miscarriage," I said, pulling away. I was getting worked up for no reason.

"Well, can you just take care of me, then? I really need you tonight, baby. Really bad." His kisses moved to my shoulder.

"I honestly don't feel up to it tonight, babe. I have a lot on my mind. It's sort of hard to get in the mood with so much going on with me emotionally. You understand, right?" This time I slid over. Away from him.

"What do I have to do to change your mind? Because I will do whatever you need."

I studied his face. What sounded like a pure offer was tainted with a hint of selfishness. It would have been great if he had meant it without wanting something in return, but that happened only in real, loving relationships.

"I just need some time to myself. A lot has gone on in the past week, and I need to take some time to process it all. From losing my own baby to my husband telling me his heart is with another woman—and, oh yeah, she *is* having his baby—I definitely need a woosah moment."

I sounded as stupid saying all of that as I felt. Who in their right mind would be going through all of this for a front? For money? Two fools.

"I understand," he replied.

We both sat in silence, not sure what to say next.

I broke the silence after a few moments. "So when is your baby due?"

His face hardened. I knew this was probably not the right time to bring this up, but then again, it would never be the right time.

"Allyson, I already told you how far along she was, remember? But she is due in five months."

I guessed my memory was still on vacation, because I could not recall him saying that. I guessed I had successfully blocked it out of my mind.

I sat in silence before I abruptly began to laugh. "You never planned on telling me, did you? If I had not gotten pregnant myself, you were going to keep it a secret." I laughed again, shaking my head in disbelief.

"Allyson, what do you want me to say? Hell, I did not know what to say to you then, and I don't know what to say to you now. Truth is, I do care about you. A lot. I married you for business and for selfish reasons, but you are a good woman. And as much as I have tried to deny it because of the circumstances, I do love you."

Wow. He said it. Just when I thought he was a heartless, cold, selfish, self-absorbed man with a little boy trapped inside, he actually showed some emotion. I was stunned.

He continued. "But I cannot lie to you. I am not *in* love with you. I am in love with my first love. I always have been, and even if we are never together, I probably always will be. When she got pregnant, my emotions were a mixture of excitement and despair. While I wanted to totally devote myself to her and be the man she needs me to be, I have already created a life with you that I can't change. . . am not willing to change."

A few drops of rain fell on my parade. In one breath he had declared his love for me, and in the next breath he had declared it for someone else.

"What is your heart telling you to do? Would your perfect world consist of paying me off and being with her?"

"She wouldn't take me back, anyway."

So he had tried to go back.

"And why not?"

"I hurt her deeply. And it didn't help it any when you and I got married. That was the nail in the coffin for her."

"Apparently not, because she is pregnant with your child. So that means she slept with you about six months into our marriage. She is not over you."

"No. Does she want to be with me? No again."

"Here is what I know. When you love someone, you do any and everything possible to show them. And when you are in love, you do any and everything in your power to be with them. You two are not together, because you have not shown her she can trust you. You have not done all you can to prove to her that she is the one you want—the *only* one you want. Because if you had done everything, even if her head tells her otherwise, her heart would not be able to deny you."

I could not believe I was actually giving him—my husband—tips on how to reunite with another woman.

He looked into my eyes, with tears forming in his own.

"This is why I love you. I have treated you like the dirt I walk on, and yet you remain so nice to me. You remain a friend to me. That is why it's not easy to just disregard you and walk away, as if you mean nothing to me, even if the contract was not in place or I was not concerned about losing my church. Not many women can handle hearing their man tell them they are in love with someone else." He paused. "What kind of woman are you?"

"A woman who believes in the power of love."

"You deserve so much better than me. You really do. I could never pay you for what you have done for me. That is why I am here to stay. No matter what."

I weighed his words before silence captured us again. I laid my head on his shoulder and put his words on repeat in my mind. I wished we could just stay in this moment forever. It was so nice to feel loved, wanted . . . appreciated. The sense of emptiness I'd been feeling had been replaced. The void I'd felt had been filled.

I had some decisions to make.

Either I was going to continue my quest to get him to fall *in* love with me or I was going to figure out a way to set him free from the captivity of his own heart.

Chapter Ten

With everything that had been going on lately, I was in desperate need of relaxation, and the perfect solution to fix such a problem was to enjoy a full spa day.

With my hair flowing in the wind, I whipped my car into the parking lot of the St. Regis Hotel. One of the plus sides of my jacked-up life was being able to have weekly visits to the spa. The shopping was great, too, but going to the spa did it for me.

"Mrs. Ward, welcome back. You look absolutely beautiful, as always. Will you be joining us today for lunch or for your weekly spa appointment?" the lead valet attendant asked.

I flashed him an appreciative smile. "Thank you, Lee. I think I will do both today. I'll be here for a few hours."

"Yes, ma'am. Enjoy."

I strolled into the lobby of the hotel and, as usual, took a moment to exhale and admire the beautiful decor. The grand staircase that flanked the left side of the foyer was always delightful to gaze upon. In my opinion, the St. Regis was by far the most elite and gorgeous hotel in all of Buckhead.

A butler approached me. "Will you be lodging with us, or are you here to enjoy one of our other luxuries?"

"I am going to have lunch at the bar, and then I have an all-day appointment at Remède."

"Okay, madam. Please enjoy," he said as he walked away.

I made my way to the St. Regis Bar and could hardly wait to find me a dark corner so I could enjoy one of my guilty pleasures—the West Paces Mary. It was the hotel's special version of a Bloody Mary.

"Good afternoon, ma'am. My name is Calvin, and I will be your server today. Can I start you off with a beverage?"

"Yes, I would like water with extra lemons and a West Paces Mary. For lunch, I would like the grilled chicken Caesar salad with cranberries."

"Yes, ma'am. And which dressing would you prefer for your salad?"

"Raspberry walnut vinaigrette."

"Got it. I will put this right in. If you would like anything else, just let me know."

"I will. Thank you."

As the server walked away, I pulled out my cell phone and decided to kill some time checking my Twitter and Facebook accounts. I scrolled my Facebook Timeline and News Feed to catch up with the happenings, the news, and the drama of everybody's day. Some tweets and posts made me laugh out loud, and others made me shake my head. Some people did not understand the purpose of social media and used both Twitter and Facebook to air their dirty laundry and tell all their business.

"Here is your West Paces Mary, ma'am. Enjoy," Calvin said as he placed my drink down. "Can I get you anything else right now?"

"No, this will do it," I said, taking a sip of my delight. I took a few more sips and focused my attention back on my phone.

"Excuse me. Is this seat taken?"

I did not even need to look up to know who the voice belonged to. My insides quivered, and my hands began to shake. It couldn't be him. I put my game face on, because there was no way I was going to give him any sign that just the sound of his voice gave me an anxious feeling.

"Dr. Carson. What a surprise it is to see you. What on earth are you doing here?" *Is he following me?*

"Mrs. Ward, what a surprise to see you as well. I am here for a meeting. The medical conference is next week. And what about you? You and the husband having lunch?" he asked, looking around.

Cute. He could have just asked if Byran was here.

"No, I am here alone. I come here weekly to visit the spa."

"Are they good? Would you recommend it? Well, I guess that is a redundant question, seeing as you come here weekly."

I laughed softly. "I definitely recommend it. I love, love, love Remède," I said enthusiastically.

"Do they take walk-ins, or is it by appointment only?"

"I am not sure. I have a standing appointment."

The server returned to deliver my salad. "Does everything look okay with your salad?" he asked.

"Yes, Calvin, it does. Thank you."

"You're welcome." He turned to Seth. "Sir, can I get you anything?"

"I will take a shot of your best top-shelf vodka with a very tiny, and I do mean tiny, splash of cranberry."

"Yes, sir. I'll be right back," Calvin said as he went to go and fulfill Seth's request.

"Hard day already?" I asked.

"Not really. Why do you say that?"

"Vodka shots? This early?" I asked as I took a bite of my salad.

He laughed, and for the first time I could see him outside of his profession and just as a man who was sharing a light moment with me.

"Don't get the wrong impression of me. I am not an alcoholic," he said, chuckling. "I drink socially. And since you are drinking the West Paces Mary, why not have a straight vodka shot? Your drink is just a remix of a Bloody Mary, and it has vodka too, you know."

Calvin returned and sat Seth's drink in front of him.

"So, about this medical conference next week . . . Are you lecturing?" I asked.

"Yes, I will be speaking to a group of young physicians just starting out in medicine. I will be answering any questions they may have about the different career options available to them as they embark on their new journey in the field."

"Sounds interesting." I took a few more bites of my salad. "How did you end up working in an abortion clinic?"

As soon as I asked the question, I wished I could take it back. His face hardened, and the light in his eyes dimmed.

"I was engaged to a woman who killed my baby, and in a sick, twisted way I wanted to take that pain out on everybody else. And so I started killing babies for a living. After a while, long after I had gotten counseling to deal with it, it became just a job. It paid the bills, and I guess I sort of got stuck. Never had the desire to switch to anything else in the medical field—until I met you. You sparked something in me, which led me to do a lot of soul-searching. So I decided to go start doing what I trained and studied to do."

"Which is what?"

"I'm a surgeon."

"Oh, wow."

"I know, right? You would have never guessed it, huh? I have been working at the clinic for only three years."

My mind was racing. "Oh, so that is why you were so concerned about me that day in your office? It brought back some bad memories for you?"

"Yeah. Like you, I wanted my baby. The woman I was engaged to wanted her career more." His face flinched, and even though he tried to hide it, I could see the mental anguish in his expressions. It still bothered him. "That is why I was so adamant about you making that decision for yourself and not for a man who is obviously too selfish and self-absorbed to see he has a good woman. Many of us single men would do anything to have a good woman."

He looked so intently in my eyes, I dropped my fork. I picked up my drink and sipped and sipped and sipped. I was at a loss for words. My hands started doing that shaking thing again, and my insides quivered more than they did when he first walked up to me. What was this man doing to me? I didn't recall ever having these types of feelings unless a man had just taken me shopping or was about to give me some good sex.

"I . . . I . . . I don't know what to say," I said, finally releasing the death grip I had on my drink. In a moment, my drink had transformed itself into something equivalent to a security blanket. "I will say I misjudged you that day at the clinic, and I am deeply sorry. I guess it is true that you cannot understand a person's *what* without understanding their *why*."

"Truer words have never been spoken," he said as he downed his shot in one gulp.

I looked at my watch. As much as I was enjoying his conversation, it was time for me to go. I motioned for Calvin to come, asked for my check, and pulled my credit card out.

"I'll get this," Seth said, grabbing the check.

"Oh, no," I protested. "I got it. It's not like we are on a date," I joked.

"We can be if you want," he said, looking deep into my eyes once again.

If this man keeps that up . . .

"If I was not a married woman, I would consider taking you up on that offer."

"You do not have to be a married woman. You could always get a divorce and marry me."

Was he serious? Okay, he was freaking me out.

His burst of laughter broke the tension of the moment. "Girl, I was just playing. Lighten up," he said, touching my shoulder.

Dear Lord, please don't let this man touch me again. I may just have to . . .

"Did you hear me?" he asked.

He said something?

"No, I did not. What did you say?"

Before he could answer, Calvin came back for the check. Seth scribbled his room number on the ticket, authorizing the bar to charge the lunch to his room.

Room 1213.

"You ready?" Seth asked.

"Yep," I said, rising from my seat. "I must say, although it was a very short one, I enjoyed this lunch with you."

I was desperately trying to mask the sound of disappointment in my voice. The last thing I needed was to sound desperate or thirsty.

"I enjoyed it as well. Can I walk you to the spa?"

I mulled over his question for a second. I wanted to scream yes, but the reality was, our church was in Atlanta, and at any given moment someone could see me and mistake an innocent walk for something more. It was one of those times when I could not afford to let my good be spoken of in an evil way. It was one of the many prices you paid for living a life in a glass bowl, where everyone could see your virtues and your vices.

"I don't think that is a good idea, Seth. I mean, I would love for you to walk me there," I confessed, "but I just do not want to risk anyone seeing us and mistaking us for a couple."

"I totally understand. Well, again, I enjoyed your company. Since you come here on a weekly basis, I guess I will see you next week, then." It was a statement, but his tone asked a question.

What harm could it do to see him again next week? I would be here. He would be here. Two people who happened to be at the same place at the same time. Harmless, right?

"Sure. I, um, usually come around the same time each week."

He looked down at his watch.

"So, I will see you next week right here, at one P.M. It's a date," he said, grinning from ear to ear.

He was a charmer.

"No, not a date. Just a meeting," I said.

"Meeting? What will we be discussing?" he asked, raising one eyebrow.

That was a darn good question. I had no idea, so I just smiled while I tried to quickly come up with a reply.

"A long time ago, before my life went in another direction, I wanted to become a nurse."

"Really? And why didn't you?"

"I will tell you at our meeting next week," I said. I was proud of that think-on-your-feet answer I gave him.

He appreciated it as well.

"That is a good one, Miss Lady." He looked at his watch again. "I don't want to hold you any longer. But I will say this." He leaned in closer to my left ear. "I absolutely cannot wait to see you again next week. It will be all I think about until then."

And with that he walked away.

The heat from his words set my soul and my body on fire. I was afraid to turn around and see which direction he went in, because I did not trust my feet to stay put and not run behind him. Something I could not explain was slowly taking over me, for while I truly wanted to make things work with Byran, Seth was beginning to take my attention off of home, and he had done it in a short span of time.

I waited for about five minutes before I felt it was safe to turn around. I looked down every hallway I passed to see if I could catch another glimpse of him. He was definitely eye candy to a sweet eye. Standing over six foot tall, with good, thick, wavy hair that was just long enough to run the tips of your nails through and beautiful brown eyes—he was temptation wrapped up in the best-looking complexion I had seen. Byran was fine, but he wasn't *that* fine.

I pushed open the door to the spa, signed the check-in list, and waited for them to call my name. I browsed the retail products and made a mental note to purchase some facial products that I had run out of at home. Afterward, I picked up a magazine, flipped through the pages, and tried to pretend my mind was not being invaded by thoughts of Seth. I found myself smiling for no reason.

Finally, the receptionist signaled it was time for my relaxation to begin. I could not have been happier. I was ready to rid myself of all my problems—both good and bad.

"Mrs. Ward, will you be going into the steam room prior to your treatment today, or do you prefer to get straight into the pampering?" Brittany, the host, asked.

I considered my options. My hair was already pretty much a mess, anyway, so a little steam might do me some good. It would definitely be good for my skin.

"I think I will sit a few minutes."

"Okay, well, since you are regular, you know how it works. I'll let Amanda know you are going to sit for a few before you are ready for your massage."

"Sounds perfect," I said as I walked into the ladies' locker room. I selected a locker and placed my purse inside. I undressed down to my panties and bra, hung my clothes on the hanger provided, put on the robe and slippers, closed and locked the locker, and placed the key in the pocket of my robe. I pulled my hair high up on my head into a ponytail holder and walked out.

The steam room was just a few doors down. I hardly ever went in there, because no one seemed to ever be in there at this time of day to chat with, and I had a phobia of passing out and no one being around to help me. It was a crazy notion, but most phobias were. Today I needed to cleanse my pores and let the mist refresh me, and just maybe some of my personal steam would be left inside.

I opened the door, and a gust of vapor slapped me in the face. Hardly able to see, I walked to the bench and sat down. I stretched my legs out and was just about to lean my head back against the wall when I heard a voice. His voice.

"Steam does the body good, huh?"

I sat up and squinted in an effort to try to see him better in the midst of the haze.

"Seth?"

"Yes, it's me. In the flesh." He laughed.

"Wha . . . wha . . . what are you doing in here?" I asked, half excited and half annoyed. Didn't this man know I was trying to run away from him?

"You always stutter when you get around me. Or do you do that around other people as well?"

"That is not important," I shot back. "What are you doing in this steam room? I thought you had a meeting."

I could still barely see him, but I saw him plainly when he got up and walked over to me. Now he was in full view. He sat down so close to me, his leg touched mine. I closed my eyes, because I did not even want to see the damage the heat from his touch had done to my thigh.

"You want the truth?"

"You think I want a lie?"

"Can you handle the truth?"

"I guess there is only one way for me to find out."

"Fair enough," he said and reached for my hand. "The truth is, I did not want to wait until next week to see you. I want to spend the rest of this afternoon with you."

"How did you know I would be here?"

"You told me, remember?"

"No, not *here,* as in the spa. How did you know I would be in the steam room?"

"I gave the girl at the front desk a nice little tip to tell me what services you were going to be having. When you went in to change, she told me you were coming in here."

I was infuriated. What if he were a stalker?

"I will speak to her about that. I do not appreciate her telling you without my permission where I would be. That jeopardizes my safety, among a lot of other things that are wrong with it."

"Did you know the girl who checked you in was hired not long ago as a part-time waitress at the bar?"

"No. But what does that have to do anything?"

"Well, for one, she was there working earlier and saw us having lunch together. You probably did not see her, just as I did not see her, because I was too engrossed in our conversation. But, anyway, she saw us." In my mind that was still beside the point. It flattered me in a small way that he would go as far as paying someone to find out my whereabouts, but it was also kind of creepy. In the world we lived in now, you could never be too careful.

"Okay, this is in a small way—and I do mean a small way—flattering. But I told you I cannot be seen with you. What if someone else walks in here and sees us?"

"Allyson, we are sitting in the steam room, talking. It could be a simple coincidence."

He had a point.

"But I am not worried about that happening," he said.

"And why not?"

"I bought the spa out for the remainder of the day." He said it so nonchalantly, as if that was a normal thing to do.

"You what!" I exclaimed just above a whisper.

"I knew two things. One, I wanted to spend the rest of my afternoon with you. Two, you would be worried about someone seeing you. So in order to get what I wanted, and for you to feel comfortable with me getting what I wanted, I paid for us to have the spa to ourselves."

This man was nuts. *Where do they do that at?*

"How much did that cost?"

If he did not have my attention before, he sure had it now. Was he balling like that?

"Money is not an issue with me. And it will not be an issue for you, either. So can I please just enjoy my afternoon with the beautiful woman I am sitting next to?"

I was speechless and did not trust any words to tumble out of my mouth. I was glad when he broke the silence.

"So not only do you stutter around me, but at times you lose words altogether. Are you mad? Are you happy? Tell me. What are you thinking and feeling right now?"

"I have no idea what I think or feel. A part of me thinks you are crazy, but the other part of me insanely trusts you."

"I am not here to hurt you, baby girl. I just want to love you."

Game! I knew it! It was all game. No man said that to a woman he barely knew. Obviously, he did not know what it meant to love someone, because if he did, he would not use the word so lightly.

"You do not want to love me, Seth. So just stop it, okay? You do not have to say that."

Without one word, he leaned in and kissed me until my mouth was dry and until it felt all the steam had evaporated from the room.

"I did not have to do that, either, but I did. In time, Allyson, you are going to see I am a good man and can recognize a good woman when I see one. If I for one minute thought I was coming between you and your husband, I would not pursue you the way that I do and plan to continue to do."

Either he was arrogant or very confident in himself.

"It still isn't right," I said, dropping my head. I tried to calm my nerves, but his kiss had every last one of them on the edge.

"Who are you trying to convince? Me or you?"

"It does not matter. I cannot carry on with you as if I am not a married woman."

"Okay, fair enough. Can we just enjoy the afternoon relaxing with each other at the spa? As new friends?"

Friends. That was safe, right? I found myself asking that question a lot when it came to him. But I could be his friend. Couldn't I?

"Okay. As friends."

"Good. After this, you never have to see me again."

Ha. That was cute. He knew what he was doing, and I did too. And with every second we spent together, I was starting to forget all my troubles with Byran and his baby momma. There was a new sheriff in town, and his name was Seth Carson—*Doctor* Seth Carson.

And he was rich.

Chapter Eleven

I walked into my house, still feeling like I was floating on a cloud.

The afternoon with Seth had been great. We talked about everything, from our childhood to our five-year plan. It was intriguing to hear about how he grew up in the country, planting vegetables in his great-grandmother's garden and shaking pecans from her tree. He spoke fondly about his grandmother, who had raised him in a small two-bedroom shack that was filled with love and plenty of food. His own mother had left him with his nana, as he called her, for a weekend and had never returned. Several months went by before they received the news that her body had been found in a ditch not too far from their house. She had been raped and beaten and was left for dead.

Hearing him tell the story and watching him relive it was painful. The way he described in detail his feelings as a ten-year-old losing his mother made me feel as if it had happened to me. I listened intently as he recounted his memories of learning how to be the man of his nana's house after his grandfather passed suddenly a couple of years later. He had a tough childhood and was pretty much a recluse throughout his teenage years. He did not spend his weekends going on dates like other guys his age, but rather riding tractors, feeding cows and horses, and tending to the land of his great-grandmother, Big Mama.

I enjoyed listening to him and watching him light up when he talked about his grandmother, who was now an elderly woman, sick with renal failure. It was obvious he loved her dearly and felt responsible for taking care of her for the remaining years of her life. He paid for her to live in the best senior citizens' facility that Augusta had to offer. There she received around-the-clock care, and anything she wanted or desired was at her fingertips, and if not, he provided it.

My phone buzzing on the kitchen counter stole me away from the memory of the tender moments we shared. I read the text from Seth.

I miss you already.

"What are you smiling about?"

I jumped at the sound of Byran's voice. Seth's text had taken me from reality for a moment, and I did not hear the door open or close.

"How was your day?" I said, hugging him, hoping to avoid answering his question.

"It was good. I figured I would come home a little early so I could take you out for a nice dinner and, if you feel up to it, a movie," he said, grabbing me around the waist.

Was this a dream? I could not remember the last time we had gone out on a date. He was always so busy with church or one of the other businesses that I had quit expecting to have a date life. Besides that, we had been on such business terms as of late, the last thing I was expecting was for him to treat me like a . . . wife.

"Wow. What did I do to deserve a date on a weeknight?"

"I was sitting in my office today, praying about us, the situation we are in, and all the things I have put you through lately. I felt very bad about it and was able to appreciate you in a whole different way after putting some things in perspective. Allyson, you know this, but you deserve a whole lot more from a man. Yet you have sacrificed everything you want and desire to make me happy. I love you for that."

My mother was right.

He leaned down and kissed me passionately. Then in one big, unexpected swoop, he picked me up, sat me on the island, and continued to kiss me, as if he would never get another opportunity to do so. I melted into the kiss, and before long we were taking off each other's clothes and tossing them across the room. His shirt landed on top of the refrigerator, and my skirt crash-landed in the sink. He laid me down on the island and made love to me. It was so intense, tears crept into my eyes. I could feel the warmth from his body searing me inside, in places that had not been so much as warmed in recent weeks. If this man did not love me, he sure fooled me.

His tongue explored my body with the sole purpose of pleasing me. His hands roamed in an effort to discover new spots. His gaze into my eyes was so powerful, I was forced to look away. We moved from the island to the kitchen table, and from there we concluded our love dance on the floor.

We both lay on the floor, staring at the ceiling and breathing heavily. Several parts of my body were still smoking, although the fire was burning out. All he had to do was blow on me, and I would be amped up and ready to go again.

"That was so good, baby," he stated.

"Good is an understatement. It was amazing."

"Yeah, that too." He laughed.

"A girl could get accustomed to being swept off her feet—literally swept off her feet," I said as I rubbed my finger down his chest.

We both laughed.

He grabbed my hand. "I am going to do better, sweetheart. I have made the decision to go back to treating you just as good as I did before we were married." He turned over to face me, stroked my chin, and looked into my eyes. "I promise."

Who was this man? Was this the Lord answering my secret prayers? Well, I knew one thing. The Lord sure was working in mysterious ways, because Seth Carson had crept up into my head space and was taking up a large portion of it.

My response was simply a kiss. I scooted closer to him and laid my head on his chest. If we could live in this moment forever, it would have been all right with me. The man that had come home tonight was the man I had grown to love.

The sound of the house phone ringing startled us both, because it never rang unless it was an emergency. I immediately thought about my mother, who had called earlier to say she wasn't feeling well. I jumped up and made a mad dash to answer it.

"Hello?"

"I am so sorry to call your home, Allyson. But may I please speak with Byran?" the female caller asked.

She did not need to say her name. My instincts told me who she was, and instantly my palms became sweaty and my heart began a race that could compete with the Indy 500.

"Sure. One second." I inhaled deeply. "Byran, it's for you," I said, pointing the phone in his direction.

He looked confused, as if he could not imagine who would be calling him at home.

"For me?" he said, puzzled.

"Yes, for you."

He got up from the floor, found his pants, which had landed on the countertop during our clothes toss, and retrieved his cell phone. He pushed a few buttons on the BlackBerry, and the look on his face told me he had obviously missed some calls.

He took the phone from my hand.

"Hello," he said, turning his back to me. "I am sorry. My phone was set to vibrate, but it was in my pants, and I did not feel it."

Why the hell didn't he just tell her he didn't feel it vibrating because he was having sex with me . . . his wife?

He continued. "Is everything all right?" He paused. "I will be there as soon as I can. I have to shower and get dressed, but I will be on my way."

He placed the phone back in its cradle and turned to face me. I was already boiling hot, because I knew that whatever he was about to say was going to send me to the third dimension of anger.

"Allyson, baby, I hate to skip out on our dinner plans for tonight, but—"

I cut him off. "That was her, wasn't it?"

He dropped his head. "Yes."

"What did she want?"

"She is in the hospital. They think the baby will come tonight."

"I thought you said she was five months."

"She is almost six now, but they have tried to stop her labor and nothing is working. Our son may be born prematurely."

A mixture of emotions flooded my heart, mind, and soul. While I hated to hear that a baby's life was at stake, I also hated to hear the man I loved refer to his son with another woman. I bit the inside of my lip, hoping to numb the hurt I suddenly felt.

"So you have to go there and, um, be with her, I guess?"

"Baby, I am sorry. There is no way I could have anticipated this happening. I am so very sorry."

If asked to give a dissertation on how I felt in this very moment, I would not know where to begin. While he could not help that the baby was coming early, it was his fault there was a baby at all. What was I supposed to do while my husband was at the hospital, tending to the love of his life? What was I was supposed to do while he was at the hospital, holding her hand through her labor pains? What was I supposed to do while he sat praying and comforting her? Was I supposed to sit by the phone and await his call? Was I supposed to eat dinner and pretend none of this was happening? This was just too much. I felt dizzy.

He stepped to me, and I impulsively stepped away. The man who had just had full access to my body was now a stranger to me, and I did not want him touching me—at all. I did not want him to hug me, because no hug—or kiss—was going to make me feel any better.

"Just go," I pleaded. "Go take your shower, get dressed, and be on your way. I am sure she is scared right now. Honestly, I cannot imagine how she feels. I don't know what I would do if my baby was threatening to come this early, which gives him a small chance of survival." I pushed away a lone tear that had slipped from my eyes. "Please. Just. Go."

He stepped toward me again, but I put my hand up and motioned for him not to come any closer. With his eyes he willed me to understand, and then he turned and walked away.

I wrapped my arms around my waist, leaned against the refrigerator, slid to the floor, and cried. I cried because if the truth be told, this was my fault, as I had put myself in this situation. I could just walk away, but as I was quickly discovering, you could not help who your heart loved. And when you really loved someone, even if you knew you needed to, it was not that easy to walk away. Plus, if I walked away, what would I do? What would I have? Where would I go?

I cried because I knew this was the first night of many. If the baby survived being born premature, he would have a difficult journey arriving at optimum health, and Byran would need to be there every single step of the way. I groaned as I imagined him leaving in the middle of the night because his son was sick, or on holidays because he had to share time with him. I shook my head, trying not to let my thoughts run too far into the future. For the first time in my life, I didn't want to be in my future, especially if it resembled anything of the present.

Byran reentered the kitchen, looking suave as ever. He was wearing Rocawear jeans and a Polo shirt, but even in those—his version of casual—he looked good. I could not help but get a whiff of his Gucci cologne. Anger slowly started pressing its way through me again.

"I'm not sure what to say," he began. "I don't know if I should say I will call you later with an update or if you even care to know what happens. I know this is not easy for you, and to be honest, it isn't easy for me. I have so many emotions floating through me right now. I am hurt that I have to leave you here, sitting on the floor, crying, and I am also afraid that my son might not make it. And I now know how you must have felt when you lost our baby," he said as he wiped sweat from his forehead. "I just don't know why this is all happening."

Was he serious? Maybe the stress of this had him delirious.

"Byran, it is happening because you, like many other men, are only happy when you can have your cake and eat it too. This is happening because you fell in love with a woman who you could not do right by, so you gave up on having her as you continued to love her. You tried, but you couldn't let her go. Thus, you created a mess. The problem with it all is you are married to me and are forced to stay with me and keep your image up for the sake of your career. And that Byran is the reason this is all happening." A thought came to me. "Exactly what hospital is she in? Because I know you have better sense than to be going to a hospital in Atlanta."

"Yeah, her doctor is in Chattanooga. It's about an hour and a half away from here."

"Chattanooga? As in Chattanooga, Tennessee?"

While I was hoping he had better sense than to have his pregnant mistress deliver in the city, I was amazed. They had this well planned.

"Yes. Chattanooga, Tennessee."

"Wow," was the only word I could get out.

"Should I call you when I get there?" he asked hesitantly.

Suddenly his presence sickened me, and all I wanted was for him to disappear.

Realizing I was not going to answer his question, that was exactly what he did. Without another word, he walked out the door that led to the garage. I listened as the garage door went up, followed by his engine starting and the door going down again. It was such a horrible feeling to be left alone knowing the only company you would have was the agonizing thoughts in your head.

I sat for a few more minutes before I decided to get up and out. I needed to get away from this house so I would not cry a river or, worse, turn up all the bottles of liquor.

I went upstairs to change into a cool, flowing floor-length sundress. I had taken a long shower at the spa, so I went in my bathroom and sprayed on an ample amount of my favorite perfume, Alien. I took the brush and brushed my hair into a ponytail, then dusted some blush on my cheeks and some M•A•C gold dust on the areas of my chest that were exposed. Satisfied with my look, I grabbed my Versace purse and went back downstairs to get in my car.

Not sure which restaurant I would end up at, I opened my sunroof and was on my way. I found myself on I-85, heading north toward downtown. I was in the mood for some good seafood, and Legal's crab soup was calling my name. I pulled my Versace sunglasses from my purse, put them on, and leaned my seat back a little to enjoy the ride. With each mile, I felt a little better. I turned my audio system on, and the sounds of Anthony Hamilton came blaring through the speakers. By far, he was my most favorite neo-soul artist, and I settled into a peaceful state. His voice was the perfect blend of sultry and soothing—just what I needed.

I looked at the clock, and it was just after seven. The traffic was mild and moving right along. Just as I was approaching International Boulevard, which was the exit I took to go to Legal Sea Foods, I changed my mind and decided that what I wanted was a piece of cheesecake from the Cheesecake Factory. I took the Peachtree Street exit and headed that way.

I drove into the parking lot of the Cheesecake Factory, got my ticket from the valet, and went inside. I could hardly wait to order a glass of Moscato. Any relaxing methods available to me tonight would be taken full advantage of.

I gave the hostess my name and took a seat in front of the cheesecake display case. My mouth began to water as I took in all the delicacies. Looking at the various cheesecakes made me want to skip dinner and go right to dessert.

Finally, my name was called, and I was escorted to a table on the patio. I was relieved to be dining outside. Fresh air was good for anyone who was perplexed in any way about anything. The light, crisp air was refreshing as it kissed my face. The hostess sat me down at a table near the road, which was perfect because I always enjoyed people watching and had the ideal seat for it.

The server came and took my order, and before long I was feasting on my favorite dish—the Chicken Madeira. I was well aware that after I digested it, it was going to spread evenly between my thighs and my butt. Even knowing that, I took bite after bite until it was halfway gone. By the time I ordered dessert, my body was screaming and begging for me to stop. I had stretched my stomach to its limit, but there was nothing better than comfort food for the comfortless.

As I left the restaurant and got back in my car, the thought of going home to my problems rushed to my mind. The bliss I had felt while dining was now seeping away through the crack in my car window.

The last place I wanted to go was home.

The last place I was going to go was home.

I took a left on West Paces Ferry Road and drove into the driveway of my next destination.

"Good evening, ma'am. Will you be staying overnight with us?" the valet attendant asked.

"As a matter of fact, I will," I replied.

"Enjoy your stay with us."

"I plan to," I said, passing him a twenty-dollar bill.

With no overnight bag and a newfound confidence to take a huge risk, I made my way to the hotel's elevator. Once it opened, I stepped inside and pushed the button for the twelfth floor.

Surprisingly, I was anything but nervous as the elevator went from floor to floor. Once it stopped, I got off and took the journey to the room.

His room.

Room number 1213.

Watching him sign that check earlier at the bar had proven to be a good thing, I thought as I stood outside of Seth's door, knocking.

No answer.

I knocked again.

Just as I surmised that maybe he had gone out for the evening, and turned to walk away, he opened the door.

"Allyson?" He leaned his head out and peeked around the corner. "I cannot believe you came here. You're not worried if someone sees you? Wait a second. Are you okay?"

"I will be just fine if you let me come in."

He moved out of the way, and with the two steps it took me to enter his room, I stepped into the land of no return.

The game was about to change.

It had already changed.

Chapter Twelve

My eyes flung open.

The sound of my phone buzzing woke me from the most peaceful sleep I'd had in a long time.

Wait a minute. Where am I?

I sat straight up in the bed, only to realize that I was in Seth's hotel room. I glanced at the digital clock sitting on the nightstand next to me and discovered it was well after three o'clock in the morning. I pushed my hair away from my face and picked up my phone.

Ten missed calls, three voice mails, and fifteen text messages. All of them were from Byran except two. They were from my mother.

I decided to read the text messages first.

Message #1:

Babe, I have been trying to reach you. I am starting to get worried. I understand that you are upset, but please at least reach out to let me know that you are okay. Not sure you want to know, but the baby is here and he's a little fighter. Get at me.

Message #2:

Allyson, I have called you five more times since that last text message. WTH is going on? I don't want to assume the worst, so please hit me up to let me know you are good.

Message #3:

> This is selfish. Why would you have me worry like this? All you have to do is simply respond by saying you are all right. This is childish, Ally.

The other messages were similar—more rants. He had some nerve to be making demands of me. He needed to concentrate on his other family and leave me alone. I was right where I wanted to be, just as he was. But knowing him the way I did, he would soon have people out looking for me. I sent back a simple message.

Byran, I am fine. Glad your baby is hanging on. Prayers are with you. . . .

I put the phone back on the nightstand and looked over at Seth's side of the bed. He was not there. My heart dropped. Had he left me here?

I pushed the covers back and got out of the bed. The bathroom light was off, so I knew he was not in there. I opened the door that led from the bedroom to the living room and found the same thing. . . . The lights were out.

I walked over to the lamp, but before I could turn it on, I could see Seth's silhouette in a chair next to the window. A hint of the moonlight was shining on just a corner of his face.

"Allyson, your phone has been going off all night," he said.

"Yeah, it woke me up a few minutes ago," I replied as I took a seat on the couch.

"Your husband?"

"Yes."

"I'm sure he must be worried sick about you."

"I sent him a text just now and told him I was fine."

"So, Allyson, what's the deal? You were very vague when you got here. Don't get me wrong. I am glad you came, but I have been wondering what took place that led you here. It is obvious something happened, because you cried yourself to sleep. What did he do?"

I honestly did not know how to explain such a ridiculous situation to anyone outside of my mother. She understood my reasoning behind being with Byran, but no one else would. I also wasn't sure how much I could trust Seth with my innermost feelings and thoughts.

"Do we have to talk about this right now? It's almost four A.M. I just want to go back to bed."

"You cannot run forever, darling. You have to face your feelings, your doubts, as well as your fears. It is only when you face them that you can begin healing."

"Whatever you say, Dr. Phil," I joked.

"Do you know why I did not sleep with you tonight, when you got here?"

I was hoping that we would not have to talk about that, either. I had felt rejection in a major way when he refused my advances.

"No, I don't. Why?"

"When I make love to you, Allyson, it will be because you want to, not because you are hurt. Seeing a woman cry does not make me feel good. Having sex with you tonight would have made me just like the men you are probably accustomed to. I am of a different breed. I could easily sex and cake you, but I'm not. You will be my woman when I do either. I respect you, and while I would love to do nothing more than lay you down on the very couch you are sitting on, kiss you, and remind you of places on your own body that you have probably forgotten existed or did not know existed, I can't.

"I am sure you have heard it said that good things come to those who wait. So after having thought of you all day long, I have decided to wait. Because what I do know is this. You will open your eyes one day and know your worth. And that will be the day you will become my lady."

He must have sensed I had nothing to say to that. He continued. "Now, I need for you to tell me what is going on with you. If you are going to be running to me in the middle of the night, you can at least talk to me. Open up."

"I am married to a pastor," I began.

"There are worse things. Continue."

"And the truth is, our marriage is really a scam. We got married for business reasons, and it seemed like the perfect thing to do at the time. He needed to get married quickly in order to qualify for the church he wanted, and the woman he wanted did not want him. I was not getting any younger and wanted to live a certain lifestyle that he could afford, so we jumped the broom. End of story."

"And somewhere between then and now you started actually loving him, but the feelings were not mutual?"

"Couldn't have said it any better."

"You cannot make a man love you, Allyson. That is one thing you must know about a man. We can live with you, have sex with you, and buy you the world, but our heart can be at another address."

"Don't I know it," I said solemnly.

"I get it. So your arguments have been about another woman—a woman he *is* in love with."

"Are you some kind of psychic? How do you know these things?"

"A psychic? No. A man? Yes. And to be honest, most men think alike. However, not all men act alike." He paused for a minute. "Nothing is going to change, darling. You will always be chasing after a man who will always be running from you. He probably loves you on a friendship level but nothing more."

This man was Dr. Phil *and* a psychic in one body. He was dead on it.

"It gets worse. The woman had his baby tonight."

Hearing myself say the words was like taking the knife out of my heart and plunging it back in—deeper this time.

"She had his what?" He sounded as much in disbelief as I actually was. "Wait a minute. Let me see if I understand you correctly. The woman—the other woman—that he is really in love with had his baby . . . tonight?'

"You have indeed comprehended well, sir. That is exactly what I said, and that is exactly what I meant."

"Whoa. Who does this guy think he is? You were in my clinic about to get an abortion because he did not want the child he created with you because he already had got someone else pregnant?"

"You are right again."

"Damn. That is the sickest thing I have ever heard in my life. Who does that? And you mean to tell me this is the man you love? Surely your feelings have to be strictly held in place by the motivation of money, because you cannot make me believe you would love a man who treats you like the dirt he walks on. You have to know . . . Please tell me that you know you are worth so much more than that."

While his words were the truth and nothing but the truth, hearing them arranged in that way made me feel like the fool I was acting like. Why did I always play the fool?

"Can we go to sleep now? I just want to disappear from reality for a few hours before I have to face it again."

"Come here."

"Excuse me?"

"You heard me. Come here."

I reluctantly got up and went to where he was sitting by the window. He pulled me down into his lap, leaned me over so my head would be on his shoulders, and wrapped his arms around me.

"Your heart is safe now. Go to sleep."

This man was slowly breaking me down. I was a bipolar catastrophe, and he treated me as if it were perfectly normal. I was certain that one day the tears would not fall, but it would not be today or right now. They fell freely, without hesitation, all the way down the center of my breasts. They flowed until my heart felt some relief. They flowed until sleep overtook me.

A knock at the door, followed by the sound of the doorbell, startled me.

I gently shook Seth, who was still holding me.

"Seth," I said softly, "someone is at the door."

He opened his eyes, focused in on me, pulled me closer, and kissed me softly on the lips. "Now, let me get up and see who this is knocking at my door."

I stole away to the bedroom. I looked at the clock on the nightstand and realized it was shortly after eight o'clock and I needed to get going. I went over to the side of the bed I had slept on before falling asleep in Seth's arms and sat down. I picked up my phone. Five missed calls from my mother. Three from Byran. A few text messages from friends. I cleared the notifications, got up, found my shoes, and went into the bathroom to wash my face.

"Allyson, where are you?" I heard Seth ask.

"I am in the bathroom. You don't mind if I shower, do you?"

He walked into the bathroom and slipped his arms around my waist. I looked at our image in the mirror.

We would make a great-looking couple. He kissed me on my neck, and chills screeched down my spine and made their way around to the center of my womanhood. I stepped forward, away from his embrace. If he was determined not to make love to me, there was no reason I should catch on fire with desire and be consumed.

"What do you want for breakfast?" he asked.

"I really do have to get going. I need to—"

"Need to what?" he interrupted.

Truthfully, I had no idea what I was about to do, other than go home, change clothes, and do some retail therapy. I had considered going to the church to work on my first women's conference I was trying to organize. Byran had told me some of the ladies in the church had been asking him when I was going to become more active, so I had decided to begin planning something that would appease them. I had no clue how to do such things, but I figured I could not go wrong with incorporating things I loved, such as fashion, food, and money.

Seth did not wait for me to respond. "You can leave after breakfast."

"Seth—"

He interrupted me again. "In the morning," he said, "do you like pancakes, waffles? What?"

In the morning! Is he crazy?

"Pancakes."

"Bacon, sausage, eggs?"

"No eggs. Grits, bacon, and apple juice."

"Got it. I am going to order this food, and then I'm going to make a run. I will be back in about an hour or so."

"Since you have to leave, do you want to use the bathroom? Because I can step out."

"This is a two-bedroom suite. I will just use the other room. I got an upgrade because when I got here to check in, they had allowed one too many late checkouts, and there were no rooms ready. So take your time."

With that he disappeared on the other side of the door. I went and sat on the side of the oversize Jacuzzi tub. The bathroom itself gave me a relaxing feeling of euphoria. The soft shades of vanilla and caramel were soothing, and the granite and marble mix was elegant and first class. Whoever designed the bathrooms had women in mind. It was simply beautiful.

I got up and turned the water on in the shower. I let my dress hit the floor and stepped under the pulsating spray of hot water. The water felt good against my skin, and I closed my mind and imagined all my problems, pains, disappointments, and failures were being washed away down the drain. I allowed the water to nourish my body for several minutes before I decided to get out. If I stayed in much longer, my skin would begin wrinkling.

I stepped out, grabbed the towel, and dried off. I sat down in the chair that was placed at the vanity, and grabbed one of the complimentary lotions out of the basket that held the other complimentary things. I also reached for the remote and aimed it at the mirror. No matter how many times I had stayed at the St. Regis, the TV behind the mirror was still by far my most favorite amenity.

The TV was tuned to the Food Network, and the Neelys were cooking up one of their famous dishes. I loved watching those two. They were a husband-wife cooking team who believed the love they shared was the secret ingredient in all their dishes.

I smeared lotion over my arms, legs, stomach, and other places I could reach on my own. A thought came to me as I did that. It would be so nice to be in a relationship with a guy who would do simple stuff, like put lotion on my back. I stopped momentarily to ponder the thought.

The doorbell to the suite rang.

The food.

I pulled down one of the two robes that were hanging on the wall, slipped it on, and made my way to the door. I opened it when I saw through the peephole that breakfast had indeed arrived.

"Mrs. Carson, I am here with your breakfast," the butler announced.

Mrs. Carson. Had a nice ring to it.

"You can put everything on the dining table."

As he placed the food on the table, I went and retrieved a ten-dollar bill from my purse. Once he had finished, I passed the money to him.

"Oh, no, ma'am. I cannot accept that. We have already been paid in full, and Mr. Carson has already taken care of the gratuity," the butler said with a smile.

"Well, all right then. You have a great day."

"You too, Mrs. Carson. Please call us if you should need anything else."

"I will."

I closed the door behind him and got straight to business. I was starving for some reason and was planning on savoring every bite.

The sound of my phone interrupted my delight, and I went and grabbed it. It was my mother calling again. She never called this many times unless something was wrong, so I picked up.

"Hi, Mom."

"Allyson Kristina Ward, where are you?" she asked, clearly angry.

"That is not important. Is everything okay? Why have you called me so many times?"

"For your information, your husband is worried sick to death about you!" she exclaimed.

"Well, has he keeled over yet?"

"Allyson Kristina Ward!" she exclaimed again. "What on earth has gotten into you? You are speaking as if you have no sense at all."

"Mother, is *this* what you wanted? To tell me that Byran is worried about me? Because if so, I am enjoying a very nice breakfast and I really want to continue doing so."

I bit off a piece of the bacon.

"I am appalled right now. You act as if it is okay for you to disappear and not tell anyone where you are."

"Did Byran tell you where he is?"

"Well, no. He just said he didn't know where you were."

"He is at the hospital with the love of his life and their new son. Oh, and that would be in Chattanooga, Tennessee."

The silence was deafening, but I waited for her response. I drank some of my juice and then shoved a spoonful of grits into my mouth.

"I, um, had no idea," she said quietly. "He called me over and over, asking if I had heard from you, and I told him no. He never once told me what was going on. If I had known, I would have told him that you were going to react like this. You always run when things get to be too much for you."

"I texted him and told him I was fine. And I *am* fine. As a matter of fact, I am better than fine."

"Where are you?"

"Again, that is not important. I am where I want to be right now, and will probably be here for the rest of the day. So, Mother, if he calls back, will you please tell him to stop calling me? I have absolutely nothing to say to him."

"Yes, dear. I am sorry I called so upset. I, too, was sick with worry when I could not reach you. I thought something had happened."

I knew she meant no harm, but it was just the wrong day . . . the wrong time.

"No problem, Mom."

"Will you be going home today? Because you know Byran sent someone over to your house after you refused to take his calls, and he knows you are not there. He also knows you did not stay there, Allyson. And if you are with some man, just be careful, honey. The last thing you want to do is get caught and screw up your financial future because you are hurt and upset right now."

Any understanding I had before flew out of a closed window. She had some nerve. How could she overlook the pain I was feeling and be more concerned about me screwing up my contract?

"Mom, I have to go. Because we both know this is not about me as much as it is about you. Not once did you express your concern about how devastated I must be right now. You are concerned only with your own financial future, because without me, you would not have one. Well, you need to be scared, Mother, because right now I don't know what I might do. I am sick of always being the one sacrificing for everyone else."

"Do not be a fool, Allyson. If you mess this up, what will you have? You are not accustomed to a mediocre lifestyle. You would be forced to get a job and work by the hour. Can you handle that? Can you handle not having your weekly shopping sprees and spa appointments? What about not having that expensive weave you wear or the purses you carry? So while you are trying to put it all on me, you and I both know that at the end of the day the only reason you are in the situation you are in is because you have a love for material things . . . just like your mother. So my advice to you is to go home and make things right with Byran. And if you are with some man, I hope you have sense enough not to get caught and ruin the reputation of your husband and his church. That would kill him."

"What about what's killing me?" I screamed. She was relentless. "Never mind. You don't have a clue, Mother. Ever since Daddy walked off and left you for that other woman, you have been the coldest individual I know. You raised me to be selfish, just like you. And I did not realize until now that the only person who has suffered is me. I have cheated my own self out of happiness. You are right. I'm lying in a bed I made for myself, but I will not stay in it. Somehow, someway, I am going to figure out how to get myself out of this mess."

I heard the key activating the door.

"Mother, I have to go. Don't call me. I will call you. Good-bye," I said, hanging up the phone, not allowing her the opportunity to say another word.

Seth walked in with shopping bags. He left me to go shopping?

"Everything all right? You look frazzled," he said as he kissed me on my cheek.

"Just a little fight with my mom, but all is well." I pointed to the bags. "So you leave me here to enjoy all of this wonderful breakfast while you steal away to shop?" I asked playfully.

"I would have taken you with me, but seeing that you did not even want to be seen walking with me yesterday afternoon, when I offered to walk you to the spa, I knew better than to think you would walk around with me in Phipps Plaza."

"Phipps Plaza?" I asked, smiling. I liked him all the more.

"Yes. You do not strike me as a Marshalls or T.J.Maxx kind of girl. Am I wrong?"

"Not at all. You are absolutely, one hundred percent correct," I said, cheesing.

"I know. So, since you are not leaving to go home until tomorrow morning, I figured you would need a few essentials. Undergarments, a new dress, shoes. Well, you didn't need shoes, but I saw the perfect shoes for the dress I purchased, in Jimmy Choo. Just had to get them."

"But how did you know what sizes to get?"

"You are the exact same size as my ex-fiancée." He stood with his head cocked to the side, as if he was sizing me up. "You are a size ten in a dress, size eight in shoes, a thirty-six B cup, and a size five in panties. Am I wrong?"

What in the heck?

"Um, no, you are right again," I said, practically speechless.

"I know." He motioned to the food. "Are you done? Did you get enough?"

I looked at the pancakes, which I had barely touched. I really wanted those above anything else, but the conversation with my mom had somewhat killed my appetite. Besides that, they were cold now, and there was nothing worse to me than cold pancakes or pancakes warmed up in the microwave.

"Yes, I am done."

"Okay, go and get dressed. I want to take you for a ride. And before you protest, there is no need to worry. The windows on my car are tinted. No one will ever know you are in there."

I laughed. Already he knew me too well.

"Okay, but believe it or not, I am still sleepy. Can I take a nap first? Afterward, I will go wherever you want to go."

"Okay, fair enough. I could use a little more sleep myself. In a bed this time. I enjoyed holding you in the chair, but I don't have the body I used to have. These old bones need proper rest, in a proper resting place."

"Understood," I said, holding in laughter.

I walked back into the bedroom but decided to brush my teeth again before escaping to la-la land. I had been so grateful earlier to find a complimentary toothbrush in the basket with the other items. No matter how cute you are, there is no need to walk around with breath that smells like a seal's behind.

The TV was still on in the bathroom, but I was not fond of *Iron Chef*. So I turned the channel to CNN instead.

"We now take you back to breaking news out of Augusta, Georgia. One of the town's most popular abortion clinics has been bombed by a group of protestors. It is presumed that everyone who was inside is now dead. A woman, who has not been identified and who was seen walking into the building when the bomb inside went off, lies in critical condition at the Trinity Hospital of Augusta. We will bring you more information as it comes in," the news correspondent said right before they went to a commercial.

"Seth!" I screamed.

He rushed into the bathroom where I was.

"Allyson, what's wrong?" he asked nervously. "Are you sick? Did you fall?"

"Your clinic," I said, pointing to the TV. "It's been bombed."

Chapter Thirteen

We rode in complete silence the entire way to Augusta. Seth had insisted I stay in Atlanta, claiming it would be too dangerous to expose me to a group of protestors who might try to attack him once he arrived on the scene. But there was no way I was going to let him go and face one the worst days of his life alone. Outside of losing a business, he had lost his entire staff to such a senseless act and would need someone there to support him. I prayed silently that God would be with us and would help us navigate through whatever we were about to walk into.

As we approached, we discovered that the road that led to the clinic was blocked by a hoard of police cars, ambulances, fire trucks, and both local and national news trucks. That was one thing I had not considered when I made the impulsive decision to come along. There was no way I was going to be able to escape a roaming camera or an overzealous reporter looking to talk to anyone connected with the doctor who owned the building that had been bombed.

Seth must have been reading my mind.

"I am going to drive around the block. I had no idea there would be this many reporters here. You don't need another problem, and I don't want to be worried about having to kill one of these idiotic protesters if something happened to you. So I'm going to get out a couple of streets over and walk to the clinic. I want you to go to this address." He took out a notepad from underneath his armrest and scribbled an address on it.

"Are you sure you are going to be okay? I really don't want to leave you here alone. I mean, what if something happens to you? What am I supposed to do then?" I asked, tears forming in my eyes. "What if one of those stupid people tries to do something to you?"

His response was a kiss on my forehead. Then he said, "I am going to be fine. This is not up for debate or discussion."

"But if I have your car, how will you get there?"

"You are worried about the wrong thing. I will get there. Now, when you get to that address, tell them you are there to pick up Louella Todd. She's my grandmother. I want the both of you to go to this bottom address. When I get home, I want the two most important people to me right now to be there waiting for me. This is going to be a tough day for me."

I wrapped my arms around his neck and squeezed him, as if I was never going to see him again. He kissed me quickly on the lips.

"I gotta go, babe. I will see you soon."

He opened the car door and got out. I sat and watched him walk away before I, too, got out and went to the driver's side. I got back in the car and closed the door. I looked around the console to try to familiarize myself with his car—a customized 2013 Jaguar XKR-S.

I put the first address in the GPS and took off. Just as I drove away, I looked in the rearview mirror and saw a few reporters running toward the car. Thankfully, I drove away at the perfect time. I leaned my head back against the headrest. What had started out as a peaceful morning had turned into a nightmare on Main Street.

The directions led me to the Peace Like a River Senior Housing Facility. It was a tall brick building sitting in the middle of several acres of plush green grass surrounded by a beautiful array of colorful flowers. To the right of the building was a large lake with park benches and rocking chairs around it. Just looking at the property was relaxing; it almost reminded me of how my day had begun.

I drove up to the security gate. Seth had not given me any instructions about how to get past security, and I was sure he had not had time to call and let them know I would be coming. I sighed in frustration as I let the window down.

"How may I help you, ma'am?"

The security guard was a fragile-looking white man with huge glasses. They were so big, he could probably see Russia from where he was sitting. I laughed at my own silliness. But if Sarah Palin could see Russia from Alaska, then I was certain with these bifocals, he could see it from Augusta, Georgia.

"Yes, sir. I am here to pick up Ms. Louella Todd," I said, hoping he would not ask me any more questions, because I sure did not have any more answers.

He looked all around before he leaned closer to his window and began to whisper. "How is Dr. Carson? Everybody around here has been talking about what happened over yonder at his doctor's office. He all right, ain't he?"

"He's fine," I whispered back.

"He ain't hardly fine. I been working at this here old folks' home for near 'bout fifty years, and anytime he send somebody round here to pick up his grandmother, it mean one thing. He worried 'bout something. He want his grandmama there when he get home because she is the only person in this here world that can calm him down." He looked around again. "And maybe you can, too. Ever since that crazy fiancée of his put him through all of that drama, as you young people call it, he ain't been right. So unless you some kin to him, he must be finding the strength to move on with his life."

"Well, I will let him know that you asked about him."

"Yeah, you do that." He paused, leaving me to wonder if he was going to let me through or not. Then he said, "So is you kin to him or not?"

I laughed, because old people were just old people, whether they were black, white, blue, or yellow. They were all messy and nosy—but in a good, old-person type of way.

"No, I am not related to Dr. Carson. He is just a good friend of mine."

"I have met some of his *good* friends. Like I said, I been working at this here old folks' home near 'bout fifty years, and ain't none of his friends ever been trusted to come and get his beloved grandmother. And I for sure ain't seen any of his friends driving his car. So you more than a good friend. You somebody special, little lady."

I could not help but smile. He was wrong, because we really were nothing more than friends, but I was sure it would not take much to become more than that. But right now my focus was on getting Ms. Todd.

"Well, thank you kindly."

"I ain't gonna hold you. I know you trying to get in there and rescue Ella from these nosy folks that live here." He looked around again before he leaned over to whisper. "I gotta warn you. She can be a little tough cookie. Ms. Ella don't play 'bout her grandson. She loves that man like her own child and will hurt anybody who tries to hurt him. If you don't believe me, just ask that last little heifer he called a fiancée. We ain't heard a word from her, so if you see her, you ask her 'bout Louella Todd. I don't know it to be true, but the word round here is Ella broke her broomstick on her back and then ran over her with her Hoveround. Now, I didn't see it, but that's just what I heard from these nosy folks round these parts."

I laughed hysterically. *Hoveround? Broomstick? Too funny.*

"I will be sure to keep that in mind, sir."

"Well, it's been nice chatting with you, li'l lady. I hope to see you round here again. You the prettiest li'l butter pecan thang I done seen in a long time. A healing sight for these sore eyes," he said, smiling for the first time and revealing one solid gold tooth.

A white man with gold in his mouth? Say it wasn't so!

He activated the gate, and it rose to let me through. I waved at him as I drove away. I could only imagine what all he knew and had seen in the time he had been working here. I would love to have a conversation with him on a day I had nothing to do. I had a feeling I would spend the entire time laughing and splitting my side. He was a hoot.

I drove up to the building, and to my surprise there was a valet attendant. I had never seen a valet station at a senior housing facility, but then again, I had never been to one. I stepped out of the car.

"Hello. How long will you be visiting with us today?" the attendant said.

"I am just here to pick up someone. I don't think that will take a long time."

"Who are you here to pick up?"

"Ms. Louella Todd."

"Oh, Ms. Willie."

"Excuse me? No, I said Louella."

"Louella is her daughter's name."

Why did Seth tell me Louella? Why did the security guard go along with it?

"Louella is the code name for us here when Dr. Carson sends someone to get her and he hasn't called ahead to let us know. We know to let her go if someone asks for Louella. That's why Ben down there at the gate let you in. Otherwise, he would have talked you to death and sent you on your way," he said, laughing.

That makes sense. I was wondering why I was let in so easily. Anybody could have been driving a car like his.

"Plus, it also helps that you are driving Dr. Carson's car."

"How do you know this is his car?"

"You are such a lady," he said, snickering. "Look at the rims on the tires. His initials are on them. This model car is only custom made. Plus"—he walked around to the back of the car—"it says 'SC' on his tag," he said, pointing to the license plate.

I walked around the car to check it out, and sure enough his initials were not only on the rims but also on the tag. "I never paid attention to that," I said.

He laughed again. "Well, I'll see you in about an hour."

"Oh, no, I am just here to pick her up. We will be right back down. You can keep the car running if you would like."

This man really loved to laugh, because he did it again.

"You evidently have not met Ms. Willie. She is a feisty old lady. And she is going to take at least thirty minutes to pack her things. She has to have everything perfect and just right. You will see. Good luck," he said as he walked away.

I walked into the foyer, and it mirrored a five-star hotel. The decor, the furnishings . . . were exquisite. I was very impressed. I surmised that Seth had to be spending quite a bit of money for his grandmother to live here. None of the residents were walking around alone. They each had a staff member, dressed in a white nursing uniform, escorting them around. I spotted the check-in desk and went over to sign in.

"Hi, I'm Julie. How can I help you today?" the receptionist asked.

"Hello, Julie. I am here to pick up Ms. Louella Todd. Actually, Willie Todd, but I was told to say Louella."

"Okay." She placed a clipboard in front of me. "Sign in for me, and I will call up and let her and her nurse know you are on your way up," she said and then walked away to pick up the phone.

I did as she asked and then placed the clipboard back down on the desk.

She returned. "I will just need a copy of your driver's license and you can go right up."

I took my driver's license out of my wallet and passed it to her. She disappeared into a room to the make the copy. I saw the LED light flashing on my BlackBerry. I pulled it out of my purse immediately, thinking I had missed a call from Seth. I looked at it, and it was just Byran. I opened the text message screen and saw that two of my friends were in Atlanta and wanted to hook up with me this weekend. Three other texts were from Byran.

Message #1, 11:59 P.M.:

Once again I tried calling you and no answer. Hit me back.

Message #2, 12:37 P.M.:

How long must you ignore me? Please call me. I have something to tell you.

Message #3, 1:05 P.M.

Allyson, this is serious. I need you to call me immediately. Fine if you don't want to know what's going on as my friend, but as my wife and per our contract, you need to contact me ASAP.

"Here you are, Ms. Ward," Julie said, passing my driver's license back to me.

"Thank you."

"Ms. Todd is waiting for you. Take those elevators directly behind you to the fourth floor. She is in apartment home four-twenty-four."

"Thanks. Have a great day," I said, turning to walk away.

"You too," she replied.

As I got on the elevator, my nerves began to overtake me. I'd had an image of a quiet, sickly lady in my head when I set out on my way here, but both Ben and the valet guy had convinced me otherwise. I had no idea what to expect.

The short elevator ride ended way before I wanted it to. I went in the direction of her apartment and stopped in front of her door. I wiped my sweaty palms on my dress, exhaled, and tried to remove any thoughts of Byran, which were slowly trying to plague my mind. The door opened just as soon as I lifted my hand to knock.

"Ms. Ward, I am Suzanne, Ms. Todd's nurse. How are you today?"

She was a full-figured woman, large enough to rival any linebacker, with red hair and, most shockingly, a gold tooth. What was it about these white folks in Augusta with gold teeth? Were they all stuck in the nineties?

"I am fine. How are you?" I asked, extending my hand.

"We give hugs around here. This is the country, and I can tell you are a little prissy," she said as she pulled me to her and squeezed me so tight, I thought my uterus would pop out of my nose. "So good to have you come here all the way from Atlanta to pick up Ms. Todd for Dr. Carson."

How did she know I was from Atlanta?

"Do I know you? Or a better question is, do you know me? How do you know I am from Atlanta?"

"For one, Julie called up and gave me your information. But also I recognized your name. I used to live in Atlanta, and I visited Cornerstone a few times."

Oh, Lord. Here we go. The last thing I needed was someone recognizing me. Yet I put on my first lady demeanor and flashed my generic first lady smile.

"It is such a pleasure to meet you. Thank you for visiting Cornerstone. And anytime you are ever in the Atlanta area, I hope you will come back by and visit with us again."

That was the same line I gave all the visitors.

She, however, did not like the impersonal treatment. "Look, you can save all of that for someone else. I don't need a speech," she said and moved out of the way to let me come in. "Ms. Todd, your ride is here."

"Well, she will have to wait a minute, because I ain't quite through getting my things together. Come on in here and have a seat, honey. It's gone be a minute," a short, dark skinned, petite woman said. "Don't just stand there. Go on and sit down."

I did as she asked me to do. She was a darker version of Seth and did not look sick at all. She appeared to be as healthy as me.

"Ms. Todd usually likes to have a warning before Dr. Carson comes or sends someone for her. But in light of everything going on, she understands he wasn't able to do that," Suzanne said, not knowing I had already been warned that it would take a while.

Ms. Todd stopped packing to ask, "Where is my grandson? Is he all right?"

"He is at the clinic, and yes, ma'am, he is fine. At least it seems that way to me."

I wanted to add that I was really worried and had been concerned about leaving him there alone, but I did not want to give the wrong impression—especially in front of Suzanne.

"Uh-huh. Now, who are you? You work for him, or you one of his patients?" Ms. Todd asked.

Before I could get a response out, Suzanne beat me to it.

"Ms. Todd, this is Pastor Byran Ward's wife. Remember me telling you about the church I was visiting before I moved here? Well, it's such a small world, because this lady is that pastor's wife. Strange, isn't it?"

Suzanne was messy, just like the other folks around this place. I could tell she was hinting at something, but I refused to give her any satisfaction. My mother had always taught me if you cannot prevent yourself from being exposed, expose yourself before anyone else has the opportunity to do it.

"She is right, Ms. Todd. I am a friend of your grandson, and he and I happened to be at the same place when the news broke on CNN. He was visibly shaken, and I was very concerned about him driving all this way alone, so I came with him."

"I see," Ms. Todd said and resumed packing. I looked at what was in her bag, and it seemed as if she was planning to stay at Seth's forever. She had enough clothes in there to last a couple of months.

"Do you need help with anything?" I offered.

"She doesn't like for anyone to bother her personal things. She will manage just fine," Suzanne said. I could have been reading into it, but I gathered that for some reason Suzanne didn't too much care for me.

"That's fine. I was just offering," I said as nicely as I could. She needed to back down, because I was definitely not the one she wanted to start a war with.

Ms. Todd suddenly stopped packing and fixed her eyes on the flat panel that was hanging on the wall across from her bed. "Suzanne, turn that up," she snapped.

We all turned our attention to the TV.

"We are back on location at the abortion clinic that was bombed late this morning. We are standing here with Dr. Seth Carson, owner of the clinic. Dr. Carson, thank you for taking the time to speak to us. First of all, how are you holding up?" the CNN correspondent asked.

"As anyone would feel, I guess. To go out of town on business, only to get back in town to find out that something terrible like this has happened, is unbelievable."

"I cannot imagine what must be going through your head right now. Outside of the destruction, you lost your entire staff in this horrendous crime."

Seth dropped his head, and I could see that he was fighting back tears. Sadness swept over me as I recalled the day I had met Cindy, his receptionist, as well as his nurse. Although Cindy was not as friendly as his nurse, no one deserved to have their life snatched away from them.

"Those girls were like family to me. I have had the same staff since I opened the clinic. I feel terrible, because I perform procedures only Wednesday through

Friday. I allowed them to come in Monday and Tuesday to give them more hours. They were all single mothers trying to make a living to support their kids." This time Seth allowed the tears to fall.

The correspondent took a moment to allow him to pull himself together before she continued. "We are deeply sorry for your loss. We talked to a few people who are familiar with you and your staff, and everyone has good things to say about you. When you opened your clinic, I am sure you had heard about other bombings that had taken place at various abortion clinics across the country. Did you ever think you might be the victim of such a crime?"

"Not at all. I still maintain my stance. Women come and utilize our services because they choose to. We do not force anything on anyone. We have had a few peaceful protesters in the past, doing nothing more than waving signs and shouting. This . . . this is shocking."

"Just a couple more questions. What do you plan to do now? Are you going to try to rebuild? We interviewed some of the locals, and we are told you had one of the most, if not *the* most, professional and nicest facilities in the area."

"I have not thought about what I will do tomorrow or the next day. I am still trying to get through this day."

"I understand. Before I let you go, have you heard any updates concerning the woman who was severely injured as she was walking into the clinic? I am told her name is Helen Reese."

"No, I have not heard any updates."

"Okay, thank you for speaking with us, Dr. Carson. We wish you the best of luck in the days to come, and again, you have our deepest sympathy."

"Thank you."

Seth turned to walk away as the correspondent ended her special report. My heart broke for him, and it was difficult holding back the tears I wanted to release on his behalf. His life had turned upside down in a matter of hours, and I could only imagine how he felt.

"Suzanne," Ms. Todd said, "get my cosmetic bag for me out of the bathroom. I am ready to go and get to my grandson."

"Yes, ma'am," Suzanne said, then went and got her bag.

"Are you ready to go, Mrs. Ward?" Ms. Todd asked.

"Please . . . call me Allyson. And, yes, I am ready when you are."

"I am ready."

She grabbed her purse and sweater and laid the sweater over her arm. She walked toward the door, grabbing her walking cane from the corner. Suzanne followed behind her with her bags, and I followed behind Suzanne. On my way out, I noticed several pictures of her and Seth sitting on the kitchen countertop. I wanted to lag behind a little to get a good look at them but decided against it.

As we walked to the elevator, Ms. Todd took slow, deliberate steps. She might look and act younger and healthier than she was, but her movements were that of a tired, sickly woman. We finally got to the elevator and rode back down to the first floor.

"Willie Jo, I am praying for your boy. I just saw him on the news. He will pull through this just fine. With the help of the good Lawd, things will work out," an older, gray-haired woman said.

"Charlie Mae, I sure do 'preciate the prayers. Keep him lifted up. We will get through this like we have gotten through everything else," Ms. Todd replied.

"I know you will. Just wanted you to know that you both are in my prayers," the old lady said.

"Mine too," a tall, slender man chimed in. "You know I love you, Willie Jo. I'd do anything I could to help you. You take care of Seth. He will need you."

"I love you too, old man," Ms. Todd teased. "And you don't have to worry about Seth. I am going to take care of him through this, just as I always have."

"How long you gonna be gone?" the man asked.

"I reckon just a few days. I can't really say right now. Got to see how long my baby gon' need me."

"You take it easy, now." The man walked over to Ms. Todd and hugged her. "Gon' miss you round here."

"Jimmy, I'll be back," she said, pushing him off. "You act like I'm gon' be gone forever."

"A day without you being round here seems like forever to me," this Jimmy person said.

"Oh, Jimmy, stop," she said, waving him off.

Suzanne pushed her big butt into the conversation. "Ms. Todd, everybody here knows that Mr. Jimmy is sweet on you," she said, laughing.

"That ain't none of your business if he is," Ms. Todd shot back.

Suzanne quickly got rid of that grin on her face. I loved it. So much so, I almost laughed out loud.

"Jimmy," Ms. Todd continued, "I will see y'all when I get back. Now, you make sure you don't forget to watch *American Idol* tomorrow night. I'll be watching it from Seth's place."

"I won't forget, Willie Jo," he said.

"All right. I'll see y'all later," she said and then turned to me. "I'm ready."

Everyone else who had gathered to express their concern said their good-byes as we walked out to the car. Suzanne, without a word, put Ms. Todd's bags in the car and went back inside. Ms. Todd climbed in the car, and I made sure her seat belt was securely fastened before I got in. The valet guy gave me the keys, and we were off to the next address written on the piece of paper.

Seth's house.

Chapter Fourteen

The winding road seemed to be everlasting, especially with the deafening silence in the car. Seth gave a new meaning to living the country life. We were so far off the beaten path, I was beginning to wonder if I had somehow made a wrong turn.

"I bet you have never been this far back in the woods, have you?" Ms. Todd asked. Those were the first words she had spoken since we left her building more than twenty minutes ago. Neither of us had anything to say—our minds were on the same thing. Or person . . . Seth.

"No, ma'am, I cannot say that I have. I was just wondering if maybe I had taken a wrong turn somewhere."

She chuckled. "We are almost there. Seth was raised in the country, on a farm, and so he duplicated his childhood habitat back out here in these sticks."

"I see."

"The only reason I do not live back out here with him is because I have to be closer to town in case I get sick."

"Ms. Todd, you appear to be as healthy as any twenty-year-old I know."

"You are too kind, dear, but Ms. Todd is a sick woman," she said, referring to herself. "I have renal failure."

"I am so sorry to hear that. Is it hereditary?"

"Well, my parents and one of my brothers died from it. After seven years, I am still holding on."

"How often do you go to dialysis?"

"Twice a week. Supposed to be three times, but ain't no sense in going that much. There's nothing they can do in that extra day that they can't do in two."

I nodded my head. "When you come back here to stay with Seth, what do you do about dialysis?"

"Seth calls a nurse in for me when I come here. There is an area set up in the house for me to take my dialysis."

Wow. Seth was becoming more attractive to me than he knew. To go to the extreme of setting up a room designated for his grandmother's treatment was honorable and admirable.

"Back at my apartment, Suzanne mentioned you are married to a pastor."

Here we go again.

"That is correct. I am."

"You must not be too happy."

"I'm fine. Why do you say that?"

"I'm an old woman, sweetie. You can't too much fool an old lady. I have been around for a long time, and I have pretty much seen it all. And by the look on your face anytime Seth's name is mentioned, I would say you are a little sweet on my grandson. Now, if you were happily married, I would be able to see that on your face too."

She looked at me sneakily. But I was going to stand my ground for right now. I decided I would work harder at not showing any emotions. Besides, what would this woman think of me having feelings for her grandson, knowing I am married?

"Seth is a good man, Ms. Todd. I will not deny that. But I am married."

"Chile, I already know you married. I asked if you were happily married. But you ain't got to answer, because I already know you are sweet on my Seth. I also know you married, but you ain't happy."

You really couldn't fool old people.

"It's a challenge, but I am hanging in there."

"Honey, all I can tell you is life is too short to live one second of it unhappy. I do understand that sometimes you have to fight for your marriage, but in order to do that, there has to be a marriage to fight for."

Truer words had never been spoken.

"Here's your turn, baby. Welcome to Carson Land."

I pulled into the stone driveway, and as far as I could see were acres and acres of green grass and rolling hills. A black wrought-iron fence outlined the property, and in the far distance I could see cows grazing in the field. I pulled up to the security gate.

"Dr. Carson, why are you . . ." The guard's voice trailed off as the window went farther down. "You are not Dr. Carson. Why are you driving his car?" he asked.

"Orlando, I'm in here," Ms. Todd said.

He stooped down so he could get a better look inside the car. "Oh, Ms. Todd, I didn't see you. How are you doing today?" he said, smiling.

"I fair well to be an old lady. How are those kids of yours doing?"

"They are fine. Getting bigger by the day."

"Good to hear it. Kinda in a hurry, son. Can you let us through?"

"Oh, yes, ma'am. Y'all take care. And please tell Dr. Carson he's in my prayers. I just got here, but I heard on the news what happened down there at the clinic. I suspect it won't be long before the media is tipped off and they find this place. But don't you worry. We will be prepared if they show up."

"I know you will. And keep on praying. We need all the prayer we can get."

He stepped back inside and pressed the button to open the gate. I drove for about half a mile before the most beautiful mansion I had ever seen came into plain view. It had seemed like the longest ride here, but now looking at this house made it worth it. Did performing abortions pay that well?

I was awestruck at what I saw. There was a lawn team working on his flower beds and shrubs, and no sooner could I open my door and get out than someone appeared.

"Mama Todd, it is so wonderful to see you, as always. We are so glad you are here," a flamboyant woman said. She was pretty, with light brown eyes. Her hair was as long as mine but wavy. "When Suzanne called to say you were on the way, I was relieved. We have all been watching the news and are so concerned about Seth. At least we have you here. You are the closest thing to him we have until he comes himself. Your presence will be soothing."

"Thank you, baby. I want you to meet, Allyson. She is one of Seth's friends," Ms. Todd said, pointing to me. "Allyson, this is Melanie. She runs Carson Land for us."

I walked over to her and extended my hand. I could have sworn I detected something strange about her, but I dismissed it. "Pleasure to meet you, Melanie."

"Thanks," she said briefly and turned back to Ms. Todd. "You must be exhausted with everything that has transpired today, and the drive here must have you fatigued as well. I know you had your dialysis this morning. I'm sure you want to rest."

"I am tired, but I refuse to put my head to the pillow before I find out how Seth is doing. I need to hear from him before I can relax."

"I know. We have all been sitting by the phone, waiting on a call. I have my phone right here," she said, waving it, "because I am sure he is going to call me as soon as he gets a minute. I am usually the first person he calls when anything happens."

"Help me in the house, baby. I want to at least rest these weary feet of mine. They don't have the same traveling ability they once had," Ms. Todd said.

Melanie nodded. "Of course."

We walked into the house, and straight ahead in the sitting room was a glass wall. Without even walking up to it, I could see the beautiful, sparkling pool that ran off into a gorgeous saltwater lake. This estate was breathtaking, to say the least. I thought I lived in luxury. Where I lived was nothing compared to this.

"Allyson, darling, have a seat," Ms. Todd said, taking a seat herself on the cranberry Victorian couch. I sat across from her in a Queen Anne chair. This entire room had an antique theme. From the Roman column candlestick phone to the vintage record player, everything about the room was a time warp, but it was superbly done.

"Allyson, do I need to call a car service for you?" Melanie asked. The tone of her voice suggested her comment was more a statement than a question. She was trying to find out how much longer I would be staying. What was with this chick?

"No, Seth asked me to wait here for him."

"I am sure he understands you cannot wait for him all night. You have a husband to get home to, right? Suzanne told me you were married."

I wished I could slap Suzanne dead in the mouth. I knew she was trouble from the beginning. And whoever this Melanie woman was, she was about to learn what it meant to stay in her place. I was tired and did not feel like verbally sparring. But speaking of Byran, I knew he had to have called by now. With so much going on, I had honestly forgotten about my troubles back home. Just as I pulled my phone out of my purse to check and see if I had missed anything, it started ringing. So instead of answering Melanie, I flashed her a devilish grin and answered my phone instead.

"Hi, Seth. We have all been so worried. Are you okay?" I glared at Melanie and secretly hoped the saliva she was gulping down tasted a little like acid.

"Yes, baby, I am fine. Did you and Nana make it to the house yet? I know how long it can take her to get ready sometimes. I was trying to wait until I thought maybe you guys had gotten there," he said.

"We are here. We arrived a few minutes ago."

"Good. At least that is one thing off of my mind."

"Where are you? When will you be here?"

"I am down at the police station right now. They are going over some details about the bombing. They have reason to believe that the protestors just happened to be there at the time of the bombing but were not actually responsible for it."

"Are you serious?"

I looked over at Ms. Todd, who had a serious look on her face. Melanie, on the other hand, was furious. She was breathing hell's flames and could probably tear Mount Everest into pieces with her bare hands.

"Yes, a bystander was filming something else on his camera phone, but he captured something that looks interesting. The fire department is still developing a report, but it appears that maybe the bombs were placed inside rather than thrown inside. The detonators were found in three different locations. One of them was in my office."

"You have got to be kidding me!" I exclaimed. "Who would be trying to kill you?"

That statement caused Ms. Todd to rise up from her seat. She was eager to speak with Seth, but she waited patiently for me to get done.

"Well, like the police said, it could have been done by one of the protesters. But there is no way Cindy would have let anyone past that reception desk, unless she was forced or unless it was someone she knew and felt I would be comfortable with going into my office."

"I am at a loss for words. I thought by now an arrest would have been made."

"Me too. This day has turned from bad to worse. It appears someone might want me dead, and if I had not been in Atlanta with you, I would have been. I had planned to get up early, before dawn, so I could make it to the office by nine. I guess I should thank you for saving my life."

I smiled but quickly cleared my face of the smile. I stole a glance at Melanie, and her anger now appeared to have turned into rage.

"I don't know if I can take that credit. So how long before you get here? Your grandmother is so worried about you." Melanie cleared her throat. "As is everyone else here."

"We will be leaving . . ."

Melanie started talking, and it took my attention away from what he was saying.

"Can I please speak to Seth?"

"Seth, Melanie would like to speak to you. I am sure Ms. Todd would like to also," I informed him.

"Let me speak to my grandmother. Tell Melanie I will speak to her when I get there."

I handed Ms. Todd the phone. "Seth wants to speak to you." I turned to Melanie. "He said he will speak to you when he gets here."

If looks could kill, I would be a dead woman. She stomped out of the room like a mad kid whose favorite toy had been taken. Childish. However, it was beginning to make sense to me. The cold air that passed between us outside was her way of marking her territory. She wanted Seth, and even though she knew I was married, I still posed a threat.

Ms. Todd spoke to Seth briefly before handing the phone back to me.

"Here you are," she said, shaking her head. "He hung up. He said he will see us soon. I just don't know who would want to kill my baby." She sat back down in the chair she had been sitting in. "I know there are some mean and vicious people in this here world, but Seth is one of the few people I know who is genuine, has a good heart, and will give anybody the shirt off his back. This is just so baffling to me."

"From what I know about him, I agree. I cannot imagine anyone wanting to hurt him."

"What in God's name is this world coming to? Innocent people lost their lives today. And if Seth had not been in Atlanta, he would very well be gone too. It gets to be too much for my little heart to take."

I moved to sit beside her. I wrapped my arms around her shoulders and silently said a prayer for Seth and for the families of the ones who lost their lives in the bombing. I did not know much about praying, but my time as a first lady had taught me a thing or two about faking the funk. I couldn't pray like others, but I did the best I could do.

"Excuse me, Mama Todd. Claudia wants to know if you would like to have dinner," Melanie said, reappearing, with a composed demeanor.

"No, I will wait for Seth."

"Okay, well, at least go to your room and kick your feet up," Melanie replied.

"I done told you I ain't going to bed until Seth gets here. Slide that ottoman over here, and let me put my feet on that," she said, pointing to a foot stool.

"Yes, ma'am."

"Melanie, do you mind telling me where the restroom is?" I said.

Before she could respond, Ms. Todd answered. "Melanie, show her to the guest room on the third floor."

"But, Mama Todd, do you think Seth will be comfortable with her being on the third floor, where his master bedroom is? I don't even have a room on the third floor." Melanie's anger was returning, and her eyes shot more hate daggers at me.

"I am positive he won't have a problem with it, because before he hung up, those were the instructions he gave me."

Melanie frowned. "Do we even know who this woman is? Why do we trust her again?"

"Melanie, you are getting beside yourself. I have never known you to be so defiant. Please show our guest to her room for the night. My goodness, it's just for one night. What is the harm in that? If Seth trusts her, I trust her also."

"Follow me," Melanie snapped as she glared at me.

We left the room and turned the corner, and a few feet away was an elevator. *He has an elevator in his house?* I was more than impressed with Seth's quality of living. The part of me who loved nice things— okay, adored nice things—was more than excited. I could barely contain my enthusiasm. If I could somehow figure out a way to end up with Seth, I would be one happy camper. My mind raced a million miles per second. Not only could this work out for me, but my mother would be happy too. Actually, this would be a serious upgrade for us both.

As the elevator carried us to the third floor, I tried to shake my head of those thoughts, because as wealthy as he was, right now he was a hurting man seemingly on the run for his life.

On the third floor was the most beautiful bedroom I had ever seen in my life. Decorated in hues of black and gray, it had to be at least the size of five of my bedrooms. I had never seen such a big room. Surely this was not the guest bedroom.

"This is Seth's room. He usually never allows anyone on this floor, so it speaks volumes that he has requested that you be on this level. Over here is the guest bedroom," Melanie said, walking me over to a bedroom that was half the size of Seth's. It had the same color scheme as Seth's room. "Actually, the room was built to be a nursery. But after things did not work out with his ex, it became an extra bedroom. The only time he allows anyone up here . . ." She paused. "Matter of fact, I was the last person to sleep in this room," she said. "Shortly after, I was hired on as the estate manager, and now I have a bedroom on the second floor." A certain sadness came over her.

Oh, I get it. She is worried I am here to replace her. She was so far off, she had no idea.

"I appreciate Dr. Carson's hospitality. I can assure you I will be gone before anyone gets up."

"I doubt that. The farmworkers are up when the roosters crow."

"Farmworkers? Roosters?"

"Yes, this is a full-fledged farm."

"Ms. Todd told me he re-created his childhood life, but I did not think she meant that literally."

"That is how they have made their wealth. They sell cows for thousands of dollars. They sell organic eggs produced by their roosters and chickens. This family is very wealthy not because he is a doctor, but because these one-hundred acres of land produce. From strawberries to steak, it is all on Carson Land."

"Wow. This is pretty amazing."

"Yeah, it is. Dr. Carson is a brilliant man. When he was building this place, he slept in the hospital where he worked. His vision for Carson Land was so great, he was willing to sacrifice until it was completed. This entire place is paid for. Debt free. Isn't that amazing?" she said.

I studied her face, and it was almost as if she had drifted into another place. She was in love with him.

"Yeah, that is pretty amazing."

She turned to face me. Her expression went from soft to hard in a matter of seconds. "So what is your story, Allyson Ward? Why are you here?"

She had just thrown the first ball. It was official—the game had begun. What she did not know is that I was the master at game playing. My current role as the preacher's wifey did not require me to play games, but if a game was what she wanted, a game was what she would get. I still remembered how it worked.

"I am not sure what you want to hear, Melanie, but I have no story to tell you. As far as why I am here, I am here because Seth asked me to be here. What more do you want to know?"

"I have seen women like you. I have had to turn away quite a few of them in order to protect Seth. You find out he is superrich, and you sink your gold-digging, crippling claws into him, and then you turn around and break his heart. Therefore, if you are here for any reason other than to be a support system for him, I will find out and I will put a stop to it. Understood?"

Wow, this chick came into the game giving her best. I had underestimated her.

"Melanie, I can assure you, you have seen no one like me. You do not know me, and I would appreciate it if you reserved your false pretenses and premature assumptions about me before you get the facts about me.

And here are the facts. Seth is a good friend of mine. I do not need to dig his gold, because I have my own gold. And the only way I could break his heart is if he gave it to me to do so. And here is something else you can be assured of. . . . If he gives me his heart, I will not break it. Last, no matter what the situation is or the circumstance surrounding it, I am not one who is easily stopped. Understood?"

Whoosh! Nothing but net, baby!

She walked closer to me and stood toe to toe and eye to eye.

"Mrs. Ward, let's get an understanding. This is my turf and—"

"I'm sorry. I thought this was Carson Land. Are you a Carson?"

"Not yet. I will be soon. It's just a matter of time," she said as she walked over to the window and looked out at the lake. "I'll be Mrs. Seth Carson really soon," she said just above a whisper.

She sounded really scary—almost stalkerish. Something about this woman gave me the creeps. I couldn't put my finger on it just yet, but I intuitively knew all her dots did not connect. Her mental elevator stopped at the second floor, where her bedroom was. She wasn't all there. I did not believe for one minute that Seth was about to marry her, but what I believed did not matter. She believed it.

"I really need to use the restroom. Can I have some time alone?" I had to get this woman away from me, and while I was good at intimidating women back in my day, this woman was of a different breed. You couldn't outdo crazy.

"This home, with the exception of the third floor, is under video surveillance—all twenty-three thousand square feet of it. Please don't let me see you roaming, Mrs. Ward."

Yeah, she was really off her rocker.

"Melanie, I just want to use the restroom. That is it. I can assure you I have no reason to roam. If I want a tour of Carson Land, I am certain Seth would have no problem giving it to me. So can I please get a few minutes to myself?" She looked as if she was ready to choke me, which meant she had given me control of her emotions. So I let her down easy. "Besides, I do need to call my husband and let him know where I am."

That statement simultaneously pleased and comforted her. If only for a moment, she no longer felt threatened by me.

"But, of course," she said, smiling. "I am not married yet, but I know I would be doing the same thing," she said in a tone that suggested we were best girlfriends engaging in girl talk. I made a mental note to talk to Seth about her when it was the appropriate time. "All right, I will leave you alone. Just get back on the elevator, and come down when you are done."

"Thanks, Melanie."

Finally she left. I immediately went over to sit down on the king-sized canopy bed, which had a beautiful satin purple, black, and ivory comforter on it. I dug through my purse to retrieve my phone. As expected, Byran had called a few times, as did my mother. I decided to break down and call Byran. Although I was still upset with him, I knew I was pushing my luck by continuing to ignore him.

I dialed his number.

"Allyson!" he exclaimed. "Where the hell are you? Have you gone insane? I have been worried sick about you."

"Byran, I apologize. There's just been a lot going on. You and this baby thing have taken up most of my head space. It really is too much for me. I just need some space—some time to process all of this."

"I understand you being upset, but you are still my wife and—"

"Wifey," I corrected.

"What?"

"I am your wifey, not your wife. There is a big difference."

"I cannot and will not have this conversation with you right now."

"All right, Byran. Why have you called me so many times?"

"You are really pushing me, Allyson."

"And you have already pushed me! What are you expecting me to do? How do you want me to be? You left me last night to go and be with another woman while she gave birth to your son. You left me. Do you hear that? You left me. What was I supposed to do? Sit at home and cry enough tears to fill up the Grand Canyon? No, Byran, you are the one who's insane."

I was breathing so heavily, I thought my heart would erupt from my chest. I could take a lot, but I was nearing my breaking point.

"You win. I am not in a position to address this right now. I am coming home tomorrow for a few hours to get some clothes and to handle a few things at church. I expect to see you there. I need some help with a few things while I am away handling the crisis here at the hospital."

"What crisis at the hospital?"

"BJ is in NICU, and his mom is in ICU. She developed an infection, and we"—he paused for a second—"we don't know if she will make it."

That was sad, but did he say, "BJ?"

"BJ, as in Byran, Jr.?"

"Yes."

"Oh," I sighed. "Well, like I said before, I will be praying for you all."

"Thanks. I expect to see you tomorrow, when I get home."

"Okay."

"I expect to see my *wife* there. Whoever this is I am talking to now, leave her wherever you are."

Sometimes you just had to know when to leave things alone. After the day I had had, I honestly had no power in me to argue and fight.

"Okay."

"I should be home by noon," he said, but my mind was in another place.

"Okay."

"I see you have few words, so I am going to let you go. See you tomorrow."

"Okay."

He exhaled loudly before he hung up. If that was his way of releasing frustration, then maybe I would try it too. Not one time did he ask me if I was okay. Not one time did he ask how my day had been. Yeah, it was time for me to exhale.

Without moving from the bed, I was able to look out the window. I was grateful for the lights that were shining brightly outside, affording me the opportunity to enjoy the astounding views of the pool and the lake. What I would not do to go for a swim or even just wade in the water.

I looked around the well-decorated room. Whoever was Seth's interior designer knew their stuff. So far everything I had seen in the house was done above par. He had spared no expense. The only thing I did not like about this room was the absence of paintings on the walls. But that could be overlooked, given the expensive furniture, the exotic trees in each corner of the room, and the huge Oriental rug in the center of the floor. The window treatments were done in the same fabric as the comforter.

Just as I was getting up to walk into the bathroom, I heard a loud noise. Initially, I thought it was thunder, but as the noise got closer and louder, I realized it was a chopper.

Oh, Lord, the media, I thought.

It was appalling to me how far some people were willing to go in order to get a story. I was willing to bet that more than a few people were parked outside the gate, hoping to catch someone coming or going.

I wondered how Miss "I Can Get Rid of Anyone" Melanie would handle dismissing them. The chopper got lower, and I realized it was actually about to land in a field about three hundred feet away. *The nerve of some people.*

As the chopper landed, I went into the bathroom to see if I could find some things to freshen up with so I would look presentable when Seth arrived. To my surprise, there was an array of assorted face washes, creams, shower gels, lotions, body sprays, oils, and perfumes on the counter. I was taken aback. Who did Seth have all this stuff for? Melanie had said he never let anyone on this level, but if that was the case, why would he need so many feminine products? The bathroom itself was about the size of my entire bedroom. It was a woman's dream. There was a huge Jacuzzi tub that looked as if it seated six to eight people, a flat panel just above it, and candles were sitting everywhere. On the vanity was a blow-dryer and finishing products, and above the vanity were bright lights and a huge mirror—perfect for doing makeup and hair.

I continued to roam around the bathroom and opened a door within it to find a closet full of gowns, lingerie, and bedroom shoes. I looked through the clothes and realized none of them had been worn. Everything, including the shoes, still had tags on it.

"You find everything you need?"

Startled, I jumped back and released a loud scream.

"Sweetheart, it's just me," Seth said.

My hand flew to my chest. He had scared the living daylights out of me.

"Seth, what in the world are you doing here?"

He flashed me the most perfect smile I had ever seen in my life. Were his teeth always perfect? "Last time I checked, I lived here."

My breathing slowed, but only for a moment, because Seth walked over and kissed me until my breathing was dependent on his.

"This is how I want to come home every day," he said, releasing my swollen lips.

"When did you get here?" I said, still caught up in a daze.

"A few minutes ago."

"Did you see the media?"

"No, I never enter the property from the front. But they told me that several trucks were starting to accumulate by the gate. I have the best security team in all of Augusta. There is no way anyone could sneak in. Even if they did, by the time they got to the actual house, someone would have caught in on the camera."

"Oh, okay. But I meant the media that was flying overhead. A chopper landed out back less than ten minutes ago."

"No, sweetheart, that was not the media. That was me."

This man was like the Mega Millions, and I had the winning numbers.

Chapter Fifteen

"Why don't you take a shower and change into something else? I have to run downstairs and talk to Nana and brief Melanie on what I need her to take care of for me. I came straight up to make sure you were okay."

This man knew exactly what to say and when to say it. The fact that he made me his priority after he had one of the worst days of his life was impressive—and heartwarming. I could easily get accustomed to a man treating me like that—especially a rich one.

"I appreciate that so much. However, I am fine. My concern is for you. Why don't you go shower and change? You can tell me what you need Melanie to know, and I'll brief her. As for Nana, I am sure she understands you want to get comfortable before you come down."

"Where have you been all my life?" he joked.

"Possibly waiting for you," I joked back. Actually, I was only half joking, because I was half serious.

"Girl, you better stop talking like that. That kind of talk will get you another ring on your finger, and this time it will mean something."

This man is about to get it.

"Go on to your room before you start something." I playfully slapped him on the shoulder. "What about dinner? Have you eaten?"

"I'm not really that hungry. This day has totally drained me. I would be handling it a lot worse if you were not here. Melanie and my entire staff should really thank you for my good mood."

"I don't think Melanie will be thanking me for anything," I mumbled.

"What do you mean?"

"She is really concerned about who I am to you, and has made it very clear that she is the queen bee around here and the soon to be Mrs. Carson. I think the only reason she is not more concerned than she is, is the fact that I am married. If it were not for that, I think she would have already found a way to get rid of me by now."

"Melanie is delusional. She is also very intimidated by any woman I have over for company. I am not a fool—I know she wants me. However, what I feel for her is like what one feels for a little sister. She is good at what she does executively, and that is as far as it will ever go."

"Speaking of company, why do you have so many female items in this bathroom?"

"To be honest, I bought all these things for the woman I was engaged to. I just never got rid of them because I knew one day the right woman would come along and appreciate my acts of kindness. I got rid of the things that she used and wore, and kept what was untouched."

"I see. Well, you have splendid taste, sir."

"I do the best I can."

"Whatever. You know you are the boss," I said, flashing my best smile. "So . . . boss, what are your instructions for Melanie? And go ahead and tell me what you want for dinner, because you will be eating something, even if it is just a fruit salad."

"Yes, ma'am," he said as he walked out of the bathroom and toward his bedroom. "Tell Melanie to tell

Claudia to make me a turkey sandwich on wheat, with lettuce, Swiss cheese, and mustard only. I want orange juice with no pulp and no ice."

"Got it. That it? No side item?"

"Baked Lay's . . . barbecue."

"Okay."

"Also, tell Melanie I need her to set up a press conference. I want no more than five news outlets there. CNN, MSNBC, NBC Twenty-six, WRDW News Twelve, and WJBF News Channel Six. Tell her that I will do it promptly at seven o'clock in the morning. Oh, tell her to make sure she calls Lance. That's my attorney. She should know this, but I do not want to do anything without him being present. Have her alert the police department. I would like someone from the investigative team to be here to answer any questions the reporters may have pertaining to the bombing. Got that?" he asked, stopping abruptly, which almost made me run into the back of him.

"Got it. Anything else?"

"Yeah, but I will wait and tell you that later."

"Go ahead and tell me now. I can remember."

"It's not about whether or not you can remember."

"Oh. Well, okay. I am going to go on down and relay these messages."

"Thank you, Allyson," he said, wrapping his arms around my waist and pulling me into him. "I know you are not my lady, but it sure does feel like it. Your outstanding support today has made me believe that love is attainable for me again. It has made me realize just how much I am missing in my life. Of all the things I have accomplished and attained, I have no one special to share them with. I hope to change that really soon."

I practically melted into his body as he kissed me on the cheek. The touch of his lips always set me ablaze. I pulled myself away, turned, and pressed the button for the elevator. I stepped inside, and as the door closed, he just stood there . . . intensely watching me. This man was all that and a bag of Ranch Doritos.

When the elevator opened on the first floor, all eyes were on me.

"Finally, someone emerges from the third floor. Allyson, darling, you look washed out. Are you feeling well? Did something happen up there?" Melanie asked.

Wouldn't you like to know. . . .

"I feel perfectly fine," I said, waving off her insinuation. "I do have some messages for you from Seth." I took a seat in the chair I'd occupied before.

"Messages? For me? From Seth?" Melanie asked, dumbfounded.

"Yes, yes, and yes. He decided to stay upstairs and change into something more comfortable, so I offered to relay any messages he had for you. I am assuming he wants you to get working on these things immediately."

She cleared her throat. "I am . . . I'm surprised he gave you a message for me. Seth knows I take orders only from him—directly from him."

"It don't matter how they come to you, chile. Just get the work done," Ms. Todd said, sounding clearly agitated. I think she had had enough of Melanie and her childish temper tantrums for the evening.

Hesitantly, Melanie responded, "Okay, I guess Mama Todd is right. What are the messages?"

She retrieved a pen and a pad from the drawer of the sofa table that was directly behind the couch. I gave her all of Seth's instructions, and she wrote them down. When I had concluded relaying his message, she disappeared into another room.

"How is my grandson?" Ms. Todd asked me.

"Surprisingly, he is handling this better than I ever could. Honestly, I think once he stops and settles down, the reality of what has happened will set in on him."

"If that be the case, I am glad you are here."

"Really?"

"Yes. My main and only concern is him. However he achieves happiness is all right with me. And when he breezed by us earlier to get upstairs to you, I could see happiness all over him. I have not seen that sparkle in his eyes in a long time. You gave him that sparkle back, baby. I thank you for it."

Wow. Without even trying, I had won over his grandmother. That was usually not something that was easy to do. I was still trying to get Byran's mother to like me. I had not even started on his grandmother yet.

"Thank you, Ms. Todd."

"Call me Nana."

Whoa. She wanted me to address her as if she was my grandmother too?

"Okay, I will call you by whatever name you prefer."

"So does my grandson know you are married?"

"Yes, ma'am, he does."

She nodded her head. "Knowing him like I know him, he probably doesn't care. I mean he does, but when he sets his mind to get something, he usually doesn't stop until he gets it. You hear what I'm saying, baby?"

"I hear you, Nana."

"So if you don't want him in your life, you need to find a way to get him out of it right now, because I don't think he's planning on going anywhere."

"To be honest, Nana, I don't think I want him to go anywhere."

Suddenly I felt the need to be transparent. One thing about talking to older people, they always seemed to make you feel comfortable with telling them all your business, and they always had a way of helping you navigate through the murkiest waters.

"That's 'cause you ain't happily married. I told you I'm an old lady. I done been around for a minute, and I know a woman in love when I see one, and you ain't no kinda ways in love with your husband. Am I right?"

"I do love him, but in love . . . I don't think so."

"If you don't know so, then you ain't."

She was right.

"I'm not. I thought I was falling in love with him, but our situation is so complicated. He makes it difficult for me to love him. No matter how hard I try—or tried—he pushed me away. But our marriage wasn't built on anything in the first place. It literally is nothing more than a piece of paper."

Every time I admitted to the stupidity of my situation, another part of me died to it. Meeting Seth had jump-started my thinking on an entirely different level. For the first time, I had a glimpse of hope that you could have a future with a man who was rich and who actually cared. All the other guys I had dated who were rich had given to me because of what I had given to them. Never had any of them given to me expecting nothing in return. Until Seth. And Seth had not really given me anything but his time, his undivided attention, and a portion of himself. He had not taken me on a shopping spree, which in times past would have been enough for me to be head over heels in love with a man. He had not wined and dined me, neither had he given me or my girlfriends all-expense paid trips to private islands—something else I was accustomed to and that would have had me doing anything a man wanted me to do. I had no access to his American Express card or his bank account. Yet I was intrigued. I was smitten.

He had given me simple things. And never in my life had simple things mattered until now.

"I don't ever tell anybody to leave a happy home or a home that is built on a solid foundation," Ms. Todd revealed. "Because even if the storm comes, a home that is built on a solid foundation will survive whatever comes its way. That's why it's so important to have the kinda love that will last a lifetime."

"Does that even exist?"

"Oh, it exists, baby. I had it with Seth's grandfather. He was taken from me early, but we had that kind of love that would still be going right now if he were here."

"If you don't mind me asking . . . what happened to him?"

"He went up North to do some work back in the sixties, and he never came back. He got into it with one of his friends, it got out of control, and that man killed my husband. I still remember like it was yesterday, the day I got the news. I could hardly believe it. But one thing that helped me get through his death was knowing he died loving me. I would be willing to bet I was the last person he thought about when he took his last breath."

She paused and stared into the abyss as the expression on her face told a story of its own. Even after all the years that had gone by, it was evident she still loved him to this day. "So you need to find that type of love. The type of love that will take a beating and get stronger and not weaker. The type of love that could be on its last breath and you beat the other person trying to bring it back to life. That is the type of love you need in a marriage. If you don't have that, you ain't got yourself nothing."

"Well, I ain't got myself nothing," I said, laughing. The Ebonics of older people was amusing.

"You need to find yourself something. Or perhaps you need to realize that something, or someone, is staring you right in the face."

"What's staring who in the face?" Melanie asked as she walked back in the room.

"Did you get everything done?" Ms. Todd asked, completely ignoring her question.

"Yes, I did. Mama Todd, I wanted to ask, are you ready for Claudia to make you something to eat?"

"As a matter of fact, I am. I will have exactly what Seth is having." She turned to me. "Allyson, you must be starving. Do you care for anything to eat?"

"No, I think I am good."

Ms. Todd shook her head. "No, you're not. Your arms and legs are too skinny and poor. You need a little meat on your bones."

I could not help but laugh. Ms. Todd was hilarious, and she was definitely from the old school. Old people believed in you getting enough to eat.

"I surrender," I said, holding my hands up, feigning defeat. "I will take a turkey sandwich as well. But I would like lettuce, cheese, mayonnaise, and pickles, if it isn't too much trouble."

"It won't be no trouble at all, will it, Melanie?"

"Not at all. I will go let Claudia know now."

Melanie scurried away like a dog that had gotten into a fight and lost.

"I don't like that girl," Ms. Todd whispered.

"Who? Melanie?"

"Yeah. There is something about her that doesn't sit well with me. I have been trying to put my finger on it, but I never can."

"What do you think it is?"

"Other than wanting my grandson to be her husband . . . I'm not quite sure yet. One thing I hate is leaving him here with her when I have to go home. She tries to pretend she likes me, but I ain't nobody's fool. That chile don't like me one bit. But the feeling is mutual, because I can't stand her, either. She ain't fooling me. She good at what she do, but I bet we would all see a different side of her if she thought Seth had someone special in his life."

"You think?"

"Oh, honey, I don't think it. I know it. That child's screws ain't all the way in. All her scruples ain't there. Seth doesn't ever want to hear me talk about her, because she's so good at what she does, but I have a bad feeling about Li'l Miss Melanie. I think before it's over, we are going to all hate the day we met her."

"Those are some strong words to say, Nana."

"I mean it. But one thing about it and two things for sure, you can't slick a can of oil. I got my eyes on her."

The elevator door opened, and Seth emerged. He was wearing white linen pants and a Morehouse T-shirt. Even dressed down from his usual slacks and button-down shirts, he looked good. He embodied sexy.

"Ladies, what have we here? Have you all been gossiping about something or somebody? No, let me rephrase that. Who and or what have you been gossiping about?"

"Son, who said we were gossiping?"

"Nana, I don't know Allyson as well as I know you, but I do know that look you get on your face when you have been gossiping."

"Look? What look are you talking about?" Ms. Todd said, feigning innocence.

Pointing to her, he answered, "That sneaky look right there. Now spill it. What y'all in here chatting about?"

This playful moment that danced between us seemed perfect. It was as if we did it all of the time.

"I don't know what you're talking about. Allyson, do you know what Seth is speaking of?"

I shrugged. "Nana, I have the slightest idea what Seth is speaking of."

"Oh, so y'all gonna leave me out of the loop? Okay, I see."

"Dinner is served," Melanie announced. "Seth, honey, I did not know you had come down. I took care of everything you wanted me to take care of per Allyson. I would still like to double-check with you on your instructions for me just in case she might have forgotten something."

"I am certain Allyson did not forget anything," Seth replied. "I can almost assure you she did not."

Melanie was taken aback. "How can you be so sure?" she asked through a sarcastic chuckle.

"Melanie, not now, okay? I have had one hell of a day, and the last thing I need is you questioning me. Please, if you want to help me, just do as I ask without question."

She walked up to him and placed her hand on his shoulder. "You are right, dear. I am totally out of place, not to mention I am being insensitive. Please accept my apology."

He moved away from her touch. "No problem." He turned to Ms. Todd and me. "Are you gossiping ladies ready to eat?"

"I thought you were not hungry," I said jokingly.

"I really am not, but you did a good job of convincing me that I need to eat," he replied.

Melanie started to pretend she was choking.

"Do you need some water, Mel?" I asked. I knew she was livid, but she was just so much fun to play with.

She glared at me. "It's Melanie, and no, I will be fine."

"Seth, baby, before we eat, I just want to say a couple of things," Ms. Todd said as she got up from the couch. "I am so glad we serve a God who is merciful, who is kind, and who is quick to step in and rescue us from the hand of the devil. You could have been dead and sleeping in your grave, but God made death get back and behave. For that reason, I believe we owe God praise. For through danger seen and unseen, He protected each and every one of us. You were raised in the church, and you have been raised to know God, and, Seth, this is a time for you to get back in right standing with Him, because if He never does another single thing for you, He has already done enough this day. You might have lost your business, but that's all right. There is something else better waiting for you."

"Amen," Melanie chimed in. "I totally agree with Mama Todd."

"Nana, you are absolutely correct. The Lord has been dealing with me recently about getting back to where I used to be when I would pray and live a life pleasing to him. Allyson can tell you I was already thinking of leaving the clinic, anyway."

"Really?" Melanie asked. "You never shared that."

"I shared it only with Allyson. But, yeah, I had been considering going into mentoring or going back to being a surgeon."

Melanie frowned. "Surgeon? That would keep you away from Carson Land even more hours than the clinic did. We would never see you."

Everybody looked at Melanie. Why did she always feel she had to take over a conversation?

"Melanie, this is a decision I have to make on my own. Anyway, like I was saying . . . Nana, I want you to know that I appreciate your prayers. I would not have made it through my life without you keeping me before the Lord. Even when I went astray and was living the life I wanted to live, you never gave up on my spirit." He walked over to her, and I saw a strong, masculine man transform into a little boy as he laid his head on her shoulder and let the tears fall.

I stood there in amazement. Although I was married to a pastor, I had never known Byran to be as transparent as Seth was tonight. Byran always seemed to have it all together. In all the time I had known Byran, I could not recall one single conversation where we talked about the Lord and living right. I could not recall ever praying with him or sharing my spiritual convictions. Matter of fact, I did not know if I was even spiritual. I mean, I did what I had to do for my role, but outside of church, I never really thought about God and how He wanted me to live. Once again, Seth had opened my eyes to something else.

"I will never give up on you, because the Lord has never given up on me. There is enough grace to cover all of us, and grace will lead us back home to our rightful place," Ms. Todd said. "We have to trust that God has a master plan for our lives, and even when we do not understand what His plan is or how His plan will work out, we have to believe that He has it all under control."

I did not realize I was crying until I felt the tears begin to cascade slowly down my face and plunge into the crease of my cleavage. I wanted what Ms. Todd had. There was such power in her words. I wanted that kind of conviction. Up until now I had just lived. I had never really thought about God's master plan for my life. My mother had taught me to live a good life, to treat people right, and I would be happy. However, I was beginning to realize that something was still missing. Somehow what I knew as living the good life was not enough anymore. There was still a void. A huge one.

"You are right, Nana," Seth said, lifting his head and wiping the residue of his tears away. "I do not know a lot of things, but I do know that Jesus saved my life today. I do know that He has a way of getting your attention. And I do know that He must love me. I will never understand why He spared me and not the girls at the office." He broke down in tears again.

We all stood paralyzed in the moment and allowed Seth to release his pain. He continued to cry for several minutes. All thoughts of dinner had evaporated, and we each went and embraced him. There was such a spirit of love in the room.

It was a love unlike any I had ever felt before.

Chapter Sixteen

"I'm going to miss you when you leave tomorrow morning," Seth said as we sat in a love seat on the balcony outside of his bedroom. "Having you near me for the last day or so has spoiled me. I feel like this is the way it should be all of the time."

Truth be told, I felt the same way. One day with him seemed like a thousand years.

"I am going to miss you too," I said simply. Since the encounter we had before dinner, I had been a woman of few words. I could not wait to get home to do some soul-searching. I had experienced something I never knew existed. For the first time in my life, I wanted a real relationship with God.

"I hope you do not become a stranger after you leave. I know you are married, and I have to respect that. Speaking of which, please forgive me for any way I have behaved that was disrespectful to you as a married woman. The kissing, the touching . . . I am sorry."

"There is no need to apologize. You have not done anything I have not allowed you to do."

"I know, but I am the man. I am supposed to set the standard and the example for any relationship you and I have. But the moment I laid eyes on you, my heart felt weak. I knew I would not be satisfied until I had you. Or at least tried to."

I smiled as I remembered Ms. Todd's words from earlier. She had said almost those same words.

"How do you know you want me, Seth? You barely know anything about me."

"A man knows, Allyson. What I see in you is a pure heart that has been tainted somehow. I don't know how you got yourself in the situation you are in, but I would be willing to bet that right now, in this very moment, if you could turn back the hands of time, you would. You are more than what you give yourself credit for. So you should not be asking how I know I want you. You should be perpetually rehearsing in your mind all the wonderful reasons any man would."

Was this guy some type of angel? Truly, he was too good to be true. No man had ever challenged me to think of myself in such a way. Most men were attracted to my outward beauty, and in turn I was attracted to their status. If they had money, they had me. But now I was inclined to believe that none of that truly mattered if you had love—and God.

"You are right. I should."

"If you decide to never see me again, I want you to remember you are worth more than any amount of money that any man could ever give you. You are worth more than rubies or any other precious stone. You are worth more than a black card, red bottoms, or any designer shoe or dress. You are worth more than a quick lay. You are beautiful. You are wondrously made. I want you to believe that and know that. I want you to keep saying that until it becomes a part of you. Do you hear what I am saying to you?"

"Yes," I said through tears.

He moved over closer to me and used his thumb to wipe my tears as they fell.

"You are too pretty to cry. You are too special to hurt."

I leaned my head into his chest and cried like a baby. A part of me felt really bad for crying, because this night should have been about him, but his words were an emotional sedative. They soothed me.

"Thank you," I finally managed to get out.

He lifted my chin and stared into my eyes. "Tell me . . . what are you dreams?"

"I don't really have any. I thought the sum of life was not struggling financially, making sure my mother was not struggling, shopping, enjoying friends, and supporting whatever dream or goal my husband had."

He shook his head in disagreement. "Nothing about what you said is a dream." He leaned into the arm of the love seat and pulled me back against him. "You told me that once you wanted to be a nurse. Why have you not pursued that?"

"What is the salary of a nurse?"

"It varies depending on what type of nurse you become."

"I can guarantee you that whatever the salary is, it is not enough to support the lifestyle I have and am accustomed to having."

"That may be true. But you cannot put a price tag on a dream. A dream is worth going after even if it pays nothing."

"No one can survive off of a dream."

"I beg to differ. I survive off mine every single day. Carson Land was a childhood dream. I grew up in the country and decided I wanted to die in the country. People thought I was crazy building Carson Land back out here in the middle of nowhere. They said people would not come all the way out here to do business with me. They said I would never make enough money to maintain this place. They said all sorts of things. And I have consistently proved them wrong. This property makes money while I sleep. If I never worked another day of my life in the medical field, I could still maintain my lifestyle."

"So why do you work in the medical field if you don't have to?"

"Because it is not about what I have to do. I love what I do. Becoming a doctor was something else I dreamt of as a child. Truthfully, if I had died today, I would have died almost empty. I have done pretty much everything I ever wanted to do. I have accomplished most of what I wanted to accomplish."

"What's left?"

"Finding a woman to share it with. Do you think I enjoy living alone on hundreds of acres of land, in a twentysomething-thousand-square-foot house? Not at all. What good is any of this if I go to bed every night by myself?"

"If you think that's bad, try going to bed with someone every night and still be alone."

"You don't have to. Life is too short to be unhappy."

"Yeah, but I am comfortable. At least with my situation I know what I am getting—what I am guaranteed. My worst fear is being broke and destitute and unable to take care of my mother. I feel like my mother has had a hard enough life as it is, and the way she struggled to take care of me when my father left is something I will never forget. I remember all too well the sacrifices she made to make sure I had not only what I needed, but most things I wanted. Thus, I make no decisions about my life that do not include the consideration of my mother. I would never admit that to her, but pretty much all my decisions in my adult life has been based on her."

"You must be an unbelievably sad woman."

I leaned up and faced him. "What do you mean? I am not the happiest person, but I am not that sad, either. You make me sound like a charity case."

"You don't know how to make decisions for yourself. You have no idea what Allyson likes. You are so accustomed to catering to other people and what they want of you and from you. Can you imagine what it would be like to make selfish decisions for just one week?"

"No."

"You should try it. For one week only, you should make all decisions based on what Allyson wants to do. Don't worry about your husband, your mother, no one. Just you."

"I would not even know where to start."

"Don't complicate it. It's really simple. All you have to do is quit thinking of anyone but yourself. That does not make you a selfish person. It just means you know how to make sure you are happy while you are making others happy."

"I hear you."

"I want you to do more than hear me. I want you to do it."

"I will try." I lay back against him. He had argued a good case and had an excellent point.

"Good enough." He played in my hair as we sat in silence.

"Seth, I am coming up to go over a few things with you for tomorrow," Melanie said. I looked on the wall near the edge of the balcony and spotted the intercom. I shook my head, because I knew it was probably driving her insane to have to sit and wonder what he and I were doing.

Seth didn't move. Instead, he continued our conversation as if she had never said anything. "What time do you want to go home in the morning?"

"I need to be home no later than ten. The thing is . . . how am I going to get there? My car is still at the hotel."

"I already worked that out. I am going to have the chopper fly you into Charlie Brown Airport in Atlanta, and a car will be waiting on you there to take you to the St. Regis to get your car."

"Seth, are you sure you want to go through all of that? I can always call someone to come and pick me up."

"I am sure, and this is the end of this discussion. I will have Jeff, my pilot, be ready to pull up around eight."

I had dated my share of wealthy men, but none of them had flown me anywhere on their private jet. Seth was really one of a kind.

"Yes, sir."

"Girl, you better be careful with that kind of talk. That 'yes, sir' business will have me reneging on everything I said earlier about respecting you as a married woman. I am just a man, you know."

"Really? I thought you were a superhero, because you sure have rescued me."

Without even turning to look at him, I knew he was smiling. *Good.* I was glad to be able to make him smile after such a horrific day.

"Seth, did you hear me? I am getting ready to come up. Is that okay?" Melanie said, slicing into the romantic moment. What could she have to tell him that was so pressing?

"Let me go and see what she wants," he said as he rose up. "Otherwise, she will just keep on."

"Okay. I will go into the guest room so you two can have some privacy."

"You don't have to do that. Whatever she has to say, she can say in front of you."

"But . . ."

"Allyson . . . not up for discussion," he said authoritatively yet lovingly.

He pushed the intercom button to speak back to her. "Melanie, you can come up. I'll unlock the elevator."

"Unlock the elevator?" I asked.

"Yes. Every night when I come to bed, I stop the elevator from coming to the third floor."

"What happens if someone needs to get to you?"

"Well, of course, there's the stairs, but they hardly ever get used."

"Gotcha."

He unlocked the elevator, and in what seemed like seconds, Melanie was there. When she saw me, the muscles in her face tightened.

"Allyson, I didn't think you were still up. Can't sleep?"

"We were talking," Seth answered for me. "What is so urgent that you had to talk to me right now?"

"Well," she said, looking at me, "since the press conference is scheduled for really early in the morning, I wanted to discuss with you some notes our attorney sent over."

Seth rubbed his hand over his head. "Are you serious? You came up here to go over some notes with me? After the kind of day I had, you want to further remind me of it by talking about some notes, Melanie? Really?"

Tears formed in her eyes, and panic swept across her face. "Seth, I am so sorry. I don't know what has gotten into me. I seem to have been screwing up all evening. Maybe the stress of this day has gotten to me more than I knew. I was so worried about you—scared that something had happened to you. Since I was on vacation for the past few days, I did not know you had left town and had gone to Atlanta. When I first got the news that the clinic had been bombed, my world stopped rotating. For a minute I could not breathe." She touched his arm. "Seth, I thought you were dead, and all I could think about were the things I wished I could have said to you."

"That is really sweet, Melanie, and I really appreciate you being so concerned. I know you care deeply for me, and that is why I trust you."

Ms. Todd's words rang in my ears. I could see right through Melanie's semi-declaration of love. I got the strangest feeling about her.

Melanie went on. "I am glad you are able to recognize and appreciate my efforts to do all I can for you, Mama Todd, and Carson Land. You guys are my life, and I haven't the slightest idea what I would do without you."

"Well, we feel the same way about you, Melanie. We are very blessed to have you."

"Really? You mean that, Seth? Because I would go through anything and take down anybody to make sure that we hold on to our bond."

"I know. But as for tonight, I just want to relax. I have no interest in rehearsing what is to be done tomorrow or rehashing what has gone on today. The only thing I do want you working on in the morning is arranging flowers to be sent to the families of my entire staff. I want you to find out if their families have insurance to give them a proper burial. If not, I want Carson Land to cover all their expenses. Additionally, I want a trust fund initiated in the names of each of their kids, and I want to donate all the money they will need in order to go to a college of their choice."

"That is such a nice thing to do. That is why I . . ." She hesitated, refraining from completing her sentence. She was about to declare her love fully but remembered I was in the room. "Okay, I will get on this first thing in the morning. The press conference will begin promptly at eight o'clock. I will get up with the roosters, so if you think of anything else you would like for me to do, just let me know."

"Thank you again, Melanie, for all your hard work and dedication to me and my family." He leaned in and gave her a hug.

You would have thought she had reverted to being a high school teenager again with a crush on the most popular guy on the football team. I studied her. She was a pretty woman. She was not too tall in stature and had a shape like a video vixen. She had every right to be confident.

"You have no idea how glad I am to hear you say that."

"Great. Have a good night, Mel."

Showing all her pearly whites, she turned and got back into the elevator. "I'll see you in the morning. Sleep well," she said as the door to the elevator closed.

"Well, that was interesting. Her declaring her love for you, and you declaring your appreciation for her. How sweet," I commented.

A part of me felt a little jealous, but I knew I had no right to feel that way. I had grown accustomed to being the object of his affection, and hearing him speak fondly to another woman made me feel some type of way.

"You have no reason to feel jealous." He had read my mind. "I said what needed to be said to get her to leave. She had no reason whatsoever for coming up here, other than to spy on us. I may pretend to be stupid, but I am far from it. So, even though I meant all that I said, I knew it was important that she hear the words now so she could relax."

"So, for clarification, you said what you thought she wanted to hear at the moment so you could get her to go away?"

"Yep. That about sums it up."

I turned and walked toward the bed. He was just like all the rest. I had to face it. I *needed* to face it. All men were pretty much the same. They were charming players, and all of them played a game of some sort. They might play on different courts, or even in different games, but they were still game players.

"You should not have played on that girl's emotions like that. I truly believe she is in love with you, and you really need to be careful how you treat her. You know, women are extremely sensitive when it comes to the men they love. There is nothing we would not do."

"What are you saying?"

"Nothing, other than for you to be careful and choose your words wisely. Women are capable of fixating on all kinds of things in their minds. Make sure you do not lead her on or give her reason to believe that the two of you can be more than you are. I had a talk with her earlier today, and she really believes she is going to be your wife one day."

"So you were serious earlier, when you said that? She said that? Please tell me you are joking," he said in disbelief.

"I vacillated with telling you, but yes, she said that and a whole lot more."

"Wow. But I have never given her any reason to believe that," he said. "I can understand someone having a crush on a person, but to create a false reality in your mind . . . that's going a bit far."

"Oh, I totally agree. Just be mindful that you refrain from feeding into her illusion. It could be the breeding ground for trouble."

"I doubt that," he said and laughed. "Whatever she feels, I am sure she will get over it once she realizes there is no chance on this side of Heaven that we will be together like that."

"I pray so," I said, but I had a feeling she was not the type of woman to take no for an answer without putting up a fight first.

In the pit of my stomach was a feeling.

And it was not a good one.

Chapter Seventeen

It was the most difficult thing I recall ever having to do. As the chopper left the ground, I felt as if I was leaving a part of me behind.

We had all gotten up at five, and at six, we had enjoyed a wonderful breakfast buffet with everything imaginable on it. The morning had got even better when Ms. Todd imparted more words of wisdom to me. But nothing could top the moment when Seth and I hopped on a golf cart, and he took me on a short tour of Carson Land.

We rode over the rolling hills, allowing the early morning mist to kiss our faces. The cool air filled our lungs as we went from one acre to another. We soon stopped to talk to the people who bred and fed the horses and the ones who took care of the cows. Seth called this part of the property Louvell's,as it was named after his grandfather who had a passion for beautiful horses. I watched the meticulous care the staff was giving the horses, and I developed a new fascination for them. I made Seth promise to give me horse riding lessons if I ever came back to visit.

We continued on a little farther and stopped to chat with the staff who took care of the smaller animals—the roosters, chickens, and ducks. But it was not until we headed over to what was referred to as the Willie Jo Gardens (named after Ms. Todd) that his eyes began to light up. The garden was breathtaking. In one section, there were rows and rows of beautiful cabbage, tomatoes, collard greens, corn, and peppers. In another section, there were rows of strawberries, watermelon, and cantaloupe. I even saw grapevines and peach, plum, and apple trees. In the back were pecan trees. It was like a farmers' market. The only thing he did not raise on his land was fish. It was remarkable. I would have never known that such an operation could generate so much revenue. My appreciation for Seth multiplied. That he not only had a vision of that magnitude but was also able to bring it to pass was altogether attractive and admirable.

If the morning was any indication of how the rest of the day would go, I was looking forward to it. As I rode in the chopper, I felt like a celebrity. The ivory leather seats against the hardwood panels were magnificent. Everything about this chopper screamed plush and luxury. I settled into my seat, closed my eyes, leaned my head back, and took in the moment as my chariot carried me home.

Because the night had run late and the morning had begun early, I found myself drifting off to sleep. However, no sooner had I traveled to the third realm of sleep than we landed.

"Ms. Allyson, it has been a pleasure transporting you to your destination today," Jeff, the pilot, said. "Dr. Carson asked me to give you this." He handed me an envelope.

I took the envelope from him and said, "Thank you."

He helped me out of the chopper and walked me over to the waiting town car.

"Louie will transport you to the St. Regis to retrieve your car. Again, it has been a pleasure serving you. Have a good day," he said, then turned to walk back to the chopper.

I got into the car and pulled my phone out of my purse just as it started to ring.

"Hello?"

"Thank God you answered the phone!" Byran exclaimed.

The panic in his voice instantly made me nervous. "Byran, is everything all right?" I asked hesitantly.

"No, Allyson, it is not all right."

My stomach dropped. Had someone told him where I had spent the last couple of days, or worse, whom I had spent them with?

"What's wrong? What happened?"

Through the deafening silence I could hear the tears. Byran never cried.

"Do you remember what happened to David's child, the one he had with Bathsheba?"

"Who is David? And I don't know a Bathsheba. Is that someone at the church?"

He sighed. "No, Allyson. They are people in the Bible."

Now, he knew I knew very little about the Bible. How was I supposed to know that David and Bathsheba were Bible story characters?

"I did not know that. What do they have to do with why you are crying? Byran, can you just please tell me what's going on?" My patience was wearing thin.

"David's child with his mistress, Bathsheba, fell sick. And no matter how hard or how much he prayed, the child still died."

My heart began beating harder . . . faster. *Please, God, don't let it be.*

He continued. "BJ . . . BJ just passed away. In my arms."

I was speechless. I'd been upset about the child, but I did not want him to die.

"I will be there as soon as I can."

"Please hurry, Allyson. I feel like I am going to lose it. I cannot call and tell anyone, because then I would have to explain too much. You are all I have. You are the only support system I can lean on. Baby, I need you."

Hearing him break down broke me.

"I'm coming, honey. In the meantime, I am praying for you strength."

"You know how to pray?"

If it were not for the gravity of the situation, I would have been offended. I let him slide.

"Yes, I am learning. I may not know how to pray like other people, but I do the best I can."

"Oh, okay. Thank you. Allyson, I really believed he was going to be fine. He developed an infection last night, but even with that, he fought through it." He broke down again. "Do you know what today is?"

I scanned the memory tapes of my mind. It was not his birthday, it was not our anniversary, and since I knew very little about his parents, I knew he was not referencing anything that pertained to them.

Suddenly I remembered. It was the ten-year anniversary of his brother's death. This could not get any worse.

"Yes, I know. I am so sorry, Byran. This is so unfair. But, as you say in your sermons, all things work together for the good. I know it does not look like it right now, but somehow this is going to work out to your benefit."

If I were not the one talking I would not have believed I was just quoting a scripture. Being around Ms. Todd and Seth had impacted me greatly. More than I must have realized.

"I do not want to hear a breakdown of a sermon, Allyson. I do not want to hear anything about God right now. I just lost my son, and I am angry. I am hurt. So please keep whatever spiritual jargon you have learned to yourself right now. I just need to talk to my friend."

But God is still worthy to be praised even in the midst of a trying time.

"I apologize. I will be there as soon as I can. Text me the address, and I will be on my way within about twenty minutes."

"Okay," he said, sounding deflated.

"Oh, and, Byran? Where is BJ's mother? Is she going to have a problem with me being there?"

"Allyson, you are my wife. She understands that."

"I will see you soon," I said just as the car pulled up to the St. Regis. I tried to tip the driver, but of course, Seth had already taken care of it. So I rushed over to valet, gave them my claim ticket, and waited for my car.

My phone rang again.

"Hello?"

"Allyson, did you make it home okay?" Seth asked.

"Yes, I am standing here at the valet, waiting for them to bring my car around. How are you? How did the press conference go?"

"It went as planned. Answered a few questions . . . You know how it goes." He was trying to sound like himself, but his voice indicated something was wrong.

I tried to lighten the mood. "I know you miss me and all, but you don't have to be so down about it," I joked.

He chuckled. "You are right. I do miss you. A lot. But that isn't why I sound down."

I knew it. Something was wrong.

"Well, spill it. What is going on?"

"The one survivor of the bombing, Helen Reese, just passed away."

Was this the day of death?

"Oh, honey, I am so sorry. Did you know her?"

"She was a regular patient. Matter of fact, you may remember her. She was in the clinic the day you came in."

"Wait a minute. The older lady I was talking to in the waiting area?" I remembered her and the conversation she and I had that day. She was a sweet lady who just wanted to be loved.

"She wasn't all that old. She just looked like that because life had beaten her down. It had drained her of the joy she had. She was a sweet woman. Every time she came in, I tried convincing her to keep her baby. Many days she would come in just to talk, and unlike many other doctors, I listened to her. I let her vent."

"Why was she there?" I asked as my car came up. I tipped the driver and hopped into the driver's seat. "There is no way she could have been pregnant again that soon."

"Of course not. She came by the clinic every single Tuesday morning to bring us a batch of her homemade blueberry muffins. She innocently walked into a death trap. My heart is so heavy right now. I feel responsible for all of this happening. Remember that day in the office when you told me I take innocent lives for a living? That very thing has come back to bite me. Innocent lives were lost yesterday at the place I took lives every day."

I could imagine him sitting in a chair with his head lowered. I wanted to track down Louie and have him track down Jeff so I could fly to be by Seth's side. But I knew I had a responsibility to go and be with Byran.

"You cannot blame yourself."

"Oh, but I do. If my ex-fiancée had never killed our baby, I would have never killed thousands more."

"Seth, you have to let that go." I connected the Bluetooth in my car and maneuvered my way onto the expressway, heading north on 75. Funny how the opposite direction, 75 South, would have taken me to where I truly wanted to be . . . Augusta.

"I know I do, babe. But right now I am harboring a lot of guilt."

"I couldn't tell you where it is located, but somewhere in the Bible is a scripture that talks about when Jesus sets you free, you are truly free indeed."

Did I just say that?

"John eight and thirty-six."

"Excuse me?"

"That's where that verse is located. In John, chapter eight, verse number thirty-six. I am so proud of you, Allyson."

"For what?"

"You may not see it, but there has been a change in you, and I want you to keep it up. Do not let anything or anyone steal this from you."

"I am not sure I can quite define what *this* is."

"It doesn't matter. You will understand it one day."

That I wouldn't doubt. The happenings of the last forty-eight hours or so had been enough to set anybody on the right path.

"Well, keep me in your prayers. I am headed to Chattanooga, Tennessee. My husband lost his son."

"My goodness. I am so sorry to hear that. I will definitely keep you, more so than him, in my prayers. You are a good woman to even go there to try to console him. Keep in touch with me, okay?"

"You don't have to worry about me doing that. To be honest, I cannot imagine you not being in my life in some way."

"I am glad to hear you say that, because the feeling is mutual."

We said our good-byes, and I concentrated on getting to Byran. As I drove, my thoughts turned into prayers. I prayed for Byran, his deceased son, and the child's mother. I prayed for Seth, Ms. Todd, and the families of those who had lost their lives. I was stunned by the death of Helen, the woman who had impacted my life with one conversation, and my emotions were swinging back and forth between pain and sorrow. She would never get the opportunity to experience real love again. She would never get the opportunity to know that wounded women could still win in life, and move beyond the hurt and disappointment to become something great. She would never get the life she deserved.

Thinking about her, and how short life really was, sent my thoughts in another direction. In the direction of my own life. I began to ask myself questions.

Am I going to continue this front and stay in a makeshift marriage for money?

What is really the true essence of love?

My phone rang, and I saw on the display screen in my car that it was my mother. I pushed the button from my steering wheel that enabled me to answer the phone.

"Hello, Mother."

"Hi, darling. How are you?"

"I am fine. Headed to Tennessee to be with Byran."

"Did something happen?"

"His son died."

"Oh, my Lord!" she exclaimed. "I am sure he is a nervous wreck."

"To say the least. I knew he must be desperate, because he never cries or breaks down in any way. Besides that, I am about to come face-to-face with the woman he is truly in love with, and only a tragedy such as this could have arranged this meeting."

"Well, now is not the time to look at it from that perspective."

"What perspective? I am looking at it from the perspective of truth. If this had never happened, I doubt very seriously I would have ever found out who she was or what she looked like. But none of that is important. I am not going to allow that negative energy into my spirit."

"I agree with you, honey. Did you enjoy your time away?"

"I did."

"Wonderful. I knew once you were able to take a little time to think, you would be just fine. Sometimes things that catch us off guard will make us feel as if we have been sucker punched. In those times, we must take a minute to gather ourselves and refocus."

"That is very true, Mom. So how have you been? Are you and Ms. Sarah staying out of trouble? I hope you all are not keeping up mess down there at the senior activity center."

"For your information, I have not been to the senior center in the past few days. As a matter of fact, I have not seen Sarah in about the same amount of time."

Sarah was my mother's best friend. They had been friends for many years and had seen each other through the birth of children, the demise of marriage, and the death of their parents. Their friendship had survived the best and the worst of times.

"Is she sick or something? The two of you are always together, shopping or causing trouble for the other bingo players at the center."

"No, she isn't sick. We have just been missing each other."

I knew my mother. She had the same routine and the same schedule every day of the week and every week of the year. Something was up.

"Mother, what are you not telling me?"

"Dear heart, why on earth do you think I am withholding something from you?"

"Because you are. So, unless you are about to tell me somebody died, then come on out with it. What is this secret you are holding?"

"Secret?"

My patience was wearing thin. "Mother!" I shouted. "What is it?"

She paused before she answered. "Darling, I wanted to sit down and have lunch with you. That is why I was calling today, but when you said you were on your way to be with Byran, I decided not to mention it. It is a shame you know me so well."

"Mother, you are stalling. Out with it. No chasers. No beating around the bush."

"I am seeing your father again."

I almost choked on my own saliva. "You are what?"

"I am seeing your father." I could hear the hint of happiness in her voice.

I was speechless. More than that, I was confused. My father was married to the woman he had left my mother for.

"Mom, how did this happen? When did it happen?"

"I ran into him at the mall."

She was lying.

"What mall, Mom? Dad doesn't go to malls in Atlanta. He lives in Birmingham."

"Okay, you got me. He came by the house," she said.

She was lying again. *Ugh.*

"If you are not going to tell me the truth, we can hang up."

"Oh, all right. I went to hear him preach," she confessed.

"You actually showed up at one of Dad's preaching engagements? Mom, I cannot believe you. Why did you do that? Were you trying to look desperate on purpose?"

"It wasn't like what you are thinking."

"Then what was it like?"

"Sarah called, being messy, one day and said, 'Your baby daddy is preaching now, and he is going to be over at Second Mount Bethel.' She also informed me that she overheard Ruby Dee and Ira Jean talking down at the center, and she said they said he and Melissa had split up. So I went to see for myself."

It was hard listening to my mother talk about he said, she said stuff at her age. *But wait a minute.* My father was preaching now?

"Since when did Daddy start preaching? He never once mentioned that to me."

"That is exactly what I said! I was amazed. So, Ally, you know I had to go and witness this for myself. I had no idea he even saw me. My plan was to ease in the back, hear him preach, and leave. But as I was walking out the door, an usher walked up to me and gave me a note from him."

"And the note said?"

"He wanted me to meet him at the Waffle House around the corner."

"I see."

"So we talked and caught up on the last twentysomething years. It was my first time really talking to him since the day he left."

"And what did he have to say for himself?" I was starting to get upset. Who did he think he was to try to come back around my mom after twenty years? It took some time for me to warm up to him after he left us, but over time I learned to love him dearly as a father, but I never wanted him to be in my mother's life as anything again.

"He actually had a whole lot to say."

"And you fell for it?"

"It's not about falling for anything, Allyson. I just heard him out. I listened to his explanation as to why he chose Melissa over me, and so on."

She was trying to brush it off, but it would not be that simple for me.

"And what was his reason?"

"Your father was young when he and I married. We were both raised in the country, and when we moved to Atlanta, there was more to do, and more to get into. He got caught up in the streets, and he said over time he fell in love with her because of how she made his flesh feel. But she never really had his heart. She never had all of him, the way I did."

"And you believed that lie?"

"Yes, I believe him."

She had to be kidding.

"Mother, you have taught me all my life about guarding my heart and not falling for lies. You even told me once that men were not worth the fecal matter of a dog. Your mantra has been, get the goods without giving up too much gold. Now you are on this phone, telling me you believe some put-together lie Daddy told you about leaving us because his flesh was out of control. For the love of God, Mother, give me a break. My view of love is flawed now because of the things you taught me. But I guess you have had some sort of epiphany."

"I know it is a lot for you to take in because of the bitterness I have infused into you over the years. But is it ever too late for a person to get it right? No, it is not. And I want to make the rest of my life the best of my life." She paused. "Allyson, I apologize. I have not always taught you the right things about relationships or love, but it was because of a bitter root within me that needed to be plucked out."

"Let me guess. Daddy plucked it out?"

"Talking with him for the past few days, and I mean really having in-depth conversations, began the process of me healing. For all these years I thought your father was too selfish to care about anything or anyone but himself. I thought what we had meant nothing to him, because he left me to struggle and take care of us."

"This is exactly why you should not entertain anything he is saying. I can understand you all having a conversation in hopes of bringing some closure to an old relationship, but to say that you are now seeing him . . . Mom, that is a bit much."

I was really upset because most of my life I had made my relationship decisions with her in mind. The sole reason I was in this mess with Byran was that she encouraged me to do it so I would not end up like her—broke and broken. I had succeeded at one half of it. I was far from being broke as long as I was married to him, but I had failed miserably at preventing brokenness.

"I know it is difficult for you to understand. It would be for me, too."

"You have no clue how difficult it is. I am stuck in a marriage that isn't worth the certificate that proves it. I tolerate, and have tolerated, emotional abuse from men who cared nothing about me because my eyes have always been on the money, as well as making sure you were taken care of. You will never understand the emotional debilitation I have endured as one man after another went through my body. Or the psychological breakdowns I suffered through thinking I was not good enough as they dropped me and moved on to the next woman once they were done with me—once their purpose had been served.

"You cannot possibly know what it feels like to give up on having true love or to convince yourself of the falsehood that love is embodied in a man showering you with material things, when it should be the merging or collision of two souls who would rather die than be apart."

The only thing I could hear were the cars zooming by on the interstate. The moment was so intense, neither of us could find more words to say. My mother had just admitted to me that everything she had taught me about love was wrong.

I had not paid attention to the time, so when I saw a sign that said I was only twenty miles from Chattanooga, I was relieved. I needed to take what little time was left of the drive to get my head together. Absolutely too much had transpired, and it seemed I was getting hit with one thing after the other. It was like trouble woke up one morning and set its entire agenda around plaguing me. But surely, there had to be a flip side to trouble, right?

"Mom, I am almost there. I will call you later, when I get to the hospital and find out what is going on."

"Okay, darling. If I had known this conversation would go in this direction, I would have not brought it up. But I wanted you to know from me what was going on. I apologize from the bottom of my heart. I never knew I was hurting you so deeply. I pray you find it in your heart to forgive me."

"I forgive you, Mother, because I know enough to know forgiveness frees the forgiver. Holding on to stuff is like drinking poison and expecting it not to have an effect on you. What I must do now is put some things in order in my own life. You made a decision for yourself to do what was best for you, not being concerned about what I would think, or anyone else for that matter. It is time I do the same thing. I cannot continue to live for the money, the cars, the houses . . . nothing. If I have to lose it all in order to gain my soul, my peace, and my happiness, then I will have gained what matters most."

"I agree with you one hundred percent. I hate that you had to come to this conclusion on your own and that I failed as a mother to teach you such a core principle. But as I have found myself saying, late is not as bad as never. You are still young, beautiful, and you deserve all the happiness in the world. If I could reverse your sorrow and replace it with joy, I would."

I sighed. It was not her fault. I should have taken over my life a long time ago. I should have set my own standards. I should have followed my own heart and adhered to my own set of rules and convictions. But I had followed the voice she gave to me. But now I had to find my own.

I drove into the Erlanger Hospital parking deck, was blessed enough to find a space close to the front, and I parked. Before getting out, I decided to check myself in the mirror, and just like I thought, my face reflected the quantity of tears I had cried. I reached into my purse and pulled out my M•A•C compact. I dabbed the sponge into the foundation and proceeded to mask the evidence of my anger, hurt, and frustration. I smeared a little Viva Glam V lip gloss on my lips so they would pop, and with my hands smoothed down the loose hairs that were trying to escape from my ponytail. Satisfied with my express makeover, I stepped out of the car. The banana-colored DKNY sundress I was wearing from the closet at Seth's house made my skin look radiant. The six-inch Prada heels and sunglasses—also from the closet—matched the dress perfectly. I used to hear old people say there was no reason to look like what you had been through. Emotionally, I was harboring a national disaster, but on the outside, I looked as if I had just stepped out of June Ambrose's fashion house.

I entered the hospital, not knowing what to expect. I would soon be laying eyes on the "other woman." Technically, I was the "other woman," because even though I was married, the other woman in my mind was the one who was good enough for everything but truly falling in love with. And that would be me. Nonetheless, with each step, I walked with my head held high. I had discovered so many things about myself over the past few days, and Byran was about to meet a different woman than the one he'd left balling on the kitchen floor. Oh, no, I had connected with a different part of me. As I thought about it, it was interesting how my mother and I had come, through introspection, to two different conclusions about our lives.

"Allyson," I heard someone call.

I turned around to see a worn and weary-looking Byran coming toward me from another direction. I went to meet him, and the closer I got, the less I recognized him. I could tell he had been crying and not sleeping, as the bags under his eyes held the evidence. I hugged him, and he laid his head on my shoulder and cried some more. I could feel his burden, his pain, his guilt. I could feel the weight of his son's death as his eyes poured his heart onto my shoulder. No words were exchanged—I expressed my condolences by holding him.

Several people walked by and offered their sympathy, and eventually I was able to guide him to a nearby chair so we could sit down.

"Thank you for coming," he said. "All I have been able to do since they took my son away is walk up and down these halls and cry."

I grabbed his hand. "I cannot imagine what you are feeling right now, because our baby never had the opportunity to make it as far as your son did. But I remember how empty I felt inside, because to me, that baby was still a soul."

"That is the reason this is happening to me. I convinced you to get rid of our baby, as if I had no regard for life. God is showing me how it felt to you to have to do that. I was so selfish, Ally. I was only thinking about myself and what I wanted and what was best for me. And now look. I don't have either child." He dropped his head in his hands. "This has been the worst time of my life. I don't know how I will ever be able to get over this."

"You will. It looks bleak right now because it just happened, but time heals all wounds."

He looked at me—almost as if he was staring through me. "There is something different about you. I can't really pinpoint what that something is. I just know there is a difference. You even look a little different—more alive."

"I am different. I have spent the last few days reflecting inwardly. I found out some things I do not like about myself, as well as some things that I do." I squeezed his hand. "But we are not here to talk about me. This is about you. Other than the unbearable pain I know you must feel, how are you holding up? Have you been eating?"

"Not really. This cafeteria food sucks. But I was too afraid to leave and go get something for fear of something happening."

"I will go and get you something. What is the next step? Are you all going to do a memorial here, transport the baby back to Atlanta, or what?"

"I want to have him transported back to Atlanta, but she wants to cremate him here and take his ashes back. However, I cannot fathom burning my baby."

But you can fathom having me suck up one through a vacuum? I tried to dismiss that thought.

"I see. So what are you going to do?"

"I have not made a final decision. I am going to wait until she is a little stronger—maybe tomorrow—before I try to convince her to make a decision. I just broke the news to her right before you came. She woke up asking about him, so I had to tell her."

"No mother wants to outlive her child."

A short older woman wearing a white jacket came toward us. Her tag read NANCY.

"Mr. Ward, Ms. Pace is asking for you."

"Thank you, Nancy. I will be right there," Byran told her.

"I will go and get your food while you go find out what's going on," I said.

Just as he was about to answer, I looked up to see a couple coming toward us.

"Byran," the woman called.

He stood up and hugged her. While the two of them embraced, the man who was accompanying her extended his hand and introduced himself.

"Hello. My name is Andre Pace, and this is my wife, Dorothy. We are Shatrice's parents."

Shatrice? Where have I heard that name before?

I, in turn, extended my hand to shake his. "I'm Allyson Ward."

"We know who you are," Dorothy said.

"Darling, let's not allow the nature of this situation cause us to lose our cool," Andre replied. "Nothing that has happened is this young lady's fault."

"Humph. If she had never forced Byran to marry her, he could have been with Shatrice, and my grand-baby would be alive right now. The stress of this all has killed my grandson and is trying to take my daughter, too."

Who is Shatrice? I forced Byran to marry me?

I turned to Byran, because I was certain at any moment he was going to come to my defense. But he stood quietly, hands in his pockets, not even attempting to correct this woman. I was forced to defend myself.

"Ma'am, I am not sure what you are talking about, but I did not force anyone to marry me."

"Yes, you did. Shatrice told me the whole story. Byran, please tell me that you did not have her around my grandson."

"She just got here, Mom," Byran said.

Mom?

"Anybody want to fill me in on what is going on?" I turned to Byran. "Who is Shatrice? Why does that name sound so familiar to me? And what is this lady talking about?"

"Excuse me for a minute, Mom and Pop," Byran said, grabbing my hand and pulling me from the chair. "I will be right back."

"What the hell is going on?" I snapped.

"Those are Shatrice's parents."

"And who the hell is Shatrice?"

"Remember that day you came home from the abortion clinic and . . ."

Before he could finish his statement, I reached back as far as I could, with as much strength as I could muster up, and I slapped him. For it dawned on me that this woman, Shatrice, was the woman who had come out of my house that day, whom he had claimed was a relative. But I thought his baby's mom's name was Leah?

"You led me to believe your baby's mother was a woman by the name of Leah," I shouted. "You are one sorry bastard."

He was a low-down excuse for a man, and he deserved whoever was crazy enough to be with him. But crazy had occupied me long enough. No longer would I continue to live in bondage for the sake of a dollar. I would not care if I had to go and live in a shelter. At least there I would be free.

I was done.

I'd had enough.

Taken all I could take.

He could have it all.

I wanted one thing.

Out.

Chapter Eighteen

"Girl, where have you been? Ever since you got married a year ago to that big-time pastor husband of yours, you act like you don't know a sista no more," said my childhood friend Kristal Howard.

"You know how it is when you get married and you assume the role of a wife—especially the wife of a pastor. You become too busy to hang out. Plus, Byran and my mom have this thing about married women hanging out with single women."

"Seem like to me that don't matter, because you still about to get a divorce and you have not been hanging with me."

Kristal and I had spent the last couple of hours outside discussing the happenings of my life. It had been almost two weeks since the episode with Byran at the hospital. He'd gone to church the following Sunday and announced he would be taking a couple of weeks off, which was all the better for me because I did not want to go near the church, neither did I want to be near him. He had come to the house and gotten a few of his things, and I had not heard from him or seen him since.

"So, this agreement y'all have . . . how are you going to get out of it?"

"Well," I said, "I have been looking at the details of the contract, and I cannot imagine what I must have been thinking at the time I signed it and so—"

"I know exactly what you were thinking," Kristal interrupted. "Racks, on racks, on raaaaacks," she joked. "I would have been thinking the same thing. If a man came up to me today, tells me all I have to do is accompany him to events, give him sex and sexy pictures when he wants them, girl, I would scream a yes to him too. Trust me, you do not have to worry about explaining anything to me, because where I am from—the hood—what you did is what we call 'come up.'"

"The come up?"

"Girl, yes. The come up."

"I do not even want to hear an elaboration on that, so I will just leave that alone," I said and laughed. "As I was saying, the only thing in my contract that gives me an out without me having to get up in front of people and embarrass myself by admitting to some sort of infidelity is—"

She interrupted again. "What about his infidelity?"

"Can't prove it. I have no solid evidence, and when the baby died, so did my living proof."

"Just get up and tell people that you want a divorce. If you put it on yourself, then it wouldn't make him look bad."

"To him it is worse, because it is going to appear he did something to me or that he did not know how to be a good husband."

"He did, and he doesn't," she shouted.

"Yeah, but to stand up and say I want to divorce him without giving an explanation is along the lines of defamation of character because of what he does. The church will then begin to scrutinize everything he does. Right now they are lenient because those in leadership who are married with families understand the dynamic of the balancing act. Although he was spending most of his spare time with Shatrice, in their minds he has been taking the past year to get established as a new husband."

"Yet he was laying up, playing house with another woman." She sucked her teeth. "These pastors are something else, child. I hope I don't end up with one, because I will be redefining the role of what it means to be a first lady. Honey, I would be up in that church, setting things straight, and if he wanted to act a fool on me, I would show him how big of a fool I was."

I laughed hysterically at her because I could envision her tussling with the men snatchers in the church if she thought one was after her husband. She was a true size eighteen, wore micro braids, had long fingernails, and sported gold rings on every finger. I would pay big money to see a showdown between her and one of the deacons or mothers in the church.

"You are laughing, but I am serious," she continued. "You need to let me beat some good sense into Byran. He might not be in love with you, but he would definitely be letting you up out of this contract, and not empty handed. He owes you for taking up all this time in your life when you could have been with someone who actually loves you. I better not see that nucca in the street nowhere."

"First of all, I will pray without ceasing that God does not ever allow you to become the wife of a pastor." I laughed. "Because you would not last a day. Secondly, all pastors are not like Byran. Some are really in it for the right reasons. Byran saw an opportunity to advance, and he took it. Truth is, I did too. I should have cared more about God's people than to go along with him in some foolishness like this. I believe there are many pastors who actually care about what they are doing for God, and regardless of my situation, I believe not all of them are cheating on their wives." I sipped my lemonade. "I just happened to get a bad one from the litter."

"That is one of the reasons I don't go to church and instead sit at home and watch one of those TV pastors."

"Kristal, there is no such thing as a TV pastor. They are pastors who have a broadcast on TV," I said, shaking my head.

"Whatever. When you attend TV church, you don't have to worry about all of that drama."

"Whose broadcast do you watch?"

"Several of them. Girl, I dedicate my church hours to the Lord every Sunday."

"Church hours?"

"Yeah, like business hours, I have church hours. No matter what comes up, everybody knows not to bother me during church hours. I get up, make my coffee, and I start tuning in around seven o'clock. I catch Bishop I. V. Hilliard out of Houston, Bishop Jakes, and on the Sundays I need to figure out how to make some money, I watch Creflo Dollar so his wealth anointing will flow through the screen and fall on me." This girl was hilarious. "Then I have a little praise and worship with *Bobby Jones Gospel*, and I finish with *Lift Every Voice* with Cory Condrey—CoCo Brother, Jesus baby!"

I almost fell out of my chair when she said that. She sounded just like the people on Cory's Atlanta-based radio show who sang the jingle when he was on in the evenings.

"Sounds like you have your, um, church hours down to a science."

"Oh, yes, honey. I have to get my praise on. I figured out a long time ago that you can do a lot of things, but one thing you cannot do is make it without the Lord."

It was sad that my friend knew this and I was just learning it. Here I was, married to a pastor, but I had never seen the benefit of, nor did I know the importance of, having my own relationship with the Lord. As the days drifted by, I was beginning to see why everyone needed to know the Lord.

"I am learning that very thing."

"Trouble is the best teacher."

"Indeed it is."

"We have to figure out how to get you out of this contract. Are you sure that is what you want? You don't want to try to make it work? What if he gets rid of Shatrice?"

"He can keep her, get rid of her . . . not my concern. I know I deserve better, and it is more than he can offer. He can offer me all the things money can buy, but he has no clue about the things money can't afford. Because what I want is priceless."

"I hear you, girlfriend."

"Besides, you cannot change the nature or the heart of a person. Only God can do that. And to be honest, I am not sure if he even talks to God except on Wednesdays and Sundays, when it is time for him to preach. I never paid attention to this, but we have never prayed together. We don't have conversations about the Lord outside of church. Is that not strange for a pastor?"

"I would say that it is. But maybe he just wanted a reprieve from church when he got home."

"A reprieve from church, yes. But a reprieve from God too? I am not saying that because I have had a spiritual awakening over the past couple of weeks, I know everything there is to know about God. All I am saying is, any man of God should have a relationship with Him every day of the week and not just the days you go to church. And the relationship should carry on into your household. I read over in the New Testament that a man needs to be able to rule his own house before he can rule the house of God, which in my opinion, starts with total submission to God. And this house was not submitted in the first place."

Kristal stared at me as if I was growing a second head.

"Why are you looking at me like that?" I asked.

"I am amazed at what you are speaking. I have known you for many years, and I have never known you to talk about God this much. A change truly has come over you."

"It has. I do not quite know how to explain it, nor do I know just yet what it means. All I know is I do not ever want to wake up not feeling this way."

"Good for you, Ally. Good for you." She picked up her punch and took a sip. "Now, enough of all the Jesus stuff. I want to hear about this doctor you mentioned earlier. What's his name again?"

"Seth. Seth Carson."

"I wish you could have seen the light that shone in your eyes when you said his name. This man must be pretty amazing, because I have heard you talk about a lot of guys, but none of them made you beam." She sipped her punch again. "I think someone has fallen in love."

Seth and I had spoken every day since I arrived back in Atlanta. He had made it through the funerals for his staff and had even attended Ms. Helen's memorial service. That had taken a lot out of him. Thus he had been spending a lot of time on Carson Land, burying himself in the things that made him happy. He had also canceled his appearance at the medical conference he was supposed to be attending in order to take time to breathe after the devastating loss of his friends and business.

Ms. Todd had gone back to her apartment, and from what I could gather, life was getting back to normalcy somewhat. Seth was debating about doing some public speaking at a few pro-life events to give his testimony about how and why he started performing abortions. I missed him terribly and could not wait to see him, but in spite of his efforts to come visit me and his offers to have the chopper come and pick me up, I decided against a visit. The next time I went to him, I did not want to be running away from something, but instead I wanted to be running *to* someone.

"I don't think I am in love, or even falling in love, for that matter, but I do feel very strong feelings for Seth."

"I am sure him being rich helps to cultivate it."

"You know what? Initially, I was fascinated by the amount of wealth he had. But if he called me right now and told me he had lost it all, I would not care. I like him as a person, and what he has, has nothing to do with it."

"Okay," she said, leaning in to touch my forehead. "Where is my friend? Allyson, are you in there?" This time she pretended to knock on my forehead. "I am getting ready to call nine-one-one, because something is wrong."

I brushed off her comment. "I am serious, Kristal. This man is so wonderful."

"Uh-huh, he might be wonderful, but you cannot sit here and make me believe you are not turned on in the slightest bit by the fact that he is rich. Don't play with me, Ally. I don't care how saved you are now. You know good and well money will make an ugly man look good. Don't tell me riding in that chopper didn't have you feeling some type of way." She gave me the side eye.

"Well, yeah, it was nice," I said, smiling.

She clapped her hands loudly. "I know it did. You ain't got to lie to me. Remember, I am your hood friend. You can be honest with your girl. A Cadillac is a whole lot better than a Caprice any day of the week. And, Lawd, a chopper? Shucks, you done struck the gold for real this time."

"But that is what I am saying. I was not digging for gold when I met him. I was not digging for anything. Now, back in the day . . . different story. 'I ain't saying I was a gold digga, but I shole wasn't messing with no broke nigga.'" Kristal got a kick out of me quoting that line from Kanye West's song.

"Here is what you need to do. You need to either go where he is or have him come here, and the two of you need to figure out together how to get you out of this mess. From the little you have shared with me about him, he seems to be a very smart man. He will know what to do."

I mulled over that idea. It had never occurred to me to talk to Seth about it. I had wanted to handle this on my own since I had gotten into it that way.

"Maybe I will do that."

"Really though . . . what is the worst that could happen? Byran lose his church? Couldn't he get another one somewhere else? Actually, that might be good for him, especially since he is in love with that Shatrice woman. Maybe they can skip town, go somewhere, and live happily ever after."

"I wish it were that simple. Byran is infatuated with being a pastor—a mega pastor. He is one of the only ones from our generation who has achieved this enormous ministerial success. Losing this church would mean he would have to start all over, and he is definitely not willing to do that. It has been proven that anytime a pastor gets a divorce, a large percentage of his church walks off, unless it is somehow proven that it is the fault of the wife."

"Which is rare."

"Exactly. So if I left, so would a lot of his members. Plus, he told me when I mentioned divorce last week, it was not an option. The only way he could remain at this particular church is if he were married. The moment he announced a divorce, they would begin working on a severance package, and then a church meeting would be held to vote him out."

"Allyson, that is not your problem. I understand you feel somewhat responsible for this mess because you readily agreed to it in the beginning, but things change. People change. What worked for you then does not work for you anymore."

"The agreement was not set up for change. He asked me plainly if I could live the rest of my life according to that contract, and I said yes. He even gave me thirty full days to think about it before I signed it, followed by another thirty days to cancel for whatever reason. Once the engagement was announced, there was supposed to be no turning back. There was no way of escape."

"There is always a way of escape. We just have to pray and ask God to show us what it is. There has to be a way for you to get out of this."

"I know," I said, defeated. It was all so depressing to me. I hoped that I could think of a way soon, because there was no way I could go another year like this. No. There was no way I could go another month like this. Something had to give. "Maybe I will reach out to Seth and see if he has any suggestions. However it goes down, it will not be pretty."

"Maybe we can just arrange for Seth to come and kidnap you. You said yourself that Carson Land was out in the middle of nowhere. So if he comes and takes you there, who would find you?"

"Girl, his little nosy estate manager, Melanie, would be in all kinds of knots. It would not take a full hour for her to announce to the world where I was—especially in the case of a kidnapping. Not only is she a problem, but she is cool with his grandmother's nurse. I am sure at some point I would have to go and get his grandmother or something, and that nurse would sing like a canary."

"But if he knew the circumstances, I am certain he would ensure you never had to leave the land for anything. He sounds like the type of man who would love nothing more than losing himself in his own man-made world. He would probably build whatever was necessary in order to make sure you were safe and that nobody would find or bother you. Your mom and friends would have to have a secret chip placed in their hands or something to be identified when they came for a visit."

"You are so dumb, Kristal!" I shrieked. "Where do you get this stuff from? What in God's name have you been watching on television? You talking about me arranging my own kidnapping to go and live on a farm—basically disappear from plain view—all because I am trying to finagle my way out of a marriage." I got up from the table and went inside to the kitchen. She followed behind me. "You are something else. People only feel the need to plan their own kidnapping, Kristal, when they feel threatened by someone. Byran would never touch me, but I am trying to figure out a way to leave whereby his reputation will not be tarnished, and I won't have a lawsuit or have my life played out in the media."

"The media? You think the media will care?"

"What!" I exclaimed. "Yes, of course they will care. Even if we did not get national media attention, we would surely get local attention. Byran is young, successful, and he pastors a mega church. If this is not handled perfectly, as I already said, it could be the end of his pastoral career. No one wants to hire a pastor whose name is attached to any type of scandal or disgrace."

"As far as I am concerned, he took that chance when he got Shatrice pregnant."

"I agree with you."

I sat down in one of the chairs at my bar and began peeling an orange. I popped a slice into my mouth and started thinking of all the possible divorce scenarios and their ramifications. Even if my name was sent through the public's shredder, I could recover from that. I was not a public figure outside of being married to Byran, so what harm could it do to me? The only person who would be affected would be him. The question was . . . did I care enough to care at all?

"I am going to call Byran and see if we can work this out."

"Good luck with that. Anybody who has been as selfish as he has been doesn't strike me as the compromising type. But prayer changes things, right?"

"Right."

Kristal checked her cell phone. "Honey, chile, I gotta run. I have a hot date tonight."

"With who? You mean to tell me you sat here and let me dish out all my dirt and you held back on me?"

"Your life is much more interesting than mine."

"I still want to know what's going on with you. Who is the hot date of yours?"

"You remember Popeye from high school?"

"Are you talking about Popeye with the pop eyes?"

"Allyson, he does not have pop eyes!"

"Yes, he does have pop eyes. He looks as if something has him caught off guard at all times." I demonstrated how his eyes looked, and she fell over on the bar, laughing so hard.

"All right, all right. His eyes are big. But his heart is bigger, and it's about the heart, right? He is such a good man."

I snickered. "If you like it, I love it. Whatever floats your boat, I am cool with it. One good thing about dating a man with big eyes is that it does not matter where you are headed in life. He will see it." She playfully slapped me on the arms. "Ouch! What was that for?"

"You are dead wrong for that. You know he can't help his eyes are like that. He was born that way," she said, sounding serious. This time I fell across the bar, laughing. "Besides, you didn't hear me talking about blind Bartimaeus when you were dating him."

I hollered. "Hunter Ingram was not blind—well, not totally blind, anyway. He was really cute without those bifocals."

We spent the next fifteen minutes laughing at the defects of our former boyfriends before Kristal took off to meet her big-eyed man. I did not know how much I had missed having girl talk—something she and I used to do on a weekly basis before Byran came into my life and consumed all my time. Until now, I had failed to pay attention to the fact that somehow in the midst of me merging my world with Byran's, he had become my world and I had lost myself in the process.

But it was time for all of that to change. Seth had long ago challenged me to begin making my own decisions, and that was exactly what I planned to do from this day forward. No one—including Byran—was going to stand in my way.

Chapter Nineteen

I turned right on Baker Street Northwest and pulled into the parking lot of the Hilton Garden Inn. I was meeting Mom for lunch at Legal Sea Foods—one of my all-time favorite restaurants.

"Mrs. Ward, where have you been? I haven't seen you in a few weeks," said Merlo, the West Indian valet attendant. "I missed you around this place."

He was such the charmer. "Been missing you too, Merlo. I promise to do better, okay?"

"All right now, I am going to hold you to that. I need to see your beautiful face at least once a week."

"Gotcha."

"Oh, and Mrs. Ward?"

"Yes, Merlo?"

"Please don't tell Pastor Ward I talk like this. He got my buddy fired for complimenting you."

What?

"Is that what happened to Simeon?"

"Yes, ma'am. But he meant no harm by anything he said. He would never disrespect you."

I could not believe Byran had someone fired from his job for something so trivial.

"Give me your boss's number, Merlo. I am going to put in a call to him and see if I can get Simeon's job back."

"Oh, Mrs. Ward, he would be so happy. He has four children, and his wife doesn't work. He really needs a job, Mrs. Ward. He would probably kiss your feet if you were able to do something."

"I will do anything I can to help."

"Thank you, ma'am. Enjoy your lunch."

"I will."

I headed inside and got on the elevator to go up to the second floor, where the main dining room was. I could already taste the famous crab soup that I was going to order, along with the Louisiana Catfish Matrimony, mashed sweet potatoes, and braised greens. I had skipped breakfast so I could have a big lunch, and I was going to savor every bite of it.

The elevator door opened on the second floor, and Amy, the manager, greeted me. She was always so accommodating and treated me and my guests like royalty.

"Mrs. Ward, it is so good to see you. How is Pastor?"

"He is well. I will let him know you asked about him."

"Please do. We miss seeing him around here too. Well, let me take you over here to your table. Your mom and dad are already seated."

"Excuse me? Did you say my mom *and* dad?"

"Mmm-hmm. They have been here about ten minutes."

Unbeknownst to Amy, I was fuming. I had planned to have lunch with my mother and her alone. She never once mentioned my father would be joining us.

I walked up to the table, and my father stood to greet me.

"You all enjoy your lunch," Amy said as she walked away.

"Baby girl, you look radiant today," my father said. I could tell he was nervous, unsure how I was getting ready to respond.

"Absolutely stunning," my mother added, piggybacking her compliment on my father's.

"Thank you," I said dryly.

I sat down and took a sip of the water that was on the table to wash down the choice words I wanted to spew out at my parents for not telling me we would be having a "family" reunion.

Angela, my favorite waitress, came and took our order. Seeing that I ordered the same thing almost every time, when she came for the order, she already had my crab soup with no parsley ready and steaming hot for me. I could have hugged her for this today because it gave me something to focus on other than my parents sitting across the table as a couple.

I grabbed one of the rolls, spread butter on it, and dipped it in my soup.

"Darling, are we going to sit here in silence for the entire lunch?" my mother asked.

"I don't know, Mother. Perhaps you can tell me since this event is your brainchild."

"Actually, this was my idea," my father said, speaking up.

Now, that surprised me. My dad was like me in that he was not too fond of surprises. Masterminding this little surprise lunch was a departure from his typical behavior.

"May I ask why no one deemed it necessary to let me in on this? I mean, do I not have a right to know that I would be having lunch with *both* of my parents?"

"Does it make a difference? You do love us the same, correct?"

My dad's tone suggested he was attempting to pull rank, which was not the best thing to do right now.

"If you thought it did not make a difference, then why didn't one of you inform me this was taking place? Because the truth is, you knew it would make a difference. You knew I would be opposed to it, and that is why you let me walk into this ambush."

"Ambush? Allyson, you are taking this a bit too far, dear," Mom said.

"You all sneaking around and tricking me into having lunch is too far, Mother."

Angela came back with our drinks, and once again I was grateful for her. I was getting ready to say more than I ought to say.

When Angela walked away again, my dad continued. "Sweetheart, we wanted to talk to you . . . together. We knew that if we had told you prior to you getting here, you would not have come. Your mother told me about the conversation the two of you had the other day, and I felt it was time that we sat down like a family and discussed some things."

Ten . . . nine . . . eight . . . seven . . . six . . . five . . . four . . . three . . . two . . . one . . . Ten . . . nine . . . eight . . . seven . . . six . . . five . . . four . . . three . . . two . . . one . . . I had to count down to calm myself. *Like a family?*

"Dad, I mean this with the utmost respect. We are not *like* a family. We are *not* a family. In case you have forgotten, you left our family to go and be with Melissa and the family you made with her. Have you any idea how you hurt Mom? Me? Have you any idea how we struggled when you first left? Before you decided you wanted to send something our way?"

I paused to give him time to respond. He remained quiet.

"You were not the one who had to watch Mom try to drown her memories of you with bottles and bottles of Riesling and white zinfandel. It was me, Dad. I had to watch her. You were not there when she was struggling to keep the lights on, working here and there, practically begging for money so we would not be in the dark and so we would have food in the refrigerator. When you walked out on us to hold on to what you had with that other woman, we were the ones left to suffer. We barely had a car to ride in, and Mom struggled to work because she could not find anyone to watch me, so many days I had to stay at home by myself because she could not afford to send me to a babysitter.

"So don't you dare sit here in my face twentysomething-odd years later and tell me you want to sit down *like a family* and discuss anything. As far as I am concerned, we do not have a family. I love you and I love Mom, but as I told Mom, she would be a fool to listen to anything you say in reference to why you left us that day. Nothing stopped you from coming back home to us. Matter of fact, I heard Mom a few times asking you—practically begging you—to come home. But you chose to stay where you were. So now that things have fallen apart where you are, you want to come back to the woman you knew loved you no matter what you did?"

I must have been talking louder than I realized, because I looked around and people had begun to stare in our direction. It was not my intent to air our dirty laundry in a restaurant, but his comment had triggered something in me. Flashbacks of Byran telling me he was in love with another woman at the restaurant in the Bahamas surfaced.

"I am glad you shared that with me. I never knew how you felt."

"You never asked, Dad."

"Let me say this. You have every right to feel the way you do, Allyson. I made some very immature decisions when I was younger. I gave up what I knew was real in order to chase a wild fetish that was not real. It was good for a while, but the older I got, the more I longed for the authentic. The type of love that was pure up until I contaminated it with my buffoonery. I honestly ran because I did not want to face the mess I had made. With Melissa, she was a part of the mess, and two messy people together seemed like the best thing for me.

"I stayed gone because I never thought your mother would truly love me again the way she had loved me before I messed over her heart. I thought if I treated her like crap she would move on . . . but even to this day she never did. So when I saw her at the church that night, I knew it was a sign from God. I knew it was my second chance at finally loving her—loving you—the way I knew I could. The way I wanted to. The way you both deserved."

Saved by Angela. That girl was like an angel—she appeared at the perfect moments. She placed our entrées on the table, and instead of resuming the conversation, we sat in silence and ate our lunch. The food was delectable, as usual, but no matter how much I tried to, I could not enjoy it as much I usually did. Seafood and tired excuses from a runaway husband did not mix well.

My mother finally broke the awkward silence. "Allyson, how is Byran? He called me a few days ago and asked me to talk to you. He wants you to reconsider the divorce."

"That is not going to happen." I shoved sweet potatoes in my mouth.

"I see. Have you at least tried to talk it over with him?"

"What is there to talk about? I am not going to be like you. I refuse to live another day of my life unhappy because I have given someone the power to control my happiness. I will not find myself in my fifties, waiting for him to have a Damascus road experience and come back apologizing for all the years of my life he wasted trying to make himself love me. I would rather find true love now. I would rather find someone who would prefer to die with me than live a single day on earth without me."

She lowered her head as my words sank in. I think she was beginning to see that her hold on me was loosening. Nonetheless, it was strange to see her cower so easily. I was accustomed to my mother being much more feisty, controlling, and aggressive. I was not sure if I liked this new persona she wore. I sat back in my chair and observed both her and my dad. It seemed as if his presence soothed her. She had a new glow, one that I could not recall ever seeing. It was almost tangible. Was that what love looked like?

"Ally, we are not expecting you to embrace the idea of us getting back together immediately. We both understand your perspective on it. However, when you get to be our age, you fully learn the lesson you seem to have already learned on your own. We now realize we took for granted something we can never get back—time. I, for one, do not want to waste another day saying 'What if?' and 'I wonder why.' I want to live fully and completely happy." He turned to look Mom in the eyes. "And your mother makes me both complete and happy."

Mom looked as though she was smitten. A girlish grin turned the corners of her mouth.

"How is Mom supposed to feel secure in what you are saying, Dad? What if you wake up one morning and realize you two really are two different people and she does not make you as happy as she is making you now? Who will be there to pick up the pieces of her broken heart this time? Who will dry her tears this time?"

"I trust your father," my mom said. "I know he is not a perfect man, and I do not expect him to be. We have both changed and are not the same people we were twenty years ago. We have both grown up and do not have time to play the games we used to play with our hearts. As your dad said, we are now on the other side of time, and it does neither of us any good to waste it."

I pretended to play an invisible violin. "That's sweet." I wiped my mouth with the linen napkin. "I wish the two of you the best remaining years of your life." I signaled for Angela to come to the table. "Can you bring the check, please?"

"Okay, Mrs. Ward. Will it all be on one check?"

I nodded. "Yes."

She left to go and get the ticket.

"Allyson, you do not have to take care of ours," Dad said.

"Dad, I cannot speak for your financial situation because I do not know what you have or do not have. But as for Mom, I am quite certain she is running pretty low. I have not made a deposit into her account in a couple of weeks, and the way Mom loves to shop and spend money, I am sure that money is already gone."

"Well, I am back now. You do not have to take care of your mother anymore. That is my job," he insisted.

"It has been my job for quite some time now. Mom got hurt on a job more than ten years ago and was not able to work again. It has been my doing that she lives the lifestyle she lives. Mom has now learned to appreciate the finer things in life, and I seriously doubt she is willing to digress to average." I pulled out my credit card. "Go ahead, Mom. Tell him. Tell him that you are addicted to shopping sprees, designer labels, fine dining, and yearly vacations. Tell him how happy you get when you get to a perfume counter and a new fragrance is out. So I hate to break it to you, Dad, but she has become extremely high maintenance over the years."

"I have changed," my mom said quietly.

"Ha!" I said too loudly. Mom was on a roll today. "Mom, are you serious? You mean to tell me you have given up your love for expensive things too? Wow, this has been a very enlightening day."

Angela came, delivered the check, and took my credit card. I pretended to be occupied with something on my phone, but I peered across the table at them again, and a certain sense of sadness washed over me. They looked as if they had found the missing piece to each of their puzzles, but I was sad because they had allowed twenty years to go by being too stubborn to try to finish what their love had started. As I continued to examine them, I watched their body language. Mom brushed something off of Dad's face, as if she had never stopped doing it. He pushed hair out of her face, as if he had been doing it all along. I had to admit they seemed happy together.

"Mrs. Ward," Angela said, "your card was declined."

"Excuse me?" I said, smiling. "There must be a mistake. Run it again."

"I tried three times."

I took the card from her. "Oh. Okay, try this card." I handed her my black card. Black cards were never declined.

I looked into the questioning gaze of Mom and Dad—particularly Mom.

"Sometimes the magnetic strip gets deactivated," I asserted.

"Yeah, that has happened to me before," Dad said. "I was down in Florida once and—"

"Mrs. Ward," Angela interrupted, "I am sorry, but this one was also declined. Is there another card you would like for me to try?"

My head was spinning out of control. My hands became a sweaty mess, and the contacts in my eyes were drying out by the second at the embarrassment. I inhaled a deep breath and slowly exhaled.

"I have cash." I reached into my purse and pulled out the cash needed to pay the check and passed it to her. "I am so sorry for the trouble, Angela. I do not have the slightest idea as to why my cards are being declined."

"It's no problem. There must be something wrong with our reader."

I snapped my fingers, as if she had just come up with the perfect explanation. "You are exactly right. That is probably what it is. Well, thank you for your patience."

"Again, no problem. I will be right back with your change."

"You know what? Since you have gone through so much trouble . . . keep the change."

Her smile of gratitude was worth the trouble of my cards declining.

"Are we done here? I need to go and check on my accounts just to make sure," I said.

"Of course, honey," my mother replied. "Before we depart, I want to say one final thing. I am sure I can speak for your father when I say in spite of the nature of our conversation today, we enjoyed spending this time with you. I know we cannot eradicate a twenty-year issue with one lunch, but we are hoping this was a start."

"There are some things about myself that I am working on. I am trying to learn how to live a Christian life, and sometimes I get it right and sometimes I get it wrong. I am not saying that I will not ever get to the place where I can accept you two getting back together. It is just hard for me to embrace right now. Mom, I just do not want to see you hurt again. That is my only reason for protesting this in the first place. In the same manner in which you all have proceeded to go on with your lives and live in total bliss, by all means continue to do so. I will soon get over myself, and maybe we can find a way to create a new normal—together. But this is the best I can do. I cannot pretend I am head over heels about it, but I can tell you that I would be willing try one day."

Mother smiled, as did Dad. I could see on their faces they had accomplished what they had set out to do.

"That is all we wanted—for you to try to understand why we wanted to be together again. We cannot ask for anything more right now," my mother noted.

"Good." I got up from my seat. "I really do have to go now. I will call you guys later, okay?"

"Please call me if you need anything, Ally," Dad offered.

"I will."

They rose from their seats also, and they each kissed me on the cheek. My mother went a little further and embraced me. I stood there as frozen as an ice cube, trying to determine if I should hug her back. I could not remember the last time my mother had hugged me for no reason. Hesitantly, I wrapped my arms around her and included a pat on the back for good measure. I definitely had to get used to this motherly love, the lessons, and the concern she was dishing out these days.

We exited the restaurant, got in our cars, and went our separate ways. I grabbed my iPhone and scrolled my contacts until I came across the number to the bank. The first card that had been declined was our bank card. Byran very seldom made large purchases without at least first letting me know, but even beyond that, he would have had to buy a house and a couple of Bentleys for the card to be declined for $68.80.

"Thank you for calling Bank of America. This is Leslie speaking. How may I help you?"

"Yes, I am calling to check the balance on my account, as well as to get the most recent withdrawals and purchases."

"Okay, I will be glad to assist you today. May I have your account number, please?"

I gave her my account number.

"And will you please verify the last four digits of your Social Security number?"

I gave her that as well.

As I waited for her to pull the account information up, I concluded in my mind that all was well and that a mistake must have been made on the restaurant's end.

"Mrs. Ward?"

"Yes?"

"The balance for the account number you gave me is zero."

I swerved over into another lane, and a motorist blasted their car horn at me. Did she say zero? I laughed softly, sure that she had misspoken.

"Zero?"

"Yes, ma'am. It says here that a withdrawal in the amount of $823,947.16 was made this morning."

"Can you also check the other accounts I have? There are two more checking accounts and one savings. I don't have the account number to any, and I don't have a check card either."

"I need your full Social."

I gave her my Social and waited for what seemed like the longest five minutes of my life as she looked up the other accounts.

"Ma'am, those accounts have all been emptied out as well."

"So you are saying I have no money?"

"All the accounts you have with our bank reflect a zero balance."

Air! I need air!

I was struggling to breathe as I fumbled trying to let the window down and remain focused on the road. This could not be happening.

"How can someone just walk into a bank and withdraw all of my money?"

"Well, not just anybody can do that, Mrs. Ward. Only authorized people on the account can withdraw funds or make any kinds of changes."

Huh?

"What are you saying? Are you suggesting I am not the victim of identity theft, but that someone who was authorized to withdraw the money is responsible?"

"Yes, that is what I am saying. You are definitely not the victim of identity theft, Mrs. Ward. Mr. Ward came into the bank and signed to withdraw all the money from the accounts."

Byran did this?

I was fuming.

Why would he do this to me?

"How is it that he is authorized to do that without my permission?"

"He is the primary account holder. You were just an authorized user on the accounts. And because he is the primary, he can do what he chooses without your knowledge or cooperation."

"So are those accounts closed?"

"No, he did not close him." She paused, but I could tell she wanted to say more. "Listen, I could get in trouble for saying this, but you seem to be taken aback and caught off guard by this. I have been right where you are. My ex-husband did the same thing to me. Mr. Ward did not close the accounts. He withdrew the funds and placed them into another account that he is the sole user on. At any given moment, he can make one phone call and transfer all the funds right back to their respective accounts. I could be wrong, but this looks to be some sort of blackmail tactic. Have you two been fighting lately?"

Was the bank teller getting in my business?

"That is not important. I need to go so I can make some other phone calls. I do appreciate your time and assistance."

"You are welcome. I apologize if I offended you in any way."

"No, you are fine. As you can imagine and have already said, I am appalled by this information. I need to go and handle it. But thank you again for your assistance."

I ended the call and immediately dialed Byran. His phone went directly to voice mail. I tried four more times, to no avail, so I resorted to sending him a text message instructing him to call me ASAP. I knew he would get the text because his phone was glued to him at all times.

My phone ringing startled me. I looked at the number and recognized that it was the spa. I had totally forgotten to call and cancel my appointment.

"Hello?"

"Mrs. Ward, hi. We were just calling because you did not show up for your appointment today. Because you are a weekly client of ours, we are going to wave the fee for no-show and no cancellation. Would you like to reschedule?"

"Can I call you back? I am in the middle of something very important, but I will most definitely give you a call to set a new time."

"Sounds great. We look forward to hearing back from you."

I merged onto I-285 and headed toward Cornerstone. My assistant had informed me earlier today that Byran was in the office and would be there until five o'clock. I looked at the time on my phone. It was only shortly after two.

My efforts to not speed failed miserably as I raced through traffic and darted in and out of lanes. Anger was the fuel that pumped the blood through my veins. I was convinced that Byran had completely lost his mind. Within twenty minutes, I drove up to the campus of the church. I saw Byran's Ferrari parked in his designated parking space. I parked in my space next to him and all but ran through the administrative office doors.

Renae, with her worrisome self, happened to be standing at the receptionist desk when I walked in. *Lord, please give me the grace to deal with her today.*

"Well, First Lady, it is so good to finally see you back around this place. We were beginning to wonder if you had abandoned our pastor," she said, looking back at Eula, the receptionist. "We do hope everything is all right. Some of the women of the church have been offering to assist Pastor in any way possible since you have not been here. I also know the deaconesses are pretty upset that you stopped working on the women's conference."

I put my hand up to stop her from speaking.

"Renae, I got this, okay? Whatever is or is not going on with Pastor and me is our business. But nothing is going on that anyone here in this church should be concerned about. As for all those who are offering help, by all means let them help. Anything their hands find to do, they should do it with all their might."

I brushed past them, leaving them standing there gazing at me like a deer being blinded by headlights.

I went toward the wing where our joint office was located. I plunged into our office suite with the force of an unstoppable train.

Damita jumped up from her desk.

"First Lady, you scared me," she said, her hands rushing to her chest. "Are you okay? You look as if you could rip someone's head off right now."

Byran emerged from his part of the office. "She probably wants to rip off mine." He smiled. "Damita, can you please give us a minute in the suite alone? Block all calls and visitors. Thank you."

She immediately grabbed a stack of folders, placed the phone on voice-mail mode, picked up her purse, and fled the office.

Byran turned and walked back into his part of the office. "So you ignore my calls, you ban me from my own house, you forsake your duties here at the church, and the only way I can get your attention is to block your access to money." He shook his head before he turned to face me. "Allyson, Allyson, Allyson. You, my dear, are predictable. I knew if nothing else, money would get your attention. It worked in the beginning, and it still does."

"How dare you do that without at least telling me?" I demanded.

"Let me guess, you were out somewhere shopping and got embarrassed because your card was declined."

"No, you are absolutely incorrect. I was eating lunch with my parents, for your information."

"Your parents? As in both of them?" he said, shocked.

"Yes. There is a lot going on you know nothing about. You are so consumed by yourself, you have no time to think about anyone else. But let us not get off the reason I came here."

He walked over to his desk and sat down. "Oh, yes, the reason you are here. Have a seat, Allyson." His tone immediately went businesslike. I sat down, ready to hear this explanation, and all I knew was it had better be a good one. "Do you think you can forfeit your responsibilities to me as my wife and still spend my money? The agreement was for you to fulfill the duties of the contract and you get paid. But when you decided you were going to go against the grain, I had no other choice but to cut you off.

"When you start acting like you have some sense, I will have the money sent back to your accounts. The only thing is I do not trust you anymore. So you are going to have to prove to me that I can trust you again before your access is fully restored. So if you convince me today that you are ready to resume the agreement, I will put a little money in your account. All the bills are paid, and food is in the refrigerator at home, so I figured a couple of hundred dollars per week so you can get little personal items you may need, along with gas for your car, should suffice.

Did he say a couple of hundred dollars? My spa appointment cost that much.

He continued. "You will be the one to determine how long this lasts. Show me better, and I will show you the money."

My right leg shook violently. Did this man have the nerve to sit in my presence and talk about trust? I scratched my head in confusion.

"So it is fine for you to do whatever you want to do and get away with it, but I do something you consider not right, and I have to suffer for it? Do you know I could go out there right now and reveal this entire ploy?"

He laughed. "What are you going to say?"

"That this entire marriage is a sham. That you married me only so you could become the pastor of this church."

"I would not advise you to do that, because you are going to make yourself appear stupid. What woman marries a man on a premise like that other than one who is just as money hungry as he is? See, the people around here love me so much, even if you stood up and said something like that, they would not believe it. But, hey, if you want to try it, go right ahead."

"Have you forgotten that I have a copy of the contract? All I have to do is get up and present my evidence."

"You *used* to have a copy of the contract. That one you had locked in your safe in your closet . . . I have it."

I had to bat my eyes really fast to prevent the tears from falling. He had thought of everything.

"Well, how do you think your little parishioners will feel about your affair with Shatrice and your son, BJ?"

His nostrils flared, and the vein in his neck appeared. I had struck a nerve.

"They have nothing to do with this issue between us. The best thing for you to do is leave them out of this."

"Or what?"

"I am serious, Allyson. Do not bring them into this. My son is deceased, for God's sake. Let his soul rest in peace. As for Shatrice, she will never open her mouth to tell anything. If she had wanted to do that, she could have done it by now."

"You do not know what she will do. You can never put anything past anybody. The same way I never thought you would do this to me, you have done it. I was a good wife, wifey, whatever the hell I was to you. You said so yourself. You have continuously laid my heart in the road to be run over like road kill. You took my emotions and played with them, as if I were some type of electronic video game. And you call yourself a man of God? I know men who are not pastors who have a better relationship with God than you do. Greed has driven you to this. If you don't be careful, Byran, you are going to wake up one morning and you will not have a thing. Yeah, you may keep this church, your businesses, and your money, but you will lose the more important things . . . the things you cannot buy."

He sat looking at me, as if I were speaking a different language.

"That was a real good speech," he said, clapping. "You sound as if you have finally cracked open the Bible you carry in here every week for show."

"Your entire life is for show. You knew when you met and married me, I barely knew anything about God and what it means to live right. And it took someone else to help me realize it. What you do not understand is you can take the money, but you cannot take what is in my heart. Keep your money, Byran. Keep it all. I may not be able to live the type of life I have adapted to, but there is something on the inside of me that tells me I can make it. I will be all right. You, on the other hand, unless you change, you will not come to a good end, because your heart is not right."

"Please spare me any more of this sermonic plague. Stick to what you are good at it, which is giving men what they want in exchange for what you want, because preaching is not your thing, love."

Was he slick calling me a whore? Was that how he saw me?

My pride would not allow him to see me break down, but I wanted to go curl up in the corner and emotionally dump it all. He was right. For years I had behaved like a whore. I went into relationships with men based on the amount of money they had and what they could do for me. When they gave the money, I gave my body. Somehow the notion that I had acted whorish had escaped me, because I felt that since I was in a relationship, it was different. But this situation had taught me you could even be married and have whorish ways.

"I want a divorce, and I am going to file for a divorce."

"No, you will not. You are not going to embarrass me or put me in jeopardy of losing my church. I will not allow you to do that."

"It is not up to you. You can have it all. You owe me nothing. I will submit to you in writing a statement that says I give up any rights I have to anything. I just want my life back. I want to be free."

"When you signed that contract, you signed your life away. However, I am not a hard man to work with. Fine . . . if you want the divorce, but I will not let you out of this contract for another four years. On our fifth anniversary I will give you your life back."

"Four more years dealing with you? I do not think so."

"You have no choice, Allyson. Listen, be grateful that I am willing to work with you. I gave you plenty of opportunities before you made this deal to back out, but you did not. Now, woman up and have some integrity. I will have my attorney revise the agreement to reflect an expiration date."

This was turning into a bigger nightmare.

"Why four years?"

"In four years my probationary contract here will have expired, and I will have gotten this church to where I want it. I will have made sure they cannot vote me out, no matter what happens. So until then you are stuck with me. But, honey, you will be just fine. You give me what I want. I give you what you want."

"What I want is to be rid of you. And, Byran, getting rid of you is what I will do."

He leaned forward on his desk. "Let me be very clear, darling. This marriage will not expire for another four years." He got up from his seat and walked to the front of his desk and leaned back against it. "Otherwise, it will be until death do us part."

The look he had in his eyes scared me. Was he this coldhearted and cold-blooded?

I stood up in the face of his intimidating scare tactic. "If God be for me, He is more than the whole world against me."

I picked up my purse and left him standing there with his ego to keep him company. I realized this was not my battle to fight. When I got myself in this situation, I had no knowledge of who God was. But now I had gotten a small inclination of His power, and I was going to let Him take care of this.

I was beginning to know it mattered not how you started, and that the real testimony was in how strong you finished.

And I planned to finish strong.

Chapter Twenty

"Hey, Louie. How have you been?"

"I've been good, Ms. Allyson. How about you?"

"I am well. Ready to get out of Atlanta," I said as I stepped into the limo.

"Jeff is already at Charlie Brown, waiting on us," he said.

"Perfect."

My phone rang.

"Hey, sweetheart."

"Hey, love. Has Louie gotten there yet?" Seth asked.

"Yes, he's here. I just got into the car."

"Great. Nana and I are waiting on you."

"Oh, you went and got Nana?"

"Yep. I told her you were coming for a visit, and she demanded I pick her up. She really became fond of you when you were here."

"Wow. I am humbled by that," I said, beaming. "I am excited to see the both of you as well. I have missed you."

"Trust me, we missed you too. And don't you worry about a thing. We are going to work this out. We will figure out a way to get you out of this mess."

"Thank you, Seth. I owe you big for this."

"You owe me nothing. I hope to prove to you one day that I am not like the other men who have been in your life. I want nothing from you. Period."

"I appreciate that."

We arrived at the airport, and I saw Jeff standing next to the chopper.

"We just got to the airport. I guess I will see you in a few," I told Seth.

"Looking forward to it. Claudia has prepared lunch for us. Hope you like chicken Alfredo."

"Oh my goodness, I absolutely love chicken Alfredo."

"Me too. It is one of my favorite dishes. All right, I will let you go so you can board."

"Okay. See you soon."

We disconnected, and I got out of the limo and went to the helicopter. Louie carried my Louis Vuitton luggage to Jeff, who placed it on the chopper. I felt sorry for them because I knew my bags were very heavy. While I did not plan to stay with Seth permanently, I had spent the past few days packing all my belongings, and a lot was crammed into those bags.

I was grateful that Byran was still not staying at the house. He was no doubt spending most of his days and nights at the hospital with Shatrice, who was still battling the infection, which had now spread throughout her body. I saw it as a blessing and got rid of any evidence that proved I had ever lived in the house. I took down our wedding pictures; I even packed up the dishes that belonged to my great-grandmother. All of what I came into the marriage with was either in the bags I had with me or at my mother's, in storage. Kristal had come over to help me get it all done expediently.

I could not explain why I felt compelled to make a move so quickly, but I had the strangest feeling that if I did not get out of there, things would get worse. When I got ready to leave the house, I left the house keys, the keys to both of my cars, the bank and credit cards, the checkbook, and anything else that connected me to Byran on the counter.

None of it mattered anymore. I no longer cared to gain the world and lose my soul. My plan was to get my divorce, go to school for nursing, and earn an honest living, like most Americans. Thankfully, I had no children to factor in, and that made it easier to pick up and walk away from my life as I knew it—forever.

So I was on my way to Carson Land to figure it all out. Once I was settled in my seat on board the chopper, I retrieved my iPad from my bag and pulled up the PocketSword app. I had never been one to read the Bible, but lately all I wanted to do was read it. The words seemed to come to life right before my eyes, and it seemed that every time I started reading, I would always start with a passage that spoke directly to me. The book of Psalms was my favorite. I had heard Byran tell the Bible Study class once that if you were newly saved, Psalms was a good book to start with, so I was yet to move away from it.

When the app came up, it was still on the same passage. Psalms 61:1–2, I had read this morning. *Hear my cry, O God; attend unto my prayer. From the end of the earth will I cry unto thee, when my heart is overwhelmed, lead me to the rock that is higher than I.*

I felt peace in my heart as I read it again. Next on my list to read was Psalms 37. My dad had suggested it when I called to let him know I was leaving. He said I would find comfort in the words, and comfort was what I needed.

Fret not thyself because of evildoers, neither be thou envious against the workers of iniquity. For they shall soon be cut down like the grass, and wither as the green herb. Trust in the Lord, and do good; so shalt thou dwell in the land, and verily thou shalt be fed. Delight thyself in the Lord; and he shall give thee the desires of thine heart. Commit thy way unto the Lord;

trust also in Him; and He shall bring it to pass. And he shall bring forth they righteousness as the light, and thy judgment as the noonday. Rest in the Lord, and wait patiently for him: fret not thyself because of him who prospereth in his way, because of the man who bringeth wicked devices to pass. Cease from anger, and forsake wrath: fret not thyself in any wise to do evil. For evildoers shall be cut off: but those that wait upon the Lord, they shall inherit the earth.

Dad was right. I felt comforted. Again, it was like God himself was speaking to me. Why did I not read the Bible before? I turned to another chapter I had spent the past couple of days meditating on.

The Lord is my light and my salvation; whom shall I fear? The Lord is the strength of my life; of whom shall I be afraid? When the wicked, even mine enemies and my foes, came upon me to eat up my flesh, they stumbled and fell. Though a host should encamp against me, my heart shall not fear: though war should rise against me, in this will I be confident. One thing have I desired of the Lord, that will I seek after; that I may dwell in the house of the Lord all the days of my life, to behold the beauty of the Lord, and to inquire in his temple. For in the time of trouble he shall hide me in his pavilion: in the secret of his tabernacle shall he hide me; he shall set me up upon a rock.

And now shall mine head be lifted up above mine enemies round about me: therefore will I offer in his tabernacle sacrifices of joy; I will sing, yea, I will sing praises unto the Lord. Hear, O Lord, when I cry with my voice: have mercy also upon me, and answer me. When thou saidest, Seek ye my face: my heart said unto thee, thy face, Lord, will I seek. Hide not thy face far from me; put not thy servant away in anger: thou hast been my help; leave me not, neither forsake me, O

God of my salvation. When my father and my mother forsake me, then the Lord will take me up.

Teach me thy way, O Lord, and lead me in a plain path, because of mine enemies. Deliver me not over unto the will of mine enemies: for false witnesses are risen up against me, and such as breathe out cruelty. I had fainted, unless I had believed to see the goodness of the Lord in the land of the living. Wait on the Lord: be of good courage, and he shall strengthen thine heart: wait, I say, on the Lord.

I closed my eyes and leaned my head back to allow those words to penetrate my spirit. I could feel the peace of God traveling through my body. I did not know how it was all going to work out, but I knew it was going to. I had nothing to my name but my clothes, shoes, jewelry, and a few other things, but I did not care. I had joy and an expectancy no one could take away.

I opened my eyes to see that we were approaching Carson Land. I had never really paid attention when we took off a few weeks ago, but as we descended, seeing Carson Land from this vantage point was spectacular. The sun was bright, and the rays caused the lake to sparkle like a flawless diamond. The entire property was awe-inspiring.

We landed on the pad, and I could see Seth waiting. He was dressed in a white dress shirt and jeans. He looked as perfect as any man could look. I could hardly wait to get out and run into his arms.

Jeff opened the door to the chopper and said, "Once again, it has been a pleasure to serve you, Ms. Allyson."

"Thank you, Jeff. You are the best pilot I know."

He grinned like a Cheshire cat. Funny how a compliment can go such a long way.

Because of the engine, I barely heard Seth when he welcomed me. We stood for several minutes hugging each other. Finally, we let each other go, hopped on the golf cart, and rode up to the house. We walked in, and both Ms. Todd and Melanie were waiting.

"Allyson," Ms. Todd said, grabbing me for a hug. "I am so happy to see you, my darling."

"My, my, my, Mama Todd. I don't recall ever getting such a greeting from you," Melanie said, interrupting the moment.

"Melanie, can you go and see if Claudia is ready to serve lunch?" Seth interjected.

She scurried off—more like stomped off. I would never get why this girl was so childish.

"It is so good to be here. When I stepped off the chopper, I felt as if I was back where I belonged," I confessed.

"God has a way of working things out, baby," Ms. Todd said. "There is a way you can't go under, and when He ordains for something to happen, it has no choice but to be so."

"You are so right. I want to thank you, Nana, Seth, you too. . . . It is because of you all and that night we were all standing in this very room that I came to the conclusion that I needed to get to know God. Since that time I have been reading my Bible and praying like never before. When I reflect back on it, if none of this had ever happened, I would not have recognized I needed the Lord in my life. So, again, thank you for leading me to Christ in a real way."

Ms. Todd grabbed me again around my neck. "Chile, you just made me happy down in my sanctified soul."

Both Seth and I laughed.

"Sorry to break up you-all's 'Kumbaya' moment, but lunch is served," Melanie announced.

"You know what? It is a pretty day today, and it's not too warm. Why don't we eat outside, by the lake?" Seth suggested.

"Sounds like a great idea to me." I turned to Ms. Todd. "What about you? Do you feel up to being outside?"

"I feel as good—if not better—than you, honey. I got a little pep in my step, girlfriend."

We laughed again.

"Mel, have Claudia and the others bring everything down to the lake," Seth said.

"I see you didn't ask me if it was okay with me, too, so I guess I will just follow suit," Melanie replied.

"Huh? You are eating with us? I thought you said you were behind on some things in the office," Seth said, genuinely sounding confused.

"I am, but everybody has to eat lunch, right?" Melanie was clearly trying to mask her anger.

"Oh, you can eat in your office," Seth told her.

"But you hate when any of us eat anyplace other than at a table. It has been your pet peeve since I have known you," she countered.

"Melanie, can you just please ask Claudia to bring the food out? And I know what my pet peeves are. But I am making a special exception for you today, and I am telling you that you have permission to eat in your office today."

Without a word, Melanie walked away, and we went out the back door and got back on the golf cart to ride to the lake. As we rode away, I looked back, only to see Melanie standing in the door, watching. That girl really gave me the creeps.

"It really is such a beautiful day. Seth, it was such a great idea to eat out here. The water only adds to the tranquility I feel right now," I said.

He squeezed my hand. "It is my prayer that you feel this for the rest of your life."

"Mine too," Ms. Todd chimed in. "I hope you stay around, Allyson, because I am going to need someone I can trust to take care of my Seth when I leave."

"It's not like you live that far away from here, Nana. You are only about twenty-five minutes or so away," I replied.

"No, I mean when I leave to go home—to my heavenly home."

"Don't talk like that. You are going to be around for many more years to come," I told her.

"Yeah, Nana . . . we don't want to hear you talking like that today. This is a great day to enjoy good food and an addition to our family," Seth said, looking over at me.

"I am not trying to scare you. But Nana won't be around here always. One of these days I'm going to leave this ole body behind and go home to be with the Lord. And, Seth, I want to know when I leave here, there is somebody who loves you just as much as me and will see to it that you are taken care of in the same manner in which I have seen to it all these years. That's all I am trying to say. I'm not predicting my death. I am just saying I don't want to leave here worrying about you."

I nodded. "I understand what you are saying, Nana. I can assure you as long as there is breath in my body, Seth will be taken care of. I owe him so much for taking me in like this and helping me until I get established and on my feet. I will see to it that I have his back at all times."

"Thank you, baby. I believe you. He needs a woman like you in his life. I hope I live to see that happen."

We arrived at the lake. In the distance I could see two more golf carts heading our way. We would soon be eating, and no one was more ready than me.

"Seth told me about your situation," Ms. Todd continued. "Back in my day, we would send somebody to go teach him a lesson, but I understand things are so technical now. But too bad you don't have any brothers to go over there and knock some sense in him. My brothers would have taken him down a dark road and beat the fool out of him, took his clothes and cell phone, and made him walk butt bare naked to the nearest house to get help."

Seth and I burst into laughter. Ms. Todd was hilarious. "Yeah, I am sure that would have taught him to think twice before he screwed over anyone else," I said, barely able to contain my laughter. "I wish it were that simple. He refuses to give me a divorce for another four years, but I refuse to wait four years for it."

"I know that is the truth and nothing but the truth. You need to get rid of that man right quick and in a hurry. He is no good for you or nobody else," she said.

"We are going to figure it all out over the next couple of days," Seth assured her. "Because they have a documented agreement, he could sue her for thousands and thousands of dollars if she proceeded with the divorce. He would no doubt contest it based on the agreement. Now that she has left, it is only going to infuriate him all the more. I am sure when he finds out she is no longer at the house, he will begin putting some things in place to try to get revenge."

"Seth, you better not let that man do anything to Allyson. My heart could not take it." She turned to me. "I haven't known you for very long, but I love you like you one of my own. It would just kill me if something happens to you."

"Nana, I will give my own life before I allowed hers to be in harm's way or taken."

Did he mean that?

"I know you will take care of her, son."

Claudia and the kitchen staff set the table and placed the food down. A couple of them stood over to the side to make sure we would not need anything else while we ate. We made our plates and ate until our hearts were merry. The chicken Alfredo was perfectly seasoned and had the right amount of Alfredo sauce and mushrooms. The breadsticks were hot and sprinkled with garlic salt, and the corn on the cob was a savory, buttery delight. To top it off, we had fresh squeezed lemonade—the kind that my grandmother made when I was a little girl. If anyone had ever had true homemade lemonade, they knew it was almost clear. That yellowish, , artificial lemony stuff they served nowadays in most restaurants was a far cry from the real thing. For dessert, Claudia had made a homemade banana pudding. I made a mental note to ask Seth if he had a home gym. We had done only a tour of the property, but I had planned to take a tour of the house today.

I leaned back into my chair and watched the ducks walk around the lake. They were so content with taking turns going into the water and playing. They had no cares in the world. Why couldn't life be that simple for humans?

My stomach started turning, and I began to feel sick. "Seth, I need to go back up to the house. I do not feel so well."

Instantly concerned, he said, "What's wrong?"

"I feel nauseated. I have not been eating for the past couple days, and maybe I overdid it."

"Julio," Seth called to the one of guys waiting over to the side. "Escort Allyson back up to the house." He turned back to me. "Your things are in the closet on the third floor like before. If you look next to the light switch in the guest room, there is a white button that looks like a decorative flower on the wall. It is actually a button for the intercom system. If you get really sick and need some medical attention, just press that button and we can hear you all over the property. It was installed for an emergency in case something happened on the third floor. I have soundproof walls up there, so if you were screaming or crying out for help, no one would hear you. Sometimes my phone signal goes out on the property, so if you have an emergency, that button is there."

"Oh, I am sure it isn't that serious," I said as I got on the golf cart.

Once I got in the house, I went straight to the elevator. The food was going to come up; there was no doubt about it. I silently prayed I would make it to the bathroom before that happened. I rode the elevator to the third floor and practically sprinted to the toilet. I hugged the porcelain god as I regurgitated everything I had eaten. As I sat on the floor, trying to determine what had caused my sudden bout of sickness, it dawned on me exactly what it was . . . stress. Finally getting the strength to lift myself from the floor, I got a washcloth, ran some cold water on it, and placed it on my forehead. I went into the closet where my bags were. I wanted to change into a sundress. The skirt and top I was wearing were not doing it for me anymore. When you felt sick, everything seemed wrong.

I thought about the fact that the walls were soundproof. *It must be exhilarating to get your freak on and know you can't be heard by the staff or anyone else who lived or visited here.* I giggled at that thought. I did not know what the future held for me and Seth, but if we were to ever get married, I would take full advantage of testing out the walls. To know I could scream and my voice would get lost in the walls was a turn-on.

I looked farther down the closet and realized there was a part of it I had not seen before. It actually wrapped around in the direction of Seth's room. I followed the closet to its end and noticed a little peephole in the bottom right corner of it. Curiosity got the best of me, and I got down on my knees to see what I could see through the peephole. It was a direct view into Seth's bathroom. I had not seen it when I was here before, but from what I could glimpse now, it was almost an exact replica of the bathroom on the guest-room side. The colors of the decor were different, the shower appeared to be slightly larger, as did the tub, but as far as I could see through the tiny hole, those were the only differences. Just as I was about to get up, I noticed a reflection in the mirror. I could not see who it was, but I smiled because I knew Seth would not stay by the lake knowing I was up here sick. I got up from the floor and headed toward his bathroom. But the voice I heard stopped me dead in my tracks.

Melanie? What is she doing up here?

I made a mental note to find out from Seth how to lock the elevator for the times when I was going to be up here by myself. I got a little closer to the doorway that connected the bedroom and bathroom. Melanie was deep in conversation with someone on her cell phone.

"What do you mean, they found some evidence at the scene? I thought they had closed that part of the investigation. Listen, you are the attorney. Fix this." She paused and waited for the other person to speak. "I do not care how you fix it. This was supposed to be over by now. Everybody was supposed to be dead. . . . No, no one is listening. I am on the third floor. You know these walls are soundproof. Seth, his beloved grandmother, and his new tramp are down at the lake, eating."

I almost walked over and showed her just how much of a tramp I was, but something told me to stay put.

"Lance, you and I would be living in total bliss right now if you had dotted your i's and crossed your t's. First of all, this all went wrong when you did not double-check Seth's schedule. If you had, you would have known he was in Atlanta that morning. I did my part. I organized the protestors, and your only other job was to make sure your bomber showed up to detonate the bombs. But you couldn't do that, either. So I had to go in there and do it myself. I had no idea I had left something behind. So since I held up your end and mine, you make this go away. Because I am not going down for this."

I almost fainted. Melanie was behind the bombing?

I knew something was not right about her!

I had to figure out a way to let Seth know. There was no way she was going to get away with this.

"The only way we are going to get access to any money now is to follow through with our plan to kidnap Mama Todd. Seth will pay any amount of money to protect his dear grandmother. The only problem we might encounter is this new, semipermanent houseguest. Her name is Allyson Ward. I have to call and get the four-one-one on why she is back here, but I will be rid of her in no time."

Kidnap Nana? What in the heck?

"Lance, I need to get back downstairs. I do not feel like hearing Seth's mouth if he catches me up here. Speaking of which, he is calling me now. I will call you later."

Thinking she was going to get on the elevator and then take Seth's call, I walked out of the bathroom to go sit on the bed and think this through. But she didn't and she saw me.

"Hi, Seth," she said, glaring at me as she made her way into the bedroom. "You want me to check on Allyson? Okay, I will go right up and check on her." She disconnected the call.

"You are going to pay for what you have done," I shouted. "You just wait until I tell Seth what I heard," I said as I stepped toward the door.

She blocked me from exiting the room. It was cute. I stood at least a foot over her.

"You will not be telling Seth anything." She lifted the skirt of her suit and pulled a small handgun from a holster. "This property is huge, and a girl can never be too safe when her job consists of going back and forth on it all day to make sure everyone is doing their job. Dangerous animals could pop up. Nosy girlfriends could overhear the wrong conversation. You understand, right?"

My heart was beating so fast, I could barely breathe.

"When Seth passed me up a few years ago to become engaged to that other woman, I was heartbroken. I was so in love with him. I would have done anything for him, but he fell in love with her, she got pregnant, and I was distraught. I convinced her to have that abortion, and that was all it took for her to be out of our lives. And then he started that stupid abortion clinic, and he spent more time there than he did here. I hardly ever saw him. Our relationship suffered."

"So you wanted him dead because he chose someone else over you?"

"Sounds crazy, huh? And it went from being someone to *something*. I can't seem to win for losing. I realized he did not want me and that I probably would never have him, but guess what? Nobody will have him if I can't."

I knew she wasn't quite right, but I had no idea she would go to this extreme. *Just press that button and we can hear you all over the property.* Seth's words came back to me, and I knew my only hope of surviving was tied to that button on the wall. I took a swing at her, pretending that I was going to hit her, but instead I purposely missed and hit the wall.

She laughed at what appeared to be my clumsiness. "Why are you here, Allyson? Why couldn't you just stay in Atlanta, where you belonged? You have a husband. But you just had to have Seth, and now I am forced to kill you. I knew the first day I saw you, you would be trouble for me. After we bombed the clinic and realized Seth was not in there, I was supposed to be the one to comfort him. But, no, you flew in here on your broom and saved the day. Well, at least I will be here to comfort him when he discovers you died from an accidental gunshot wound."

"He will not believe you, Melanie. If you wanted Seth, why didn't you just tell him? Why did you get rid of his other fiancée? Why do you walk around fixated on being his wife, and yet try to kill him? If he had not been in Atlanta that day, he would have died!"

"Seth has started getting distant again, and I knew some woman was the cause of it. I was fed up trying to show him how much I loved him, only to be overlooked time and time again. Do you know I was the first person to sleep in this room after his fiancée left him? Yep, it was me. I treated him like a king that night. I catered to him in every way, and he soaked up all the attention, but do you know he had the nerve to still refuse to sleep with me." She laughed and lowered her head. "Do you know what rejection feels like, Allyson?"

"Every woman has been rejected, Melanie, but that gives you no reason to become infatuated with someone and to try to take their life because they don't want you. You are a beautiful woman. You could have had any man you wanted."

"Except the man I wanted."

"Melanie, you should have just moved on." I eyed the gun. *If she lowers her head one more time . . .*

"You should have never come here. I had this all under control until you popped up on the radar. Seth has been walking around here like a kite without a sail since you left. I knew from the moment I saw you two in each other's presence, he was in love with you."

"And you cannot change that. Even if you kill me and it is ruled an accidental death, there will always be some woman you will be trying to get rid of. He is never going to want you, and you should not want to be with a man who does not want to be with you, no matter how much you love him. You have to value yourself and know you deserve to have a man who dotes over you and who would rather die than spend a single day without you."

She lowered her head just as the elevator opened. When she turned her head at the sound of Seth's voice, I tackled her to the floor. The gun went off, and a bullet went flying into the ceiling. I managed to take the gun from her as Orlando, the security guard, rushed to hold her down on the floor and handcuffed her.

"Dr. Carson, the authorities are on the way," Orlando said.

Seth looked very disappointed and hurt. "Thank you, Orlando, for responding promptly.

"No problem, Dr. Carson."

"Seth, you are the only man I've ever loved," Melanie cried and pleaded.

Seth shook his head. "Save it, Melanie."

Orlando picked her up and put her on the elevator.

"I should have listened to you," Seth said. "I am so sorry. When I heard the conversation over the intercom, my biggest fear was not being able to get here fast enough. The thought of something happening to you almost killed me as I tried to get here."

He pulled me into his arms and held me so tight, I thought he would squeeze my last breath out of me.

"I love you, Allyson. And I am going to spend the rest of my life taking care of you, defending you, providing for you . . . loving you. I am never going to let you go."

He could not see them, but tears fell swiftly from my eyes.

It was not just his words that moved me—because words meant nothing without the attachment of actions—but my spirit bore witness with his, and I knew in that moment I was standing in the arms of the man God had created for me.

It had taken me going through hell and back in order to get to him, but for this outcome, I would do it over again.

Chapter Twenty-one

"Shatrice, how are you?" I said as I walked up on the lady I had seen at my house that day.

"I am fine. Thank you. I appreciate you for agreeing to meet me."

We had agreed to meet at the Augusta Mall. I figured if she wanted to meet me, she had to come to my turf. I had been in Augusta now for almost a month and was slowly forgetting I had ever had a life in Atlanta.

"I will admit I was skeptical about this. But when you told me you could help me get out of this situation with Byran, I was inclined to hear what you have to say."

"I did not want to speak to you over the phone, because these days you can never be too careful, and one time, a long time ago, Byran bugged my phone. I have been paranoid ever since. I should have known then he was not anybody to be involved with. But, anyway, I want to help you because I wish somebody had helped me before I gave my heart to a man who really had no regard for it."

"Would you be helping me if your baby had lived?"

"Truth is, I don't know. When my baby died, I put a whole lot into perspective. I want to first apologize to you for disrespecting your marriage."

"Oh, girl, please. Byran and I did not have a marriage. It was an arrangement."

"It does not matter what you may call it. The two of you stood before God and made vows with each other, and I was completely wrong for stepping into the middle of it. I have constantly asked God for forgiveness, and believe you me, I have paid dearly for it. It is no secret, as I am sure he has told you, that I was in love with him. Byran could have told me the sky was purple and I would have believed it. He has an uncanny way of getting you to believe everything and anything he says—even when you know he's lying."

"When you love someone, you overlook the obvious to believe the unobvious."

"That is a good way of putting it. Well, when he first called me after you two got married, I had finally moved on and was beginning to get him out of my system. I could have married him, but I knew it would just be a repetitive cycle of what I was already accustomed to—him cheating. I did not want that life. I wanted to be in a faithful, committed relationship, and I knew if I wasn't, eventually I would lose my resolve and resort to his same behavior. So, when he called me, I turned him away, and then one night he showed up at my door, confessing his love for me.

"The first time, I listened and sent him on his way. Then I would wake up in the middle of the night to text messages about being his only love and how he was miserable without me. The second time he showed up at my house, I let him in. And from that night onward, I let him in. It is funny how we worked better when he wasn't committed to me. When he has to commit, we suffer relationally. Each time he would leave my house, I would sit and wonder how you felt. Even though he told me about the arrangement you had, I knew better than to believe you were over there in that house with no feelings at all. And even if you started out not really loving him, I knew over time you would begin to. When he is being himself, he is an easy person to fall in love with. His charm, his wit, his humor are all adorable traits. I think he genuinely cares about people. I just think his core problems are commitment and selfishness."

"I would have to agree with you," I said.

"So, when I got pregnant, he made me all sorts of promises. He told me things were going to be different. That day I saw you at your house, I was there because we had gone to the doctor's office that morning to find out the sex of the baby, and I had to drop him off because he rode with me. At that time, I was still going to a local doctor, and he had not gone to any appointments for fear of being noticed. I was inside your house because I had gotten sick and needed to use the restroom. I remember feeling like a load of crap when I saw the questions in your eyes. That had been me so many times when I was in a committed relationship with him."

I knew I must be completely over him, because her words did not sting.

"Did you know that was the day I went to have an abortion?"

"You had an abortion?"

"No, I went to have an abortion, but I miscarried while I was at the clinic."

"Wow. I had no idea. I am so sorry. You must have been livid when you found out I was pregnant."

"I was. It was his idea for me to get the abortion, because he told me you—the woman he was in love with—were also pregnant and that it was bad timing. So, in an effort to prove to him that I was willing to do anything he wanted me to do, I agreed to it. I was so stupid. I actually believed he would see that as being selfless and would fall in love with me, rather than being in love with you."

She dropped her head. "It really breaks my heart to hear this. I cannot believe he would ask such a thing of you. You know, part of the reason I am here is that we as women need to learn how to stick together so that this cycle will not repeat itself with our daughters, sisters, nieces, and friends. We have lost respect for one another, and we do not value another woman's relationship or emotional well-being. Somewhere along the way we have gotten so desperate to have a man, we tolerate anything."

"This hasn't just started. The Bible is full of all types of stories like this. Abraham, who loved Sarah, made Hagar the first baby momma. We could learn a lot from that story. Look how Hagar got kicked to the curb once they had gotten what they wanted from her. Sure she had some issues when it was all said and done, but if you had been used the way she was, would you not have issues too?"

Shatrice nodded her head in agreement.

"And then there is Leah and Rachel, two sisters who grew up together. Who played in each other's hair, who tried on each other's clothes, who sang songs together, took baths together, and who found themselves at odds with each over a man. The competition with women started with them. They stayed competing with each other. Leah tried to keep him by having his babies and, after a gang of kids, realized she could not. Rachel found herself envying her sister because she could not have kids. We are talking about two sisters. Not strangers. Two sisters. So how can we really expect anything more when the same situation applies to two strangers?"

"See, that is what I am saying. We have to do better. We have to change the way we women think so men will start respecting us. We are the key to what could very well start a revolution. If all women banded together and declared that we would respect our bodies, we would respect our fellow sister's relationship and marriage, we would help each other raise, teach, and train our kids. We would be a force to be reckoned with."

"It can happen, Shatrice. You should start a movement."

"I might just do that. I do not want to hear of another woman who is contemplating suicide because a man has broken her heart and she is now convinced she is nothing without him. I do not want to hear of another woman who is staying in an abusive relationship because she is getting her bills paid. I want her to know she can tap into the power, gifts, and talents within her to produce the wealth she needs to take care of her kids—herself. We misunderstood the teaching of the older generation. We were never supposed to just depend on *any* man, but wives were to depend on husbands. But unmarried women think they need a man to take care of them. Wives get that privilege, but not sidepieces, jump-offs. . . ."

"Or wifeys," I added.

"Wifeys?"

"Yes, girl. That is the new term out here floating around."

"What exactly does it mean?"

"Well, for me it meant one thing, but for most, a wifey is a woman who gets some of the benefits of being a wife without it being legal. For me, it was legal, I was married, but I did not have the respect a wife should get. I had an arrangement, which is how it is with most wifeys. They are in committed relationships, are often proposed to, and often live lives similar to a that of a husband and wife, but it is not sanctioned by God."

"Wow. I never knew that. Come to think of it, I think I have heard some men refer to their wife as a wifey, in the same manner a woman refers to her husband as her hubby. I never knew the term had a meaning behind it."

"I will never tolerate another man calling me wifey. The Bible does not speak about wifeys. The Bible—in Proverbs chapter eighteen, verse twenty-two—says that whosoever finds a *wife* findeth a good thing and obtaineth favor of the Lord. So, when a man takes a wife, in turn he receives God's favor. Wifeys don't have favor-producing ability."

"Man, this is deep."

"Yeah, people who say it jokingly don't realize what they are saying," I told her. "And sometimes we can be tricked into a mind-set. The Bible talks about husbands and wives. That is it."

"True. Maybe I should start a movement and have you teach on this."

"I would be honored to talk about this, but you already know Byran will slap me hard with a lawsuit."

"Speaking of Byran, the last thing he is expecting is for us to team up. He is so convinced that I love him so hard, I would stand for anything. And in times past, that was the truth and nothing but the truth. But when my son died, I saw it as a second chance to get my life in order without having any attachment to him. As I lay in ICU for all those days, battling that infection in my body, all I could do was pray, and I promised God that if He spared my life, I would get myself together and do the best I could to right my wrongs.

"So the first thing I knew I had to do once I got up on my feet was to pay you a visit. Byran confided in me what was going on with you two and how he was basically holding you hostage to a marriage you wanted out of and have every right to be out of. Beyond the death of my son, beyond my battle with an infection, that was the final straw for me. How are you going to make someone stay with you that don't want to be there? It is the most ludicrous thing I have ever heard. I purposed in myself I would help you."

"So what bright idea do you have?" I asked. "All of this sounds good, but how are we going to get Byran to release me from this marriage?'"

"What is the most important thing to him right now?"

"The church."

"Exactly. The whole reason he wants you to stay in the marriage is so he does not lose his church. He knows how a divorce would look, and he also knows how important it is to the leadership that he be married, which is why he married you in the first place."

"Right."

"If you expose him, it will backfire on you, and you are right. You will have a fireball of a lawsuit thrown at you."

"Right again. Therein is my problem. Besides the fact that he would contest, thereby creating expensive court and attorney fees, I have no money and he took away my access to the money."

"I am going to get rid of him for you by blackmailing him. I will threaten to expose him in front of his entire church if he does not let you out of this marriage. That will not only jeopardize his position at Cornerstone, but his reputation will be so tarnished, it would make it difficult for him to go anywhere else and pastor. Now, I would never expose him, but he does not have to know that. Because if there is one person on earth who can expose him, it is me."

"But how? It is your word against his. Do you know how many women step forward, claiming to have had a relationship with a pastor? Especially a mega pastor. Hundreds . . . maybe even thousands."

"I have proof. I save everything. Texts, e-mails, pictures. Everything."

"Smart girl."

"I know. Besides that, you do know all medical facilities are covered under surveillance, right? We are on camera countless times, holding hands, walking in and out of the building. I made friends with the security director, and if I ever need them, I could get access to those tapes. Not to mention, he made a very big mistake. He allowed me to list him as the father on BJ's birth certificate. But even if he had not, I could prove a pretty good case that he is my child's father with just the information I have."

"You are my new best friend, girl," I said, reaching over to hug her. "I am not interested in him being exposed. I could have already done that, if only out of anger. But the church in general—pastors in general—gets a bad rap. Not all churches have drama, and not all pastors are whoremongers, thieves, or child molesters. So, the only reason I am going along with this is that I do not believe you will even need to actually use this information."

"He will be blown away by the fact that I would even threaten to use it against him. I have always done whatever he told me to do. Hopefully, after this he will crawl into a corner somewhere and get himself together. He is too good at what he does to keep down this path. I love him enough to help him. Because, don't get me wrong, I still love the man. Thus me doing this to help you is my way of helping him. I hope he wakes up, because I have, and there is no way I will ever go to sleep in the bed of naïvete again."

"Thank you so much. You have no idea the stress I have been under trying to figure out a way to get out of this mess. I have been praying. My parents have been praying. My friends, everybody . . . has been praying. And the only thing that was left to do was trust God."

"When you left Atlanta, he hit the roof," Shatrice revealed. "You have no idea how upset he was. But I secretly admired you because you found the strength to leave it all without thinking about or being concerned with what others might think. But he was so upset, he could barely contain himself. Of course, when he gets upset, whoever is around him will be his target. Girl, that day you left, he had the biggest attitude. I had to practically knock him upside his head to remind him it had nothing to do with me."

"Yep, that describes him perfectly. I had to, Shatrice. I felt like if I did not leave when I did, something really bad was going to happen."

"Has he tried to reach you?"

"Of course. For the first week he blew my cell up. That is why I changed my number. The only people in Atlanta with my number now are my parents and my best friend. I also changed it so he could not track my location through GPS. Either way, even if he had found me, he would have not been able to get to me. I am heavily guarded," I said, laughing.

"When I wrote you on Facebook, I had no idea if you would write back. I told God if you did, it would be the sign I needed to confirm that I was supposed to offer my help."

"Well, like I said, I am glad you called."

"So here is what I was thinking. I am going to go to the church and have a talk with him. At least there I know he will blow up only so much. I will put it to him simply and see how it goes. I will have my proof on deck, so if I need to flash it to prove how serious I am, then so be it."

"I want to be there when you go," I said.

"I don't think that will be a good idea. Byran was really upset. I don't know what he would do if he saw you."

"I do not care. There are some things I want to say to him. I want to go."

She looked as if she was mulling over the thought. "Okay, if you insist. I am not a small person, but I am no match for him if he charges either of us," she said jokingly.

"We will not have to worry about that. I will have some people on standby if I need them."

"Oh, okay. You got a little gangsta in you, I see."

I chuckled. "No. I am just surrounded by people now who really love me and would go to no ends to protect me."

"Isn't that sad?"

"Isn't what sad?"

"That you have to have people on standby to protect you from the man who vowed to protect you for life," she said.

"Oh. Yeah, it is. But I am over that now. I am finally at peace with myself, with my life, and the people in my life."

"That is wonderful to hear. I am working on having that same peace myself. I have to first get him out of my system. I really did and do love him, Allyson."

"And you may never stop, Shatrice. But sometimes loving someone may mean letting them go. And who knows? You two may end up together again one day—because I do believe he loves you—but first, he has to learn to love himself if he will ever be able to love you correctly and how you deserve to be loved."

"You are so right."

"So when are we going to Cornerstone to confront Pastor Ward?" I asked, smiling.

"How soon do you want to be free?"

I smiled again. "I am already free."

Chapter Twenty-two

Seth and I rode hand in hand as Louie drove.

"Are you nervous?" he asked.

"Why would I be nervous?"

"A part of your life is ending today."

"It does not matter, because a new part of my life has already begun," I said as I lovingly looked into his eyes.

He kissed me on the forehead as we turned into the parking lot of the church. I saw Shatrice's Mercedes already parked there. Byran's Ferrari was parked in its usual spot. In about an hour people would be coming for Bible Study. We had to get in and get out as quickly as possible. I did not want to answer a thousand questions.

It felt weird coming to the church after having been gone for so long. When I thought about it, I never really fit in here as a first lady. I had done the best I could as a pastor's wife, but it was not something that I was meant to do. But for the sake of being with Byran, I was willing to do whatever it took.

The car came to a stop, and Seth and I got out.

"I will be right out here waiting if you need me," he assured me. "Are you sure you do not want me to go inside with you?"

"I am certain. I need to handle this by myself," I said.

"Okay, here are the divorce papers. I expect you to come out of there a single woman," he joked.

"Yes, sir," I said, smiling and placing the papers in my black leather attaché.

"If you are not out in thirty minutes, I am coming in there, Allyson. I cannot afford to lose you."

"Babe, he is not going to act a fool in the church. When we get through with him, he may never act a fool anywhere else again."

"Let's pray so."

"Okay, I am going in. See you in a bit."

I walked into the church and down the hall. I noticed that the picture of Byran and me that had once hung on a wall of the administrative wing had been taken down and had been replaced with a generic picture. As I approached our office suite, a small amount of nervousness tried to overtake me. I had not seen Byran in a couple of months, and I wondered how I was going to feel when I did.

I could hear Shatrice's voice from outside the door to the suite. I punched in the combination to the suite's lock, and to my surprise it was still the same, and I entered.

"Byran, the best thing for you to do is to give the woman the divorce," I heard Shatrice say.

"That is not going to happen, Shatrice. I am just getting the respect I need around here. People think she has not been here because she is depressed about losing the baby."

"They think she has been depressed all of this time? Surely you do not believe that. People are smart, and there is no way they believe that. They may know and are just keeping quiet about it, giving you some time to work it out."

I walked into the office. When Byran saw me, his eyes got as big as Popeye's, Kristal's boyfriend.

"Surprised to see me, huh?" I said.

"What are you doing here, Allyson?" he answered, standing.

"I came to bring you these divorce papers to sign," I said, taking the papers out.

He laughed so hard, he sat down in his chair. "Whew, you are hilarious, Allyson. Girl, you should have been a comedian. I told you I was not giving you a divorce until after four years. Nothing you can do will make me sign those papers."

"But there is something I can do," Shatrice said.

"Baby, you in on this with her?" he asked, looking puzzled. Then a thought hit him. "Oh, you want me to divorce her because you are ready to marry me. Babe, why didn't you just say so?" He broke into a wide grin. "The only problem is I still cannot marry you right away, because it will look like we were messing around all along. You do understand, don't you?"

I shook my head at his arrogance. This man needed some help.

"Byran, I am not here because I want to marry you," Shatrice informed him. "I am here to get you to sign these divorce papers and let this woman go on with her life. She does not want to be married to you, she has moved on, and you need to do the same."

"What interest is this of yours, Shatrice? What I do with my wife is my business and hers," he said, changing his tone. Once again, Byran was all about himself and would challenge whomever when necessary.

"Oh, so it is you and your wife now? What about when it was you, your wife, and me? You are a piece of work. And I realize you will throw anyone under the bus when you see things are not going your way," Shatrice observed. "So, here it is, Byran. You will sign those papers Allyson has in her hands or else."

"Or else what?" he shot back.

"Or else I am going to your church and exposing all your dirty little secrets. And even if that means people will look at me sideways for the rest of my life, as I always say . . . so be it. If it means that not another woman has to fall prey to your sneaky, manipulative ways, I will suffer the loss of my reputation."

He seemed unfazed. "Shatrice, you have no reputation, because no one knows you. Who are you? If you try to walk up and say anything in my church, before you take the third step, you will be stopped. Who do you think will believe you? I will just tell people you are infatuated with me, I rejected you, and you cannot move on with your life."

"You are so sad," I interjected. "You claimed to love this woman. Are you telling me your love has an on-and-off switch? You can just turn on her that easy because she is doing something you don't like? I can understand you doing me that way, because you admitted you never really loved me. But Shatrice? This is the same woman who you said you were in love with. Do you even know what love really is? You are looking in the faces of two women who loved you and would have done anything to make you happy. Most people don't get that in a lifetime, let alone from two people. And you are too silly and self-absorbed to see you have been blessed."

"Yeah," Shatrice chimed in. "This woman was about to have an abortion in hopes of getting you to see how much she loved you. She was willing to kill her child for you. How sick is that? Byran, can you not see the damage you have done?"

"Both of you . . . get out of my office before I have you removed!"

"We will gladly leave after you sign those papers," Shatrice countered.

He hit his desk with his hand, causing both Shatrice and me to jump. "I already told you I am not going to sign any papers!" he shouted.

"Okay, well, we tried to talk to you like adults, but you are insisting on being a tough guy," Shatrice said, getting up. She pulled a yellow envelope from her purse and placed it on his desk. "In this envelope are copies of everything I have the originals to. Text messages, e-mails, videos, voice mails, surveillance footage from the hospital and doctors' offices in Chattanooga, and a host of other things. Additional copies are with a friend who is standing at the post office right now, ready to drop them in the mail to every local radio and TV station. All I have to do is call."

He opened up the envelope and fumbled through Shatrice's pile of evidence. I stole a look at it and was surprised she had so much. She had gathered everything but a string of his hair, but then again, I would not put that past her, either.

I laid the papers I had on the desk to go along with what he already had. To his left were the nails—the evidence—that would crucify him. And to his right was the salvation—the divorce papers—that would spare him. The decision was up to him.

"Even if I agreed to sign these papers, you think I would sign them without first seeking counsel from my attorney?" he asked, still looking through Shatrice's pile.

"The papers are very simple. We do not have any kids together, and the only thing I am asking for is to be released from the deal we made, and granted a divorce. I want nothing from you," I replied.

"You think I believe that?"

"Just read the papers, Byran." I glanced at my watch. In another fifteen minutes people would begin filing into the church. I needed him to hurry and sign the papers before that happened or before Seth came storming in.

Shatrice saw me getting impatient and took her cell phone out. “Hey, girl. Are you at the post office? I don’t think Byran is going to sign these papers.”

His eyes got big again. I almost burst into laughter. For the first time I noticed how small he had gotten and how worn he looked. He had bags underneath his eyes and looked as if he had not slept in weeks.

“Shatrice, hang up the phone,” he ordered.

“Hold on a minute. Byran is saying something.” She put the phone down by her side. “Were you saying something?”

He flipped the pages of the divorce papers. There were only three, but he kept flipping back and forth. “I said hang up the phone.”

“You do not control anymore. I will hang up the phone if we have a deal. Otherwise, I will give her the word to drop those packages in the mail, and this time tomorrow night our story—our love story—will be on the local news. What will it be? Are you going to sign those papers or not? I have someplace to be, and I need to know now.”

“Yes,” he said, barely above a whisper.

“I’m sorry. What did you say?” Shatrice replied.

“Yes.”

“Yes what?”

“Shatrice, don’t push it. I am saying, ‘Yes, I will sign the papers.’”

“Girl, we have a yes, but stand by. I will call you back if something changes.” She ended the call.

He grabbed a pen from his desk and signed the papers. I grabbed them as Shatrice laid another document in front of him.

“What is this?” he asked.

“This is a gag order I got on myself,” Shatrice explained. “This document will protect you going forward and assure you I will not pop up later and try to use this evidence against you in any kind of way. I am going to sign it, and Allyson will notarize it. That is the only copy. I do not need one."

Byran looked confused. "You would get a gag order on yourself?"

"We thought of everything. We know how you operate, and we are trying to show you this is not about exposing you but about doing what is right," she explained.

She signed the paper and I notarized it, just as we had planned.

"Byran, I honestly pray you find happiness and peace within, and I forgive you for everything you ever did to hurt me," I said. "You can tell the church I was so overcome with grief, I wanted out of my marriage. I do not care what you tell them. You will be fine, because these people adore you, need you, and besides that, you are incredibly gifted and talented. I hope one day you will get the opportunity to stand before men, both young and old, and testify of the type of man you used to be, because I will pray to God every day for a change to take place in your life."

I stepped to him and kissed him on the cheek. "Thank you for setting me free. You will discover that you don't have to trick and scheme to get the blessings of God. All you have to do is trust Him."

Shatrice kissed him on the other cheek. "Good-bye, Byran. I will always love you."

We both walked out of the office and down the hall.

Two wounded women.

Two victorious women.

For we had proved it was possible for wounded warriors to win.

Chapter Twenty-three

August was a month that was hot no matter what. It was in the middle of the year between a windy spring and a cool fall. You could not escape its heat. But as I looked around at those who were closest to me, the joy I felt even in the midst of the heat was hard to contain.

"Baby girl, how does it feel to turn thirty?" Dad asked.

"Like it felt yesterday, when I was twenty-nine," I replied and laughed.

"Give it a few days. Your entire outlook on life will change," Mom chimed in.

"She is right. Girl, when I turned thirty, men started flocking to me left and right," Kristal said.

"And why do you think turning thirty had something to do with it?" I asked.

"See, men can sense that transition you go through when you exit your twenties and enter your thirties. You are more mature, you think on a different level, and you realize life is not slowing down for you. You get on your grown woman ish, and you start settling down."

"I was thinking of all that yesterday, at twenty-nine, though," I said.

"Yeah, you just wait. In a few days you are going to wake up and see life totally different. The change may have already started, but it will soon be solidified," Kristal assured me.

"I remember when I was thirty," Ms. Todd said. "I was too hot to trot. My husband could hardly keep up with me."

We all laughed.

"Is that right? What were you doing, Nana?" I asked.

"Anything I wanted to do that I was scared to do in my twenties. I had figured out I was old enough to know better but young enough to do it, anyway," she joked.

"Dinner is served, everyone," Claudia announced.

We all got up from the living room and went into the dining room, where the buffet was spread. It contained all my favorite foods, from chicken Alfredo to fried fish. . . . We had it all.

As we sat down at the fourteen-seat dining room table, I looked at the paintings on the walls. On the wall directly in front of me was a replica of the painting that hung in the bar at the St. Regis. It was the phoenix rising from its ashes. And on the other wall was a picture of James Durham, the first recognized African American physician in the United States. Two different paintings with great meanings. One said you could rise from anything, and the other said you could accomplish anything.

As I surveyed the people in the room, Seth, Ms. Todd, Mom, Dad, and Kristal, I thought about how we had all risen from something to become better individuals. We each had a testimony of endurance, survival, and restoration. Verses from one of my favorite new scriptures, Psalm 66, came to mind.

For thou, O God, hast proved us: thou hast tried us, as silver is tried. Thou broughtest us into the net; thou laidst affliction upon our loins. Thou hast caused men to ride over our heads; we went through fire and through water: but thou broughtest us out into a wealthy place.

God had indeed been good to me and those I love. My parents were doing great, and Mom was happier than I had ever seen her. As time went on, and as God dealt with me, I had to admit, the two of them were made for each other. Sometimes relationships went on a journey of separation, but when it was true, genuine, authentic love, people could find their way back to each other.

Kristal, my ghetto fabulous friend with the big heart, would be joining me on Carson Land as my assistant. I had taken over Melanie's job, after convincing Seth I actually wanted to work for anything I got. Our relationship was blooming, but I was determined not to follow the same path I had always followed. His money meant nothing to me, and if or until I became his wife, I would not spend it like it belonged to me.

Ms. Todd had finally given up the apartment at the senior housing facility and had decided to move back to Carson Land. She was still taking her dialysis twice a week but seemed to be happier and healthier being around those that she loved and cared about the most. She reminded Seth and me on a weekly basis that we needed to hurry and get married so she could live to see her great-grandchildren.

And Seth.

I looked over at him and partially listened as he talked to my mom about the strawberry patch. He was the kindest, sweetest, and most gentle man I had ever met. If I had to sit down and create a sketch or a description of a character in one of those romance novels that described the perfect man for me, he would fit it entirely. He had taught me how to love myself and know my value. He treated me as if I was as precious as the Hope Diamond. He loved over all my flaws and loved me through my failures and disappointments.

And to this day, and even though my divorce had been finalized three months ago, he refused to dishonor me by sleeping with me outside of marriage.

What a man! What a man!

All of them combined had taught me something different that I did not know a year ago, and on this thirtieth birthday I was simply grateful.

My dad tapped his crystal glass with his fork to get everyone's attention.

"I just have a few words to say about my daughter before we bless the food and eat," he said. He turned to look at me. "Baby girl, you are the light of my world, and you have been since the day you were born. My actions have not always matched what I have felt, but you mean so much to me. I want to apologize to you again for not being directly involved in your life while you were growing up. If I could get those years back and relive them, I would. But I am grateful to God that He has seen fit for us to make the rest of our days the best of our days. I am honored to be your father, and I am honored to be able to share the first birthday with you since that year I gave you that herringbone necklace."

He reached down beside his chair and retrieved a bag. "I scraped up every penny, dime, and nickel to buy you that herringbone all those years ago. It took everything I had, but I was determined to get it for you because I knew how badly you wanted it. Well, God has blessed me more since then. Thankfully, I do not have to struggle the way I used to. So today, baby, I want to replace that necklace with this one," he said, handing me a blue Tiffany bag. "Your mother told me you still had the herringbone, and I am sure when you look at it, you think back to a time when you were happy as a little girl, but the happiness slips away when you think about how I left you. I pray that every time you wear this new necklace, you will feel happiness and know that this time . . . Daddy is not going anywhere. I am here for the long haul, my sweet darling."

By the time he finished speaking, I was in his arms, crying like a baby. The Tiffany necklace meant nothing to me in this moment. This moment was all about me being Daddy's little girl again, and that was exactly what I felt like—his little girl.

When we had both found an escape from our tears, I opened the box, and in it was a sterling silver Tiffany Notes round pendant that had the letter *A* on it. It was absolutely gorgeous. I gave him another hug and composed myself the best I could.

I went back to my seat, and as if I had not cried enough, I cried more when everybody took turns telling me what I meant to them. By the time everyone had said their peace, Claudia and the staff had to take the food back and reheat it.

"While we are waiting on the food to come back out, I would like to say something else," Seth said. "I did not say much a minute ago, because I was saving my full speech for later, but I guess I will say it now." He walked over to me. "Allyson Chase, you have changed my life in more ways than you will ever know. I did not know what the missing piece in my life was until that day you walked into my office. Now that you are here, my breathing is off rhythm when you are not around. And I have concluded, if I have to go a day without you, I would just as soon disappear from earth. I would just as soon die.

"Scientists have this theory that the world came about through some big bang theory. We know that is not true. We know God created the world and everything in it. But their theory isn't all bad, because when I met you, our two souls collided, and out came this beautiful love that we share. I would be a fool to spend another day contemplating—or even praying about—my future with you. I already know what it is.

"So, Allyson Chase, let's make a deal. I have a contract right here that I would like for you to sign, and before you get upset, just hear me out. The agreement details are as follows. One, you will accept my love for the rest of your life. Two, you will love me until the day you die. Three, you will have as many of my babies as you want to have." He got down on one knee. "Tiffany has a slogan. It says, 'True love grows, year by year, hand in hand, better and better.' And I totally agree with them. So what do you say? Will you give me the honor of being my wife?"

He pulled a Tiffany box from his pocket, opened it, and removed the most flawless diamond I had ever seen. Being familiar with Tiffany, I recognized it as being the Tiffany Novo diamond. I looked at my dad, who was grinning from ear to ear. I looked at everyone else. They were giving me nods of approval.

"Somebody give me a pen," I said.

I could tell everyone was baffled. My mother handed me a pen.

I looked Seth in his eyes. "I signed my life away once before to the wrong man. But I trust you, and I know God created you for me. So today I agree to sign my life away . . . again. To the right man." I signed his mock agreement. "And my answer is yes. Yes, I will marry you, Seth Carson!" I screamed. I jumped up from my seat and into his arms.

He swung me around, almost knocking over Claudia, who was coming back into the room with the food.

"Perfect timing," I heard Dad say.

I kissed Seth until you could not tell where his lips ended or where mine began.

To God be the glory for the wonderful things He had done in my life.

Epilogue

Many waters cannot quench love, neither can the floods drown it.

–Song of Solomon 8:7a

"We have gathered here today before God and these witnesses to join this man and this woman in holy matrimony. We believe that God has joined them together and no man shall separate them. The bride and groom have written their own vows and would like to share them at this time," the preacher said.

"Honey, God has given me another chance at love. I dare not take this opportunity for granted. You are the beat of my heart, you are the melody in my song, and you are the blues in my thigh," he said as the crowd laughed no doubt recognizing that last part as a line from the movie *Love Jones*. "You are the woman who calms me and settles me when I become afraid of growing old. You are the woman who completes me—makes me whole. We cannot get the time we lost back, but we can redeem the time by enjoying the love we share now," he declared.

"Darling, I would have never thought I would find my way back down Lovers' Lane. I had given up on love. My heart had waxed cold, but you came back into my life and gave me warmth, which started my love flowing again. I wish I could tell you I had all the answers. I wish I knew what the future holds. But all I know is we are two imperfect people serving a perfect God, who makes all things new. And I am grateful that He did not restore our love, but He made it new," she said.

There was not a dry eye in the church as my mom and dad got married for the second time around. The love in the building was almost tangible.

Then the preacher said, "I want to read a passage of scripture from the book of I Corinthians, the thirteenth chapter, and verses four through thirteen from the Message version. It reads, 'If I give everything I own to the poor and even go to the stake to be burned as a martyr, but I don't love, I've gotten nowhere. So, no matter what I say, what I believe, and what I do, I'm bankrupt without love. Love never gives up. Love cares more for others than for self. Love doesn't want what it doesn't have. Love doesn't strut. Doesn't have a swelled head. Doesn't force itself on others, isn't always 'me first,' doesn't fly off the handle, doesn't keep score of the sins of others, doesn't revel when others grovel, takes pleasure in the flowering of truth, puts up with anything, trusts God always, always looks for the best, never looks back, but keeps going to the end.'

"'Love never dies. Inspired speech will be over some day; praying in tongues will end; understanding will reach its limit. We know only a portion of the truth, and what we say about God is always incomplete. But when the complete arrives, our incompletes will be canceled. When I was an infant at my mother's breast, I gurgled and cooed like an infant. When I grew up, I left those infant ways for good. We don't yet see things clearly. We're squinting in a fog, peering through a mist. But it won't be long before the weather clears and the sun shines bright! We'll see it all then, see it all as clearly as God sees us, knowing him directly just as he knows us! But for right now, until that completeness, we have three things to do to lead us toward that consummation: Trust steadily in God, hope unswervingly, love extravagantly. And the best of the three is love.'"

The audience clapped as he concluded reading a very famous passage of scripture for weddings. He then led them through the ring ceremony, the lighting of the unity candle, and the proclamation.

"You may kiss your bride," he said to my dad.

My father took my mother's face in his hands and kissed her passionately. I was almost repulsed looking at them kiss, but sitting next to me was Seth, who was the perfect distraction. He looked down at me and kissed me on the lips.

"Soon that will be us," he whispered.

"I know, and I absolutely cannot wait until that day," I whispered back.

"Ladies and gentlemen, I present to you again Mr. and Mrs. Lawrence Chase," the preacher announced.

The church erupted in applause.

I would have never imagined a year and a half ago, when I got married, that I would now be divorced and engaged again. And I certainly never anticipated my parents getting back together. A lot could happen in a short period of time. It all started with a wrong wedding and ended up with a right one.

The reception hall was elegantly decorated. I had tried to convince my mother to bling everything out, but she had opted for the simple, classy feel. She had said that at their age, a big wedding and a fancy reception were the furthest things from her mind. She was no longer trying to impress anyone but wanted to do what made her happy so she could get on with living.

"Mom, Dad, you both look great," I said as things were coming to an end. "You made me very proud today." I kissed them both on the cheek.

"We are equally as proud of you. In less than six months you will get your second chance at love, and this time, just like this time is for us, it will last," Mom said.

"I believe it, Mom. So what time do you leave for your cruise?"

"We fly out of Atlanta to Miami at six in the morning. I think the ship leaves around ten," Mom replied.

"Okay, you all enjoy yourselves. Don't come back with any babies."

"And why not, Allyson? Are you afraid you won't be the baby girl anymore?" Dad asked.

"No, I am afraid I will lose my parents in your attempt to be the new Sarah and Abraham."

We all laughed. I hugged them, Seth came up to wish them a safe trip, we said our good-byes, and Seth and I left.

We boarded the chopper and headed back to Carson Land. As I always did, I leaned my head back against the headrest and thanked God for another day. It had been wonderful.

"What's on your mind?" Seth asked.

"Oh, nothing much. Just reflecting on the day. It was beautiful. I am genuinely happy for my parents."

"Indeed it was. And I am happy for them too. Everyone deserves to feel love and be in love."

"I agree."

"What do you want to do tomorrow?"

"Sleep. I am exhausted. Between helping Mom plan her wedding, planning another one of my own, and running things around Carson Land . . . I am spent."

"I totally understand. You should be."

"Did you have something in mind for us to do? Why did you ask?"

"Not at all. I just wanted to know how I could cater to you."

He always knew how to make me smile and feel like a queen. He picked up my foot, slid my shoe off, and massaged my heel and arch. I slid down a little in my seat and relished the stellar treatment.

As I settled into the embrace of relaxation, my thoughts detoured to a replay of my life. In spite of my rough childhood, my bumpy teenage years, and my unhealthy young adult years, God had kept me. Through danger seen and unseen, He had kept me. Many times the devil could have taken me out, but even when I did not know it, I had angels watching over me.

It was unknown to me what God had in store for me, but since He had done a good job thus far at leading and guiding me, I knew I would forever put my trust in Him to continue doing so. He had turned my tears of sorrow into tears of joy. He had turned my mourning into dancing. He had restored my soul. Even when I did not know to pray, He was patient with me until I learned to pray.

Who couldn't serve a God like mine?

"What are you smiling about?" Seth asked.

I opened my eyes and looked at him. "Just thinking about the goodness of the Lord."

"A woman that prays is so attractive."

I smiled. "Is that right?"

"Yep. Complete and total turn-on."

"Well, you just wait until I become your wife so I can show you what a turn-on is."

"I was thinking. Why do we have to have a wedding? Let's get married tonight."

"Ha! Are you getting fresh with me, Dr. Carson?" I grinned mischievously.

"I'm just saying. We could get married tonight so you can back up all this talking you are doing."

"Get your mind right, mister. In due time, you will have me and as much of me as you want."

"I already have the part of you I wanted the most."

"And what part is that?"

"Your heart."